M. J. Farrell

is the pseudonym for Molly Keane. She was born in Co. Kildare, Ireland, in 1904 into 'a rather serious Hunting and Fishing and Church-going family' who gave her little education at the hands of governesses. Her father originally came from a Somerset family and her mother, a poetess, was the author of 'The Songs of the Glens of Antrim'. Molly Keane's interests when young were 'hunting and horses and having a good time': she began writing only as a means of supplementing her dress allowance, and chose the pseudonym M.J. Farrell 'to hide my literary side from my sporting friends'.

She wrote ten novels between 1928 and 1952: *Young Entry* (1928), *Taking Chances* (1929), *Mad Puppetstown* (1931), *Conversation Piece* (1932), *Devoted Ladies* (1934), *Full House* (1935), *The Rising Tide* (1937), *Two Days in Aragon* (1941), *Loving Without Tears* (1951) and *Treasure Hunt* (1952). She was also a successful playwright, of whom James Agate said 'I would back this impish writer to hold her own against Noel Coward himself.' Her plays, with John Perry, always directed by John Gielgud, include *Spring Meeting* (1938), *Ducks and Drakes* (1942), *Treasure Hunt* (1949) and *Dazzling Prospect* (1961).

The tragic death of her husband at the age of thirty-six stopped her writing for many years. It was not until 1981 that another novel— *Good Behaviour*—was published, this time under her real name. Molly Keane has two daughters and lives in Co. Waterford. Her twelfth novel, *Time After Time*, was published in 1983.

Virago publish *Devoted Ladies* and *The Rising Tide*. *Two Days in Aragon*, *Mad Puppetstown* and *Full House* are forthcoming.

DEVOTED
LADIES

M. J. FARRELL

With a New Introduction by Polly Devlin

Published by VIRAGO PRESS Limited 1984
41 William IV Street, London WC2N 4DB

Reprinted April 1984

First published in Great Britain by Collins 1934

Virago edition offset from Tauchnitz 1934 edition

British Library Cataloguing in Publication Data

Farrell, M.J.
    Devoted ladies
    Rn: Molly Keane   I. Title
    823′.912[F]   PR6021.E33

ISBN 0-86068-466-0

Printed in Great Britain
by The Anchor Press at Tiptree, Essex

The cover shows
The Bay. c 1927
watercolour on silk 21 ×20.5cm
purchased 1927
Art Gallery of New South Wales

INTRODUCTION

Devoted readers of M.J. Farrell's hunting romances—and there were many—who bought her new novel, *Devoted Ladies*, in 1934 to lose themselves in her singular and special world, that of the Anglo-Irish in Southern Ireland, and one to which she utterly belonged, were in for a rude shock when they first opened the book. And the word "rude" is used throughout the book to denote shocking and aberrant emotion. It is also used to cover feelings and behaviour far removed from the incorrigibly "natural" horsy habitat in which the heroines of her earlier books had ridden and danced and suffered the pangs of romance and the pain of loving. Those famous preoccupations of her four previous novels—horses, romance, snobbery, the world of the landed gentry in Ireland, the hunt as tapestry, the glorious backdrop to life, and the houses of Ireland lying like temples at the very heart of her books—seemed, in the initial stage of *Devoted Ladies*, to have been superseded by new and somewhat sensational interests. Her readers were transported to a fashionable flat in a chic quarter of London, to a party given by one Sylvester Browne—a jaded, gilded playwright—sounding like a fairly tiresome cross between Noel Coward and Charles Morgan with a dash of John Gielgud thrown in (who became in fact one of her great friends and directed the four plays she later wrote).

There had been a reassuring continuity in the highly successful books by this young Irish author Molly Keane, who seemed to have tumbled inadvertently into authorship—and indeed celebrity—and who kept her identity so well hidden from the general public under the pseudonym M.J. Farrell, which name she had casually adopted from a local pub sign. She felt that being a writer in her particular world would have brought ostracism. The choice of name shows either considerable naivety or a certain cunning, since as an Irish disguise it is perfect, being sexless, anonymous and carrying no overtones of gentry: and she *was* gentry, part of that small international community which was also parochial, that strange, select elite world called Anglo-Ireland, which hung poised between two cultures, sucking social sustenance and culture from the one—England—and using the other as the substructure for its easy edifice. From the beginning of what appears to be her almost unconsidered literary career she wrote about this society, taking its order for granted, in order, as the legend goes, to earn enough money to supplement her dress allowance.

Not that there *was* much money in it at the beginning. She sold her first book, *The Night of the Cheerful Countenance* for £75; her second was bought by Mills and Boon for £100. "I'd sent if off to an agent whose name I'd seen in the *Times Literary Supplement* and he'd thought it was O.K., but my feet left the ground when a publisher wanted to publish it." Its title, appropriately enough, was *Young Entry* (published in 1928) and it is an accomplished piece of writing, though somewhat repellent in the behaviour depicted in it, the unbecoming attitude of the Quality towards the subclass of native Irish on which their elaborate superstructure rested, and rested as they were soon to see, somewhat precariously. The young, upper-class women who populate it talk in a tiresome and typical way, albeit with patronising affection, about the "people" of Ireland. In this simulacrum of her real world everyone knows each other, their breed, seed and generation and as her new books appeared, a central character from one book would occasionally pop up in a peripheral role in another, adding much to the sense of exclusivity and familiarity—a club in fact, open in reality only to a certain caste; but here thrown open by a member to any reader, whatever their sympathies. It was a risky thing to do—hence, perhaps, the pseudonym.

She was always as courageous a writer as she was a woman and rider, but her literary courage sometimes seems to have more to do with not recognising the hazards of how she writes about class and sex than with negotiating or outfacing those dangers. But she was not above poking fun at herself and in the opening pages of *Devoted Ladies* there is a moment of sly irony when Sylvester Browne recalls a moment of glory on a hunting day in Ireland.

Here there is a dust of gold in the gorse the darkest day in December, and excitement is a gold cry in the wind and danger a crown. . . Such thoughts were rude and fit only for some hysterical Irish novelist writing her seventy thousand words through which the cry of hounds reverberates continuously: where masters of hounds are handsome and eligible men and desirable young girls over-ride hounds continually, seeing brilliant hunts on incredible three-year-olds: and all—after even the hardest day—are capable of strong emotion at night.

Not a bad, though superficial, summing-up of her own books—and certainly what readers might expect of them. The joke continues—a key point in the plot hinges on the rich, young lesbian heroine's reading of *Young Entry* by M.J. Farrell, which she finds among a job lot of books and being fired by a desire to go to this strange, lovely place she discovers in the book. Jessica, her tough girlfriend, pounces.

"*Jane*, who could have sent you these books? All outdoor sports, my dear. And here's one just about girlfriends—*Young Entry*; how rude! Why should they expect any one to know what they mean by their dreary huntin'-talk? Perhaps Sylvester sent them for a bit of fun. He knew I'd get a good laugh out of them anyway. . .Girlish friendship and fox-hunting—now they're eating soda-bread—what's that? Oh we're in Ireland I see. . .It's worse, my dear. It's full of the lowing of hounds and every one stuffing themselves with buttermilk scones dripping with butter. Plenty of picturesque discomfort and cold bath water and those *incredible* Irish mountains *always* in the distance."

It sounds a little as though M.J. Farrell had suffered rather at the hands of the reviewers, although in fact from almost the beginning she had had great success with her insouciant and stylish writing. In time *Devoted Ladies* was to get its share of acclaim too.

Infernally good. . .a worldly wise, witty and remorselessly cruel book. The landscapes are exquisitely done. I feel I could talk about a Farrell as one talks about a Corot. . .Certainly one of the most brilliant novels I have read in the last two years.

wrote Compton MacKenzie.

Devoted Ladies seemed to have strayed far away from those incredible mountains. The setting is chic, the tone brittle and the romantic interest hinges on the stormy relationship between a lesbian couple, one frail and dying of alcoholic poisoning, if not from her friend's pure spleen. Other cosy elements include a crudely-drawn homosexual valet and certain introspective musings about writing. Rude indeed. But for all the early change of locale and population, M.J. Farrell's fine gifts for atmosphere and description and evocation were manifestly in place and her ability to match her prose to the texture of the time and location. *Devoted Ladies*, set in the pale green and silver world of fashionable thirties London is an art deco novel. Its hue, its designs, the lines of the book, the nonchalant langour of its inhabitants, their studied attempts at decadence seem the epitome of the period. The characters appear as though about to be photographed with arum lilies in the background. Everything is glittering, reflective, hard on the surface, fluid underneath. The year that the book was written one of *Vogue's* more memorable dictates was "Your very important profile will have the windswept fleet lines of a speedboat or aeroplane" and this jaunty style exactly matches that of Jane, goofy to a degree and who with hindsight seems an archetypal image of the decade—a Mrs Simpson dressed by Schiaparelli. Jessica, her butch lover, though rather a caricature figure, is gradually, though not wholly successfully, revealed as a genuinely frightening figure from whom there can be no escape.

Molly Keane has always had a talent both for tuning

her prose to the right pitch for the emotional weight she gave it to carry and for matching her tempo to the pace of the action. In *Devoted Ladies* the surfaces and shapes of things are described to brilliant effect and the action slides along propelled by electric energy. And the book is about appearances as much as about the pain behind the surface, the violence of emotions hidden behind the *maquillage*, about how a sudden crack in the glaze can show the disturbance beneath. (Auden's lines "The crack in the tea cup, opens a lane to the land of the dead" come to mind.)

In some extraordinary way, considering how M.J. Farrell avoided much mention of sex or physical contact, there is something a little prurient in her treatment of the lesbian lovers, not unlike a child who has discovered a grown-up secret without quite understanding it. There is something a thought sophisticated about the "rudeness" so that it doesn't ring altogether true—though there is a paradox here in that she successfully shows the mendacity and shallowness of the little world she seemed to stumble on—a place where there is little truth. "I suppose I was rather curious and shocked by coming upon all that," she says. "Before then no-one thought anything of two elderly ladies setting up house together. I'd certainly never heard a murmur, though now everyone murmurs about everything. I was excited by finding out about lesbians and homosexuals. It was new. It made a subject." She adds by way of explanation. "I didn't know how to write and still don't. I found it very difficult—even the grammar. It took ages to write a sentence. My interest went in spasms, there would be a sudden arousal of

interest that took over, something new—like this—that
would be the start of a new book." But it was literally just
a start, for soon after the book opens Sylvester forsakes the
louche life of London for the rich sentimentality of his
version of Ireland and takes himself to his cousin's
crumbling mansion where he can relish the left-over
Edwardian life he finds there. Jessica and Jane follow him
and we are back home safely in the old Farrell hunting
grounds, almost as though the excursion into café society
had never happened. Devoted readers could relax.

Except of course that M.J. Farrell's houses are never
safe places, never sanctuaries, though they may appear
so. These beautiful houses lying so vulnerably open in the
haunted countryside of Ireland are full of old spirits and
tensions and moods; the accumulation of ancient passions
turns them into emotional archaeological sites, where an
outsider stepping unwarily can set off shattering
reverberations. And then too the fox is not the only
hunted creature in this hunting territory. Jane is hunted.
"Some women" Molly Keane speculates "like being
bullied", but Jane, cornered in fright and piteous
despair, realises that she, a far simpler, more ordinary
creature than she had ever imagined herself to be, doesn't
like being bullied at all. As she struggles to leave jealous
Jessica, to get to good, kind, dull, rich, manly George
Playfair (who talks to his dogs like women and no doubt
to his women like dogs—an ideal Anglo-Irishman in
fact), Jessica moves in for the kill. And the struggle
between the two forces, one passive, traditional,
conventional, obstinately strong, the other passionately
active, eccentric, darting and vicious, begins. This

engagement of power is a leitmotif in all of Farrell's books—only through such conflict can peace, or at least some kind of treaty for living, emerge.

In the book we are left in no doubt as to what would be the extent of George Playfair's recoil if he had had any conception of the real nature of the relationship between the two women. "If he'd comprehended it—if he'd been able to—a man like that certainly would never have married her" Molly Keane says. "Well, he probably would have died. He was a very innocent gentleman— but the people *were* very innocent then, people like that." So of course was she.

It was only when she was in her very late teens and early twenties, when staying with the Perry family at their home, Woodrooff, a great house in the Tipperary hunting country, that she began to find out about her own contemporary world. This beautiful and welcoming house was to her a haven, an escape from her curiously stranded existence in her parents' large house in County Waterford where her mother, a poet writing under the pseudonym of Moira O'Neill, remained utterly engrossed in her own nineteenth-century idea of the world and her father thought only of his horses and hunting. They took scant interest in their children who grew up passionate about riding but with little guidance about anything else. At Woodrooff, where she spent the greater part of six or seven years before her marriage to Robert Keane, she met a society that was new to her—cosmopolitan, fast, rich. Many of the people who came to stay there were part of, or on the fringe of, literary and intellectual London life and when she in turn went to stay with these new friends she was introduced to a semblance of the world she was to depict in *Devoted Ladies*.

Though Molly Keane's characters were never drawn straight from life, John Perry, one of the Woodrooff children (who later helped her in the writing of her successful plays) is supposed to have been the original model for Sylvester Browne; and Joan the horsy, glamorous wife of the local M.F.H. in *Devoted Ladies* was also based on a famous Woodrooff *habitué*. In real life this dashing rider was much admired by all her young acolytes who copied her ways and aspired to be her favourite. "That too was all very innocent" Molly Keane says. "There was nothing lesbian about it at all. Perhaps part of it was because there was a great scarcity of young men." Here this queen of the hunt is subtly metamorphosed into a creature of infinite self-satisfaction and affectation, maliciously pinned down for our delectation. But perhaps the most inspired word-portrait in the book is that of the grotesque Piggy, also innocent, but whose innocence is without charm or appeal. Greedy, ungenerous, lacking self-knowledge, yet pathetic in her unrequited, ignorant loyalties and her pitiable search for love, she is remorselessly presented. It is a pruned and merciless portrayal of a woman, (not alas all that exceptional in her context), who literally leaps towards love.

All the portraits, however disguised, seem so idiosyncratically recognisable that one imagines the book—indeed all M.J. Farrell's novels—must have been pored over by her contemporaries as a *roman-à-clef*. One wonders what the inhabitants of her Philistine hunting world and the fringe of literary London can have made of this artless-looking girl who cast such an artful eye over their shared territory, who wrote with such accuracy about their self-deceptions, yet who was finally so often affectionate and even tender towards her chosen subjects. And how did her old-fashioned parents react to a book like *Devoted Ladies?* "Well, people in Ireland read very little" she says drily. "I don't think my mother read any of my books. They would have worried her and she avoided worry where possible. I'm quite sure my father read none of them. He only liked Surtees and history."

The irony is that the great appeal of Surtees lies as much in his perception of life as a whole, his delivery of pertinent and devastatingly accurate observations about life in general as it lies in his exquisitely funny accounts of hunting lives in particular. In the fusion of the two, often opposing, viewpoints we are given a remarkable and vivid social history. M.J. Farrell does precisely the same. Her parents never knew what they missed—an impeccable picture of what is to us a vanished world, but still full of relevance and revelation.

Polly Devlin
Bruton, Somerset 1983

CHAPTER I

SYLVESTER was giving a party.

His guests toiled up flight upon flight of dark stairs.

Jane was so accustomed to the smell of cats and ammonia on the stairs (there was a mews below) that she hardly noticed where they left off and where the expensive smells of Sylvester's rooms began. She had been there very often this summer, for Sylvester preferred to entertain in his own rooms to entertaining in restaurants or night clubs: "It iş more me," he would say, "and much cheaper, and much better—don't you agree?"

And here his friends would agree with enthusiasm. His food and his drink were always good. Not that Jane minded about food or drink either (so long as she could have enough drink). If you have always fed on the rarer and more expensive forms of food you will, by the time you are twenty-eight, have developed an intelligence about food or else you simply won't mind. Jane simply didn't mind. And her favourite drink was brandy; brandies and sodas followed by a mass of liqueur brandies rolling pleasantly in their large hot glasses.

It was not for Sylvester's good food and drink that Jane came to see him whenever she was asked, and often when she was not asked. It was because she hoped on and on in the face of constant disappointment that Sylvester would put her in a book or in a play.

She could never realise that the people Sylvester put in his life he did not put either in his books or in his plays. When he told her this he hoped that the flattery implied in the remark about his life might assuage her dismal greed for seeing herself as she wished him to see her.

But although he spoke to her softly and cunningly: "Jane, you know I never put the people who *matter* to me in my books"; she would answer only: "Oh, you are *horrible* to me," in her rich South American voice, so teeming with feeling and so barren of words.

Yet in spite of his reluctance to enclose the substance of her flesh and her spirit forever in an aspic of words, Sylvester continued to be very sweet to Jane. Although his new revue was playing to good business and his last book doing well, the moment might yet arrive when he would require to borrow money from Jane, or at any rate make use of her cars or her houses or any of the many benefits which providence spends cn very rich young women that very poor young men may thereby profit a little.

It was two years now since Sylvester had ceased

to be a very poor young man, but he had not yet quite lost the habit. He was genuinely economical, just as he was genuinely a good writer and a competent playwright. But Jane was genuine in nothing. He believed even her complete stupidity was partly a pose of mind.

How much her affection for Jessica was a pose, a queer piece of exhibitionism, that he did not know.

Jessica and Jane were in Sylvester's bedroom now painting up their faces for the party.

Sylvester's bedroom was all shape and no colour. It was decorated in brown and grey and black. Jane always thought it inconceivably dreary, but Jessica, who thought she knew about house decoration, went into sullen rapture over the lighting. She struggled to impart her feeling to Jane in chosen difficult words. She always worked hard and deliberately for words, but Jane only said, "I'll say it's horrible; I'll always say so."

Jessica looked at Jane standing there in the colourless space of Sylvester's room. She looked at her and looked away again and back again. "She's such a good shape," she thought quickly—clothing for herself in words some indefinable excitement—"Wherever she is she makes her own pattern."

In the grey and black and brown room no doubt Jane did look well, for her lines were faintly geometric, as though flesh had been put on her body

only to be ruled off again with extreme exactitude.
Her bones were no more than small enough to
justify the theory that she was ghostlike, not
gaunt. As it was she escaped that unattractive
state of body by very little. Her coarse fair hair
was a lovely blanched colour and she arranged it
with much care like a little girl's. Sometimes when
in a particularly girlish mood she would even tie a
piece of it up with a ribbon. But it was the scar
of her hare-lip that gave to Jane's face its peculiar
and distant expression of sadness, entirely redeem-
ing her features from that dreary baby-like prettiness in which but for this they were surely cast—
this thread of a scar, pulling her mouth a little
to one side and her nose faintly crooked, was
fascinating. It compelled curiosity. First it was
faintly shocking and then it became enormously
amusing. She would paint her mouth as its lines
were, a little awry, and this was amusing too. Her
eyes were pulled rather open by the scar (if one
folds one's upper lip together the reason for this
becomes apparent) which lent them a permanent
expression as though staring with tears.

Jessica who had lived with Jane for six months
now was quite a different sort of girl. She had
been well brought up by her rich family and this,
since her brain was her obsession, she found not a
little tiresome.

Her ideas were well discovered and, if not always
original, at least generally easy to coax into im-

portance. For the discovery of ideas, their crystalli-
sation into phrases and the subsequent delivery of
such phrases at the right moment (if possible with
no one present who had enjoyed them before) she
found family life a poor background. In her
comfortable and unsympathetic home Jessica's
charm was no charm. And charm, of a dark,
compelling kind, Jessica possessed without a doubt.
But the length of its influence was a very variable
matter.

In her friendships with men as well as with
women Jessica spent herself so lavishly and so
emotionally that soon there was no more she. She
had spent what she was in a sort of dreadful effort
towards entire mental contact with the person she
loved. And having reserved no smallest ledge of
herself for herself, no foothold for the last secret
feet of her mind, she would retreat in anger and
despair from her friendships. Then cruelly, dis-
dainfully and despitefully she would speak against
such a one as she had loved.

Her dreary enthusiasms were tolerated by her
friends for the sake of those moments when, her
lips curled back from her teeth like a dog, saliva in
their corners and hysteria in her eyes she would
tell and tell and tell of that past moment in her
life; with pitiless mimicry and sure malice breaking
the one who had shared it with her on the wheel of
her words, on the wheel of her own despair.

Venice with the loved one, or a week in some-

body's yacht—she would tear their hours apart and
show, with screams of insane laughter, how this or
that had filled her lover with sentiment and enthusiasm, while for her it had been beyond
mockery.

But how would Jane have voiced enthusiasms,
they wondered, who had never heard her say more
than: "I feel horrible—fix me a brandy and soda."
Still, Jessica could be so wildly funny about the
least probable people, the tale was worth waiting
for, worth the endurance of her prolonged obsession.

Jessica was an intellectual snob. She seldom
condescended to be gay, although she would take
endless pains to be rude. She loved to express
her emotional reactions to people, food, form or
colour by word of mouth. Now she said to Jane:

"You're looking very wonderful to-night—don't
let's stay at this party too late—Look, Jane, in that
silver dress you're terribly exciting—so . . . *Blanched*,
so . . . *Tarnished* . . ." Whenever Jessica got into
difficulties for words she would create a mental
atmosphere of astericks pregnant with meaning.

Jane said: "Tarnished? Aren't you horrible to
me?" and they went down to the party.

Sylvester's party had only just begun when they
came in, so Jane decided at once that she had
come too early, which was a fatal beginning.
However, Sylvester was enchanted to see them
both. He said to Jessica:

"I hope you have something really rude and unkind to tell me, darling. We must have words together presently when these people have all arrived. I hate being interrupted when I have you to talk to."

Then he said to Jane:

"What lovely beads, Jane. They are divine, aren't they?" He took them in his hands to look at them and suddenly in his long satirical hands Jane's beads, which had up to now only looked expensive, took on a quickened look of beauty that stayed with them even after he gave them back to her.

Although Sylvester had no enthusiasms left—not even dreary ones such as gathering up etchings or rare and ugly china—although he was thirty years of age and a very tiresome young man and a moderately wealthy one, he preserved within himself a respect for things—good beads or horses galloping, properly made toast or the reason why a fly plaits its forelegs together. But he preserved this within himself, for he had a horror of the tiresomely fantastic either in life or in letters.

Perhaps Jane's scar enabled him to look on her as a Thing, faintly worthy of curiosity. Otherwise it is difficult to see how he troubled to retain her friendship—for the faint possibility of future need could scarcely have influenced him so far.

But Sylvester had not much time to spare to the girls now, for he greeted all his guests with old-fashioned politeness, and not until late in the evening did he, at his own parties, indulge in selfish converse with those of his guests who bored him least.

Jessica watched Sylvester talking to the people he'd asked to his party. "She watched him covertly," she said to herself, but, in fact, she was staring at him openly with her jaw rather dropped and her mouth rather slackened, trying for the hundredth time to put a name to that nameless quality which was Sylvester's power over others.

Of all the writers she had known he only could divorce himself from his profession and be Sylvester. Lovely and charming and almost stupid. Kind and sweet and polite ... Jessica said: "A double gin and tonic water please"—and proceeded to consider the party. She heard Jane's plaintive whine across the room: "Oh, darling—fix me a brandy and soda, I feel *horrible*." She wondered whom she was talking to, but when she saw it was only a handsome young man she felt quite easy in her mind and continued her mental analysis of those present, an analysis which she felt to be a definite importance of the moment.

Jessica was immoderately drunk by now, so drunk that she would have argued reasonably with any one about her entire sobriety. More, she would have sustained with fervour her reputation for carrying her liquor like a gentleman. She was looking splendid. Her dark eyes were full of secrets and her hands teeming with life.

"Go away, for God's sake," she was saying to a young man who had just brought her another double gin and thought he might stay and talk for a little. "I don't want to talk to *you*. I want to talk to this girl. This girl looks more like my cup of tea."

Sylvester, who knew she did not know the girl—a pretty little Hearty (he forgot why he had asked her here to-night) watched and listened with amusement. With enormous enjoyment he heard her begin to abuse his new play. She tore it competently to pieces.

"There's only one phrase in the whole thing," Jessica declared arbitrarily, "and that's the one I lent him—when the girl says: *'Bring me a bottle of beer'*—just a bottle of *beer*, utterly fed up, you see—can't you *see* it—I mean I think—I think the whole thing is in that. I may be wrong. It's just my idea. You know. But—*'Bring me a bottle of beer.'* There are people who affect one just like that aren't there? When one's with them all the time one's thinking—Christ if I had a bottle of beer instead of talking to them. It's rather how I felt about Sylvester's Piece. But of course the *lovely* thing was he couldn't see I meant that. He has quite a thing about his own Pieces—But the lovely part for *me* is I can go as often as I can bear it to that dreary

Piece and hear the girl say that every time I go—
So *lovely* for me."

Sylvester began to be sorry for the pretty Hearty
who had got herself so entangled in Jessica's merciless conversational net. Women like Jessica he
considered ought to wear some outward Sign as a
warning to those who may then pass by. A wreath
of white dahlias perhaps—or a garland, that had
been rather a pretty fashion. Anyhow this poor
girl was as bored as he was entranced. He would
gladly have gone to her relief but Jessica was
scarcely drunk enough to continue her abuse of
his dreary Piece to his face. Or perhaps she was.
No. He would not take the risk of interrupting
her enthralling commentary.

But he had hardly arrived to this selfish decision
before Jessica ceased to discuss him or any less
interesting subject. He saw her morose silence, she
could pull silence about her in sullen folds. He
observed that she permitted the girl who was so
pre-eminently not her cup of tea to manoeuvre
and escape her, and then he saw her fixed gaze
burning itself out across the room where Jane lay
placid and obviously contented in the arms of a
young man. It was obvious that he had fixed her
a good many brandies and sodas, or at any rate
brandies, for she had reached that state of polite
almost lady-like coma in which Sylvester found
her most tolerable. For then she hardly spoke;
indeed she was very peaceful and quiet in

liquor and annoyed nobody nor even demanded Love.

Why then should Jessica look upon this quiet interval with eyes of passionate gloom and why should she explain to Sylvester when he came and sat beside her the Evil and the Folly of women drinking.

"You and Jane will have to start putting things in each other's coffee," he said. For if Jessica could be tiresome and boring, then so could he.

But he saw she was in earnest. She sat twisting her great white hands (their painted nails had an obscene quality half flower half animal) together in her lap—the disarming thing about Jessica was the way in which she could produce suddenly a domestic and pathetic attitude of mind and body, such as a terror of the urge to drink, in the middle of his party—and a lap which would not have disgraced the black silk apron of a long dead housekeeper, in a Molyneux gown.

He wondered if this was the first approach of that inevitable storm which must end this curious friendship. Surely he saw a storm coming, the sky growing black and the leaves turned to a still and icy green against its darkness. Was he to be the first to hear Jessica really break forth upon the subject of Jane? What lovely words might he now gather up and keep for his private entertainment for that lovely Piece of which he would never deliver himself—not to the pen, not to the rarest friend, not for Gold—well, perhaps for *much* Gold. No. No. Never. These confidences, which he labelled with delight "Sacred and Girlish" were his own, alone and forever.

But Jessica was taking altogether too wide a view of the Drink Evil; he would endure her a little longer, but she must narrow her subject matter down to Jane and the evil effects of drink on Jane, not on a million Janes. "But now look," he said, "at Jane."

Suddenly looking anew as it were on Jane, not just seeing her mildly, he felt almost wounded by his pity for her, poor girl, as she lay on his divan, silver and bark geometrically woven in its fabric. In the mild square lighting of his room her crooked face was as though drowned in water and quite at peace. He looked at Jane as he had directed Jessica and back again on Jessica, on her consuming eyes. He felt supremely concerned for Jane, a concern which filled his mind almost to the exclusion of the hope that Jessica might pour forth to him the first fine torrents of her abuse of Jane.

"I can't bear to see her like that," Jessica went on, "half asleep—half drunk. It disgusts me. Why, I'd rather see her dead, I think." And with this she picked up a bottle of Tonic Water and made menacing gestures with it across the room at Jane.

Jane just had time to scream: "Now, Jessica,

don't you throw that bottle at me—'' when Sylvester, sitting still in a kind of entrancement from
which he could not even rouse himself in time
to catch Jessica's upthrown arm (and she had
been a noted bowler at Heather Close in her
schooldays) saw the crash of broken glass and
heard Jane scream: "Oh—you're *horrible* to me,"
as she bowed her bleeding head upon his divan.

Sylvester's friends were very polite people and
paid but little attention to this scene (although
there was not one of them who did not cherish
his impression of it). They continued to play
cards, drink, eat and talk while Jessica and
Sylvester supported Jane towards Sylvester's
bedroom, and onwards then towards the bathroom, for two of his guests were having a quiet
talk in his bedroom and Jane after murmuring,
"Oh, you *horrible* boys," staggered on to the
bathroom.

Here Jessica bathed her forehead. There was
a shallow cut slanting up under her hair and
bleeding profusely from the splinter of glass which
had struck her. Jessica's aim was not so good
as in the days when the full pitches she bowled
had been the terror of Heather Close adversaries
in the cricket field. She stopped bathing Jane's
head to tell Sylvester about this. Sylvester, who
could not bear the sight of blood curdling in
water, sat swaying backwards and forwards on
the edge of his square green bath. He was feeling

slightly sick, partly from the sight of Jane's nasty blood and partly from his understanding of that fierce instinct to cherish that Jessica—drunken, pallid and tender—displayed now as she sponged Jane's head with his favourite sponge; dreadfully protective where five minutes ago she had been to all intents and purposes a murderess. He preferred her, he thought, in the swift committal of her *crime passionnel*.

Peroxide, lint, bandages, he had to find them all in turn; and there sat Jane in the coral light of this hot green room, a bath towel fastened about her neck like a man at his barber's, her crooked mouth a little open and her whole attitude as drained of emotion as that of any woman at the conclusion of a blood quarrel with her mate. It was unbearable. But it was none of his business. Jessica would undoubtedly kill Jane before she quarrelled with her. But that was nothing to do with him. Jane might be a lot better dead, anyhow —the dreary little Piece. But that it seemed was for Jessica to decide—Jessica who said: "Sit there, my sweet, while I find our coats and then I'll take you home."

When Jessica had gone he said swiftly, although it was none of his business: "It's nothing to do with me, Jane, I know—but she'll kill you some day."

"Yes," Jane agreed, "she's horrible to me."

"But does she often throw bottles at you?"

"Oh, Sylvester, her temperaments are certainly horrible. I'm very devoted to Jessica, I love having her around, but I'm scared to death she'll kill me."

"But, Jane, you are a fool to go on living with her. Your husband even wasn't such a devastating companion."

"Ah," said Jane, "he was kind of disheartening to live with. I got sort of low-spirited always looking at him. Now Jessica—although she's horrible to me—she's a real live woman. Why, Sylvester, last week she threw such a temperament she just smashed all the china in the bathroom and then she lay and bit the bath till she broke a tooth in it—naturally she did, for my bath is a unique alabaster bath. You've seen it, Sylvester? Well, your bath is nice, you know, but mine's a very lovely bath . . ."

The return of Jessica put a stop to any further confidences and as Sylvester watched her lapping Jane in her coat and taking her away from his party he felt unwarrantably vexed. And why should he feel vexed, for it was none of his business. Not if Jessica drew a revolver from her sac and shot Jane with appropriate words: "Smile, Baby, for the last time, Smile!" and then drove Jane's expensive corpse about in Jane's expensive car till she found a convenient spot to dump it, would it be Sylvester's business. No, he would not become involved.

So resolving, Sylvester returned to his party which he found much as when he had left it. Standing at the door of the square green room (baths or rooms Sylvester liked them square and green) he gazed upon his party for a little while. Standing there fascinated him. It was like reading about somebody else's party in a book, or seeing a party on the stage. But these people seemed to him thinner, more unreal than the stage; like lovely photographs of people, they grouped themselves so dramatically, presenting such fantastic contrasts and inconceivable prototypes of Fiction in Life.

Old Veronica now, her ageless face and lovely hair, while her very bones seemed to him to creak because she was so old, so old, so weary and so untired of this contest. There she sat playing at cards, and Hubert, her love, sat playing opposite to her; Hubert with his almost auburn hair and eyelashes, fifteen guineas a time, low over his green eyes that looked blindly out on a world that misunderstood so much yet yielded so much. What, Sylvester wondered, did that hungry, creaking old Veronica find in him, Hubert, that she must bind him to her by platinum watch-chains and diamond links, and God knows what besides?

And Blanche and Stephen were playing cards with them. Why had he asked Blanche and Stephen to this party? They were so fantastically contrasted with most of the other guests. He had pitied Blanche caught in that mood of Jessica's which must net some listener to her—any victim sufficing. Now he envied her as she and Stephen sat opposite to each other losing money to Veronica and Hubert, but with that about them of which no two thieves might rob them.

Blanche, so tall and quiet and so unamusing. He saw her in the setting in which he knew her best—riding confidential hunters over an Irish country, playing very family bridge after dinner; her father, that old falcon of a general, conducting heavy post-mortems over every hand when it was played. He saw her with her dogs, very sweet, loving them without affectation; and with her young friends, so like herself: Brown hair. Brown eyes. Clean fun, and not much fun. Yes, that was true, but did it matter? The more shadowy impersonal angles from which Sylvester looked at life were brittle and fine to the danger of their complete extinction. One false word and Sylvester's fun was forever gone from him, or at any rate not to be re-captured for that hour.

But Blanche and Stephen had more, more than he and Hubert and Veronica and Jessica and Jane and all the rest of them had ever lost—for they had never had it.

Blanche had Stephen and Stephen had Blanche. They actually loved and put their trust in each other. They would marry and Blanche would

follow him to Egypt and to India (for he was a
soldier) and watch him play polo (he was a notable
polo player). Returning once in three years for a
season's hunting she would be unable to hunt
because of the child she was bearing him (Sylvester
was determined to see Blanche's fate at its darkest
and its happiest.) Uncomplaining—probably re-
joicing—she would bring forth many of these
children and rear them up towards the same
solidity of truth and happiness which she would
know all her life provided she was never so unlucky as to become for one moment the victim
of her own cynicism or her own despair.

How well it was, Sylvester considered, that there
were still many many copies of the Blanche and
Stephen picture in the world and even among his
own circle of acquaintances. He felt overwhelmed
by an enormous sense of their value. Yet the
thought of them caused him to reel with a vast
boredom. One could admire them, but one could
never compete with their company.

He looked almost with relief over to old Lady
Bracken. How he adored to see an old woman
really well made up and really well dressed. It
was as exciting to him as the flight of a bird. White
hair, a silver dress and pearls—the loveliest piece
of decoration. She was queen of all the jewelled
fishes in his green aquarium. So he saw his party
now a little distorted as though seen through water
—or, clearer still, gin—they were poised as though

hung on threads—like those fish sold outside Lords
(and other places too, of course). Yes, they thought
themselves free of his aquarium and of their own
lives, never perceiving the threads of their movements were gathered up and hitched to some reel
of fate or accident that held them prisoners in
its devices or, more terrible, in its lack of device,
proportion or purpose.

For why should Jane—poor silly—not be as
happy as Blanche? as serene as Blanche, thanking
Heaven (on a full stomach) for a Good Man's
Love? Why contrarily should she be loved and
bullied and perhaps even murdered by that frightful Jessica? Surely the thread of her fate might
be snipped, as with nail scissors, so that she could
swim away in time, back to the warm mud-flat
of domesticity.

Well, it was none of his business.

He had forgotten George Playfair. It was in
George's reluctant arms that Jane had laid her
body down overcome by the peace that came to
her through brandy. And it was George who
stood before him now—that beautiful elegant
man. George who was Blanche's friend and
Stephen's friend—who for the last week had sat
by Blanche's side while she (wrapped cosily in a
fur coat against the July weather) had watched
Stephen play his glorious part in swift games of
polo, her very soul quickening as she watched
him. George had come to his party to-night with

Blanche and Stephen. He was Stephen's best friend and liked to assume a certain mysterious nobility of character, a stern repression of untold tenderness in his relationship with Blanche. For George had loved her too. She was a sweet girl and many besides George had loved her.

But luckily for George (and Sylvester advisedly used the word "luckily") he had not discovered for himself the nature of his need until she was irrevocably another's. That she should be Stephen's, Stephen's—his best friend's—was so fittingly in keeping with the situation that Sylvester almost envied George. For is there anything in life more absorbing than faintly unhappy love? Love in which the imagination rules the senses, in which there never has been nor ever can be any purpose or actuality, only a faint unease and lovely sense of loss. In the days of his loving Sylvester would have envied George his spiritual situation. Even now he could realise with distress how wasted its nicer values were upon him.

Imagine then his sense of shock when George stood before him, a whisky and soda in one hand and a cigarette in the other, and he heard George's charming voice asking him with solid intention and interest, which was with him the nearest thing to excitement, Jane's name, Jane's address and, in fact, all Sylvester could tell him about Jane.

No doubt some cruder souls are incapable of

appreciation when their situation is one from which the finer pleasures derive. Nothing in Sylvester's former knowledge of George Playfair could lead him to suppose George guilty of any subtlety in the spending of his emotions. Sylvester, though, was an optimist over his friends. Their crudity seldom failed to disappoint him.

George and Sylvester had known and mildly liked each other from childhood's happy hours, through boyhood's days and so on up to virile manhood. For George had so far excelled Sylvester in all manly forms of sport as Sylvester had excelled George in the finer subtleties of life. Now he answered George's questions about Jane with a tender reserve so far as Jane was concerned, for she was a poor thing and unique, so Sylvester felt tenderly towards her and cared not at all whether George entangled himself for good or ill in Jane's peculiar life.

"She is a lovely girl," he said, "and her rich husband is no more. She has a lovely flat, and as for the dark girl who threw the bottle at her, she has a wild playful nature—just a hot-blooded girl."

"Hot-blooded?" George interrupted. "Do you think so, Sylvester? I should have said she was rather a prude. Well, fancy throwing a bottle at a friend just because you think she's going too far. And she wasn't—going too far, I mean. She was lying like a child——"

"Yes, yes," Sylvester interrupted him hastily. One must remember that George was a Playfair and a Catholic and a man's man. One must remember that he seldom came to London—only on occasions when his best friends were playing in international polo matches and his late loves watched them (and never a dry eye as they watched) or after the Gunner meeting at Sandown —for George, before he came into his inheritance in Co. Westcommon, had been a member of that Royal Regiment of Artillery.

Anyhow his ideas were simple and often indeed nearer the truth than other people's. Let him be left with them. So: "Yes, yes," Sylvester said. "I have a great *affection* for Jane."

"I liked her, Sylvester," George said. "I thought there was something very sweet and sincere about her. I liked the way she went home with that awful woman even after she'd hurled a bottle at her."

"Yes, Jane has a sweet nature," Sylvester admitted agreeably. "You must go and see her. She has a lovely flat," and he gave George Jane's address and every encouragement to pursue the matter farther. For though Jane had asked George to come and see her she had in the confusion consequent on Jessica's outbreak of temper forgotten to tell him her name or where she lived.

Thus Sylvester made his escape from George without disturbing any of George's nicer feelings

as a Playfair and an honourable man. For what
was the use? How explain to him that Jane's
husband and lovers and passionate friends were as
unreal as she? For first George would have had to
learn a whole new language of life and having
learnt it he would still have found Sylvester's
explanation of Jane unsatisfying. Antichrist, that
was how Jane typified all that she was to George
could George have understood about her. A thing
of the Groves. Unclean. Incredible. Yes, that
was how George would have thought of poor Jane
—and why should Sylvester encourage anybody to
think rudely of anybody else? The violence and
stupidity of men like George he found peculiarly
tiring. He saw George moving off down the
stream of the party—he would tell Blanche and
Stephen he was leaving and then he would come
back and say "good-night" to Sylvester. He would
thank him, and say, When are you coming over to
stay in Westcommon again? Hester and Piggy
are mad to see you.

It happened as he foresaw, and Sylvester
answered: "Well, I was over there fishing in
April and there was no water in the river. Also
I do so passionately repent my folly in having
given them such a very expensive and powerful
wireless set last Christmas. As their cousin and a
rich author I should have been wiser to have
given them each a rich jewel, a yacht or a mink
tie. I love staying with them and now I have

made the place impossible for myself, I regret it enormously."

"All the same," George slanted his head and smiled knowingly, "you will be over in the autumn. And I will give you the old horse and you will come out cub-hunting when hounds meet at nine o'clock. Not earlier.

"The country is in great order now," said George. "A rich man can do a lot in three seasons if he puts his mind to it. The coverts—you remember Carnarogue? Every old goat and every tinker's ass in the country wandering through it, and the gorse about a mile high? He cut it and fenced it and there's a nice snug bit of covert grown up in it now."

Yes, Sylvester remembered Carnarogue. Wild gorse on each steep side of a narrow glen. A black and high-banked little river ran down the bottom of Carnarogue. But now he saw the way out where the water spread wide and shallow—lean cattle had made a path down here for drinking. Here there is a dust of gold in the gorse the darkest day in December, and excitement is a gold cry in the wind and danger a crown . . . Such thoughts were rude and fit only for some hysterical Irish novelist writing her seventy thousand words through which the cry of hounds reverberates continuously: where masters of hounds are handsome and eligible men and desirable young girls over-ride hounds continually, seeing brilliant hunts on incredible three-year-olds: and all—after even the hardest day—are capable of strong emotion at night.

No. This was Sylvester's party—"He has a damn *beautiful* pack of hounds," George said now. And this entirely upset Sylvester again with his plans for spiritual composure—for how could any poet have conveyed more explicitly than George such severity of beauty as George conveyed in those few serious words—lovely, speedy, dangerous words. Sylvester both saw and heard beauty and speed, speed and beauty through the words, and here and now they conveyed too rude an emotion. Such ideas unbalanced his polite and fragile way of living. He cared too much about them. Gentle, charming, unsafe creature that he was, Sylvester's dearest likings were unsafe within himself. To admit his enthusiasms destroyed him —or at any rate the admission of his real enthusiasms. To be unashamedly romantical is to be too accessible to others. One must preserve one's own. So Sylvester smiled inattentively and shook his head.

It was all too remote from his party and from here and now. Besides he fully intended to be in Ireland by the end of the present week. For he was tired, just a tired old quag with his poor mind wound up like a mechanical mouse. He wondered if this dreary party he had made and called into being would ever end. How he pitied

himself and his folly and how he wished there
were more people like George who would go away
from parties when they were not wanted. Who
did not understand anything with a bitter and
pitiful comprehension but took the Janes and the
Jessicas and the Huberts and all the other "horrible
boys"—Jane called them—as they were to him and
not as they were themselves.

But now Sylvester, looking upon his friends, felt
within himself how their feet were set for ever in
a salty and burning desert (although a moment
ago he had seen them as fish swimming on the
threads of chance). Their faces were in the
shadow of Death and Sin. Deathlike were their
faces and hollow their laughter and their jokes
such thin, unhearty wit ever dependent on a gross
unkindness. Sylvester sometimes bought painted
flowers for the decoration of his room. Some stood
in a vase now, lilies painted green, and copper
lilies. They were as boring as his friends really,
and equally decorative, but now he found them
hateful. He found himself thinking passionately
of mountains unseen in the rain, of ugly roads
and drenched sheep. He delighted in the rich
sentimentality of his thoughts. Almost he felt his
exile from such rural scenes to be compulsory
upon him and this engendered a romantic longing
in his thoughts of them and induced a further
dislike of those who now surrounded him. Must
he for ever endure their antics, their praise of his

work and their immediate perception and bitter derision of his failure. Yes. He knew that so long as he lived his present life of expensive simplicity —and to be truly simple life must be exceedingly expensive—he must endure their appreciation or their pity. Here was his work and here was good money. He was not fool enough, not single enough of purpose, to leave it. He did not really want to leave it—that was it. In reality he was as great a play-actor as any of them and as afraid to be alone. To be alone without any defence from oneself is—unless one is genuine past all conceits —is to be defeated or undone. What is really one-self is so slight, so impotent, so vulgar a spirit. It is only the thing one has become that sees the awfulness of the thing one was. But what I have become, Sylvester thought, is not what I am. I am afraid—afraid for my small endeavours, for the vulgar and frail cleverness of my writings. Some day my craft will betray me. I am so full of pretences. Would that I were as George or Stephen or Blanche. Would that I were at peace, or in difficulties, or in love. My life is the reflection of water in water, as vague, as unstable and as lost and untrue.

Wholly possessed as his mind was by these reflections Sylvester still contrived to move brightly and gaily about his party. Well, perhaps neither gaily nor brightly, but more an inducer of these states in others. For those who most

frequently acclaimed Sylvester's acid wit and
biting humour were those to whose own sprightly
imaginings Sylvester was so gracefully responsive.

At last they dispersed, the gay and the sad, the
drunk and the sober, leaving him with words of
gratitude for his lovely party—rattling empty
words, death-like faces, and creaking bones.

He adored the absolute complacency of his own
revulsion from them. He revelled in his dislike
of Hubert's stilled young face, his two inches of
eyelash stiffened with a cosmetic so that they
stood out clear from his eyes. He realised
Veronica's scent in a sudden wave of dislike. Her
smooth ageless face disgusted his mind. She asked
him to lunch with her on Thursday. A new place
she'd discovered. So amusing. Good-bye, Sylvester. It's been such a lovely party.

"Good-night, Sylvester—Lovely. Lovely. I have
enjoyed myself," Hubert followed her out.

So they all went away. Old Lady Bracken was
so drunk she just went out rattling her pearls
and muttering: "Filthy crowd of people, absolutely
filthy. Can't *think* why I came here to-night."
Stephen and Blanche, looking at her and hearing
her, obviously thought the same although too
sober and polite to say so. And so indeed he knew
did everybody think who had come to his party,
but such it was to be rotten and deathlike. The
last man he said good-night to—and he was such
a clever dress designer, he had dressed most of

Sylvester's new show—had bad teeth. Very bad,
Sylvester noticed and he thought: "Filthy man!
Why did I ask him here?" And he knew that the
death and the rot were in himself too. He was
part of it.

He could not at this moment think of any one
of his friends for whom he had an honest liking,
and he was so tired, so miserably tired. Now he
must put his room in order before he went to
bed. Sylvester always did this himself; reducing
the unfriendly chaos existing after a party to his
own particular order produced a sense of dignified
restraint within himself.

He set his two Hepplewhite chairs against the
wall with loving exactitude; gathered up the
stray empty glasses with loathing and put them
in the dining-room; beat up his cushions in the
most housewifely manner imaginable; put the
two Battersea boxes that held cigarettes facing
one another upon his mantleshelf; the gramophone
records in a neat and shining pile—the two he
enjoyed most playing at the moment on the top—
then, satisfied that his room had assumed its
habitual cistern-like calm, he went to the door
to turn off the lights.

His hand was on the switch when, with wicked
and insistent uproar, his telephone began to ring.
Sylvester picked up the receiver thinking as he
did so of the dramatic possibilities of a one-
sided telephone conversation. The idea of it

always excited him on the stage or in a book. But in real life it was less frequently dramatic. Now this could only be some careless girl who had left a diamond brooch behind her. But fancy ringing up at this hour about it. Inhuman.

"*Yes*," said Sylvester, wearily, disgustedly.

"Oh, is that you, Sylvester?"

"*Yes.*"

"Oh, Sylvester—Jessica's been so horrible to me—I'm scared to death."

"What's she done now?" Sylvester saw a vision of Jane being held under the bath water till she drowned—Jane having her throat cut with the blade of a safety razor—Jessica grunting like an animal as the blood spurted forth. (*Does* blood spurt when a throat is cut? or is it just a dismal trickle?) Jessica, her murdering over, spent and cold. Sylvester saw it all, for he was incurably and insatiably romantic, strive as he would towards cynical unconcern.

"Oh, she's tough," Jane whimpered down the telephone. "Oh, she beat me. She just threw me around the place—the nasty rough piece."

"But why are you ringing me up now to tell me about it, my poor child?"

"Oh, Sylvester, I just wanted sympathy. Whatever can a girl do?"

"I should leave her before she kneels on you and cuts your throat. Or wrings your neck—I think I'd wring your neck if I were she," Sylvester added thoughtfully. He heard Jane scream—a faint excited scream.

"But I *have* left her, Sylvester—Why, here I am right out in the cold telephoning to you from a filthy public call box. I was so frightened I just put on a fur coat and ran right away."

"Well, what are you going to do now?" Sylvester was pleasantly surprised in Jane. That she should have produced moral courage in a quantity sufficient to enable her to run away from Jessica, even temporarily, was surprising to him. So ungenuine was she that he more than doubted whether she could even feel genuine physical fear. He must encourage her. Poor child. Alone in the dawn in a public call box. What a situation. He cleared his throat.

"Are you going to a hotel?"

"Why, no. I'll say Jessica'll have gotten over her temperament by now. I'll go along home again."

But the idea of such a meek return of the lamb to the shambles both devastated and nauseated Sylvester's sense of the occasion. An escape is after all an escape and does not happen every day. One must make the most of it.

"You can't go back to her," Sylvester spoke dictatorially into his mouthpiece. "Go to a hotel—you may even come here if you like."

"Oh, *Sylvester*, why I'd just love that—*Jessica*, you leave down that telephone—*Oh*, let go of my arm!—Oh, you're *horrible* to me——'' That was what Sylvester heard coming surprisingly indeed to his ear. Now there really would be trouble, with Jessica swooping, a bold hawk, through the dawn, on this poor squalling pigeon. Sylvester waited for the sound of a revolver shot that would settle Jane once and for all. Indeed and truly he would not have been surprised to hear it.

But what he did hear was Jessica's voice saying: "Go back to bed, Jane—you fool. You'll catch cold standing about in your chemise like that——" Jessica harsh and possessive but certainly not murderous in intent. And why should one stand in a public call box in one's chemise? A dark suspicion of Jane filled Sylvester's mind.

"Jessica," he said softly, "is that Jessica speaking? Where are you speaking from, Jessica?"

"Oh, Sylvester? Yes, it's Jessica speaking now. Well, where should I be speaking from? From the flat, of course. I've just sent Jane back to bed. What did you ring her up about?"

"I wondered," Sylvester answered, "whether it was *her* rich jewel that I found in my bed. A diamond brooch—a lovely wheat ear design. Is it yours?"

"No," Jessica snapped. "Good-night."

Sylvester hung up his receiver. What a disgusting little exhibitionist Jane was. What suggested these antics to her mind? This was not the first time she had lied extravagantly that she might gull him into a state of excited belief in some imminent personal danger to herself. It was an inversion of that diseased sympathy which revels in the sight, even in the infliction of pain on others, he supposed. The strange part of the matter was that there was not, to Sylvester's mind, the least doubt but that Jane did stand in some quite real danger from Jessica's violent passions. But why should he care? He felt quite nauseated as he recollected with what enthusiasm he had just offered her an asylum here in his own rooms. Terrible to think that even now she might be here, bundling out of her car in the dark; bouncing into his rooms, swaddled in the fur coat, reft from a camphor incarceration to substantiate her tale, and crying raucously: "Oh, Sylvester, I feel just *horrible*. Fix me a brandy and soda."

It was all too much for Sylvester. He felt disgusted and out-worn. Even as a Thing Jane could interest him no longer. He did not mind how soon Jessica killed her. He did not even want to hear what she should say about Jane if she should leave her. Jane was a bad nut. A shapely filbert, your tooth crashed through it easily to the dry rotten fibres inside. So dull. So boring. Not even rude.

Stripped now of all defence and of all seeming, let us consider Sylvester. One must not be harsh to him, nor must an author betray too great a knowledge, nor too one-sided an enthusiasm for

the person and character of his hero. This was
a rule which Sylvester himself had endeavoured
to follow in his books and in his plays, until one
day he found that in event only were his characters
betrayed, and as for their persons—there was never
a direct and vulgar description in the entire length
of a book. In phrases descriptive of action, yes.
Here was a trick through which a portrait might
with more subtlety be conveyed. Thus:

"Oliver lit a cigarette, his precise, ugly hands
so slow and careful over the matter that Patience
could have screamed out her disgust of him—
'Darling, I want to talk to you.' His voice and
his hands were the same—exact, incapable of
change. It was absurd to hate a man because his
voice and the shape of his hands no longer excited
you ... "Well, there you had the shape of his
hands and the sound of his voice and one had
avoided, "He had ugly hands and a dull voice.
He sat down beside her on the sofa. 'Darling,' he
said, 'I want to talk to you.' She could have
screamed: 'Oh, go *away*, you dreary ass. I don't
want to talk to you. Leave me alone——'"

Who observed or cared whether by the last or
the first phrase they learnt these things about
dreary Oliver and temperamental Patience?

To look at Sylvester was like nothing so much
as the eldest son in a Conversation Piece. You
know, the melancholy young man who has long
found fun in the village but a dismal distraction.

He occupies an important position in the fore-
ground of the picture, toying with his fowling
piece or his spaniel's soft ears. Sylvester's face
too was pale and sad and well suited to its habitual
expression of hurrying from any grave issue, unkind truth, or unpleasant decision. There was too
much thin space and too little determination of
outline between Sylvester's high cheek bones and
his long chin. Only his eyes, his dark sentimental
eyes, betrayed a gentleness of mind past any power
of his own unkindness to confound. Out of a sort
of self-defence Sylvester could be dreadfully unkind to the harmless, tiresome people who annoyed
or aggravated him, just as he was moved to absurd
lengths in his passion of protectiveness towards
them—witness this incident which had so nearly
caused him to welcome that posturing little
strumpet Jane back to his flat—and he as tired
as any dog. But to continue the frank and un-
decorated catalogue of Sylvester's appearance: he
was of middle height, gracefully made, with charming hands and feet, abnormally long and pointed
ears, which, with the addition of a short and
slightly flattened nose, gave some terrible people
an excuse to describe his appearance as "Puckish."
This shocking adjective distressed Sylvester in-
ordinately. It is not too much to say that for a
lengthy period of time it quite destroyed his calm.
His voice had no quality in it of which one could
take hold, saying: "What an ugly or what a charm-

ing voice!" It was uncertain, at times affected
and yet forever betraying him with some damned
unintended inflection into a shade of meaning
that he did not mean or had not realised he meant
until he heard it in his own voice. He had no
concentration of mind. That was Sylvester's chief
complaint against himself. He knew his plays
were bad and he knew his books were worse and
this grieved him. He could not stand away from
them accepting only the fact that they made him
good money—such quantities of money as are only
to be earned by the very good or the very popular.
No, he must put pieces of himself in them, undone
by his enthusiasm—pieces which terrified him first
by their goodness and shocked him then by their
nakedness—disgusted and heated him to nausea
and then belonged to him no more. He would
pretend blatantly about all this, pointing out one
of these dreadful pieces that were really him and
saying: "Such camp, my dear, *Lovely.*" "Now
there's an entrancing bit of trollopes for you—"
"My dear, that went with a *swing*—such *applause*—
Not a dry *eye* in the house—" and so on. Thus
he would destroy himself and persuade himself
that the truth was not in him. And if it was he
would betray it, he would not let it betray him.

But now Sylvester was asleep, lapped in crêpe-
de-chine sheets like a blonde film star. For he
loved such warm and soft and pretty things.

CHAPTER II

JESSICA stood at the foot of Jane's bed and regarded Jane sleeping.

This was the morning after Sylvester's party and Jessica felt neither very well nor very kindly disposed towards Jane.

The sun was shining warmly into the room, lighting the limp silver curtains and silvery stripped wood and searching in a deadly and accurate way into the bunch of false lilies bought in the same shop where Sylvester had bought his. There was no height in Jane's bedroom. Everything squatted on the floor. The dressing table was about twelve inches high and the stool where Jane sat to make up her face about six inches high. Her bed seemed to be made up really on the floor itself. It had oval ends, had cost the earth and was, as a matter of fact, exceedingly comfortable. A mass of small stools squatted about here and there. There were also quantities of bottles of scent in boxes of black and silver cubistic designs and shapes. Jane used buckets of scent in a year. She did everything with it except drink it. Well, she always said she didn't drink it, but she may quite likely have quaffed off an odd nip in a tooth glass. It was the sort of thing she would do and keep quiet about. There was a time when Jane filled her room with toys—

wide-skirted dolls, sad dogs, rude monkeys, but
Jessica had stopped that, no more vulgar play-
things now, and indeed Jane did not much mind.
As an affectation her toys had been rather a
nuisance. And took up too much room. How
she had once played her toy game for Sylvester's
benefit! But not one of his heroines had gone all
elfin and girlish over a teddy bear in consequence—
not one. It was hard work getting into Sylvester's
books, but Jane meant to do it some day or other.

Still Jessica stood and regarded the sleeping
Jane. Jessica's dark hair was cut with a charming
severity. If her dark face had been less heavy
and turbulent in expression Jessica would almost
have succeeded in looking as hard and boyish as
she hoped she looked. But this plan of hers had
been spoilt by God in the beginning, for He had
given her a positive bosom and massive thighs.
She was a heavy-minded woman too, without
much gaiety of spirit. It was typical of her to
break china and bite baths in moments of stress,
so did she grind her teeth into life and with as
little satisfaction to herself.

Now she felt evilly disposed towards Jane lying
there with a lead-coloured cosmetic peeling off her
face like half dry cement. The bandage on her
head reminded Jessica of last night's affray. Jane
had behaved really monstrously last night.
Stupidly drunk she'd been, not a bit amusing.

Jessica folded her dressing-gown severely about

her and knotted its belt. She had bought it from her tailor in Savile Row. Red silk with white spots and a scarf to match—this for the concealment of the hirsute virility of the male. Then she shook Jane's bed until Jane woke up. Her yawns widened the cracks in the cement on her face. She looked very ill and unattractive.

"How awful you look, darling," Jessica said as soon as she thought Jane was wide enough awake to be annoyed by what she said. "Do you feel terrible, or do you only look like that?"

"Oh, Jessica," Jane moaned, "fix me a brandy and soda. I feel *horrible*."

"Oh, God! Don't let's have any of your sickening after-the-party reactions," Jessica stormed. "You were beastly drunk last night and you're not sober yet. Can't you *say* so and leave it *alone*. Don't mess at a thing."

"I'll say I feel very sick," Jane said weakly, "... sea-sick ..." Oh, how terrible she would say she felt. A pain in her head and sick in every nerve. If Jessica didn't stop pretty soon she would be sick too, though more from spite than necessity. What Jane required was some one to Mother her. Some one to Fix her a brandy and soda and a Cachet Faivre. Some one to draw the curtains and shut out every chink of light—rather than opening them to the unkind sun. Some one to pad about and pull up the eiderdown and pat a girl on the back—a "there-there" atmosphere in fact was

what she required, instead of Jessica going on
anyhow. And wearing a dressing-gown like that
—she'd get herself talked about soon. Jane roused
herself from her queasy lethargy to tell Jessica
this.

"My God! You are filthy——" Jessica became
really pale with anger. "Is nothing clean to you—
absolutely nothing? I mean, there are some things
in life sharp and clean still; must you have your
dirty joke about them—*must* you?" She turned
away from Jane's bed with deliberate disgust.
"I'm going out to buy some moss roses," she bit
her words in rather than spoke them out.

"*Darling*, don't leave me. I'm sorry. You know
you were horrible to me——" But Jessica had
gone and Jane was left alone, which she hated.

Why buy moss roses, anyhow? They were
wickedly expensive and smelt of turpentine. Why
not buy Madam Butterfly if you wanted a bunch
of roses? Then you had a bunch of roses that
looked well, real well. Jane did not mind expense
provided she got what she wanted—or what some
one else had wanted first, but had not been able
to afford—for her money. But she was just beginning to feel a little restive over Jessica's way of
expending vast sums on undecorative and short-
lived bunches of flowers when yellow carnations
would last twice the length of time; or on odd and
ugly pieces of china which she was more than
liable to smash in one of her temperamental

storms. Woolworth china would have done as well
for that.

Had Jessica but guessed it Jane was, after six
months of it, on the edge of wondering what,
anyhow, she still saw for herself in this difficult
and passionate friendship beyond the fact that
she paid and Jessica talked. However, this was
no moment in which to ask herself such awkward
questions with such obvious answers. Jane subsided once more into torpor beneath the bedclothes, breathing a half-conscious sigh of relief
as she heard Jessica bang the door of the flat on
her departure.

One thing Jane could do well and that was
sleep. All through her unattractive and over-fed
childhood she had slept off the effects of too much
rich food and too much artificial excitement.
Through sleep she had survived the more curious
girlish excitements of her schooldays; and sleep
too had been a great help to her in her marriage
with that rich but unimaginative American Citizen
whose only enthusiasm was diving. He had died,
five years previous to the writing of this story of
Jane, in his favourite diving bell—the apparatus
which enables the diver to breathe having failed.
Jane wired to his mother: "Denver passed peace-
fully away this afternoon," and followed up her
wire by a letter in which she softened the horrid
details down as much as possible. In fact, an
impersonal reader of her letter might almost have

gathered from it that Denver was rather to be envied this fatal mishap. And with this those who knew Jane best might have agreed.

Anyhow after she had collected her considerable widow's portion, Jane had returned to Europe—Europe where she had had such fun in her finishing school, Europe of her happy girlhood—and here she rented a flat, and there a sunny villa, and somewhere else an old-world manor house. But the sanitation of the last never quite came up to her best American standards. She drank a lot and slept a lot, never ceased to struggle her way towards Sylvester's books and plays, and between her lovers and her girl friends her emotional life was far from uneventful. Nor was her social life any duller than a girl's need be provided she can pay for the amusement, food and drink of others as well as for her own.

Jane was sitting up in bed drinking weak china tea and lemon (for she did not really drink brandies and sodas quite as often as she asked for them) and melting Cachets Faivre in a teaspoon when her telephone bell rang.

"A gentleman rang up at ten o'clock, madam, but I told him you were still asleep. He said he'd ring up later." Albert, the nasty boy who looked after Jane and Jessica with praiseworthy efficiency, continued to lay out Jane's clothes in a neat pattern on a chair—vest, brassière, suspender belt, stockings, he took mild pleasure in the arrangement of these pretty things, and listened with interest to the onesided conversation. The gentleman who had rung up earlier had sounded nearly as imperative as one of those screaming girl friends of Mrs. Barker's or Miss Houpe-Boswell's—Mrs. Barker and Miss Houpe-Boswell were Jane and Jessica.

"Hullo—Yes, speaking. Yes, Jane Barker speaking—Oh, Mr. Playfair—Yes, how nice—Why, it's very, very sweet of you—I adore a polo game—Oh, *this* afternoon—Oh, *this* afternoon—well, I can't do a thing about *this* afternoon—another day—oh, the what? Oh, the finals. Oh I see—And your boy-friend is playing——"

(*Another* of them, thought nasty Albert as he squeezed out the tooth paste).

"——Lunch with you?—My dear, I'd love to—Well, Hell, but I'm in bed—yes in *bed*—Going back home to the country to-night, are you?—Oh, this is certainly sad—Oh, listen, come and lunch here—A *horrible* picnic—No, I'd love having you—Please come—*Really*—Good-bye—No, *Honest*—One-fifteen, then—Good-bye."

"Oh, Albert," Jane whined, "there's a horrible boy coming to lunch. What can we have to eat?"

Albert slipped an emerald ring off his finger; he had been trying its lovely effect as he blew the powder off of the dressing table, and considered sourly.

"I don't know, madam, I'm sure," he said at

last. "We could have managed a nice little lunch
of course if we'd known a bit sooner."

"Oh, Albert, try to think. What are you paid
for, anyhow? Is Miss Houpe-Boswell in yet?"

"Said she'd be out to lunch, madam. Gave
orders you was to have a raw egg in a little brandy,
madam. But that won't do the gentleman,
madam."

"Well, what shall we have, Albert? It's after
twelve now."

Albert softened into a gracious consideration of
the matter. "Well, suppose I mix a nice cocktail,
madam. Then two nice portions of Foie-gras
nicely served with cress. Then a good ham
omelette, madam, it's a cold day, you know, and a
nice salad followed by a nice bit of Camembert,
p'raps—what'll you drink, madam?"

"Oh, I don't *know*. I'll have a brandy-and-soda.
You might try him with a bottle of that Hock Miss
Houpe-Boswell bought from her boy-friend. Nobody seems crazy about it. It never begins to look
like getting drunk. Well, I suppose I must get up
now."

"I *shouldn't*, not if I were you, madam. I'd rest
for ten minutes after taking all those Cachets
Faivre. I'll prepare your bath, madam, and I'll
fix you a nice brandy-and-soda and you'll be
feeling grand by lunch time."

"Shall I? Well, maybe you're right. Oh, Albert,
I'm feeling——"

"Madam may be feeling horrible at the moment," Albert pulled the curtains together and prepared to hurry away, "but she'll be feeling grand soon."

"Shall I? Well, maybe you're right." Jane subsided for her ten minutes further rest prescribed by Albert. Punctually at the end of ten minutes he returned with a double brandy and a syphon of soda water. Fortified by this, Jane retired to that ornate and vulgar bathroom which was the pride of her life.

The great feature of Jane's bathroom was that none of its furnishings looked at all as though they could fulfil the functions that one expects of the furniture of a bathroom. There was nothing obvious about them. They were a long series of carefully constructed disguises, and some of the happiest inspirations for their construction and decoration had been Sylvester's.

Thus the bath was not a bath at all but a shallow pink shell, its grooved radiations like mild Beleek china made kinder to the naked body by a movable lining of green sorbo moss. The other half of the shell was as it were opened backwards into the wall hollowed to fit it, and a concealed light from behind it shed a rosy glow down upon the bather. Sylvester had particularly played with the idea of Jessica stepping (after the Birth of Venus by Botticelli) from this shell. Of taps or plug there was no sign. Nothing so vulgar. The

uninitiated might search in vain for any means
of inflow or egress for the bath-water, which, as
a matter of fact, both welled up and ran out
through a species of navel concealed beneath the
sorbo moss—it all depended on which of the three
buttons in the wall behind you pushed in or pulled
out. So much for the bath, and no wonder Jane
was proud of it.

The walls of the bathroom were hung with
tightly stretched canvas on which a clever friend
of Jessica's had painted some very funny pictures.
There was a cosy-looking arm-chair in one corner
and on a small table beside it were four little
books: *Gems from Wilcox*, I., II., III. and IV.,
Poems of Love, Death, Hope, War. The raised
cameo-like profile of Miss Wilcox on their blue
bindings was strangely at variance with the wall
decorations. But contrast, Sylvester insisted, was
the chief thing in life. And as he had only discovered the little books after much trouble and
searching of bookshops, Jane was so touched and
excited by his gift that even Jessica did not quite
dare to tear them up and put them down the
privy, so artfully concealed in the entrails of the
arm-chair. For the rest, a basin was hidden in a
spinet and cosmetics behind looking-glass doors.
The floor (of green glass) had exotic lighting and
heating below it. Altogether, as bathrooms go, it
was not to be despised. Jessica might sigh in vain
for blacks and silvers and cubistic squares and

angles—Jane would have none of them and in this
Sylvester upheld her, for his happiest hours in the
flat were spent in the devising of new extravagant
concealments and decorations.

Restored and braced by her brandy and soda,
and familiar with all the intricacies of the bathroom, Jane was soon bathed and dressed and she
walked into her drawing-room not more than ten
minutes after her guest's arrival.

"You must forgive me, please," Jane said, "I'm
horribly late." She looked charming in her clever
brown dress with her face tidily made up, her
mouth freshly painted into its scar.

George Playfair, though he hardly knew it,
disliked the drab little faces of the healthy outdoor girls he saw day by day in Ireland. He would
have said now that it was a pity Jane should raddle
up her face like this, but he really thought it bright
and lovely.

Now she was pouring out cocktails. She looked
very like an expensive photograph, with those
Auratum lilies growing in a bronze pot behind her.
Just as well arranged.

George cleared his throat and asked her if she'd
attended Ascot. Jane shook her head and said she
thought racing was horrible, which caused George
to abandon his retrospection on the Derby and
also his summary of the form for the first July
meeting at Newmarket. He asked her if she was
going to Peterboro' Hound Show, which was

rather a silly question when he came to think of
it, but the Irish have their stock summer amusements in England and it seems strange to them
that the English residents should not universally
enjoy them.

At George's question about Peterboro' Jane
thought it was time to make a decided break
away from sport. She said: No. She was going
to France, and proceeded to tell him about her
villa, a very, very lovely place where you bathed
off the rocks, and lay on yellow mattresses or blue
mattresses in the sun. She told him what cars
she was bringing out and who should travel in
which, and who she wouldn't have on any account,
and many trivial details which could not concern
him but still quite absorbed him. No one is a
bore who tells of their own affairs with genuine
circumstance and detail and of their friends with
spitefulness.

As luncheon proceeded George abandoned more
general topics of sporting conversation and told
Jane with much circumstance and particularity
of his horses, yes, and of his dogs. And he told
her of them with such simple enthusiasm that
Jane heard him with something not unlike live
and unpretended interest. Though why she
should care that Sea Urchin must, handicapped
as well as he was, have an outside chance in the
two-mile chase at the Limerick August meeting,
she could not have said. "I hate flat racing," she

told George, "but I like jump meetings real well, if
the weather wasn't always cold, or if I could see
clear to the end of the track. They took me to the
Grand National once, and I'll say it was *horrible.*"

"But in Ireland——"George said, and he painted
a pretty picture of Irish race-meetings where the
summer sun glowed and mountains were blue and
there was hardly a meeting but the Curragh of
Kildare that confined its programme to the dreary
flat racing so disliked by Jane.

"——And you need never go to the Curragh," he
assured her; and Jane thought, No, most certainly
she never would go to the Curragh. But she
listened with pleasure to all this enthusiastic and
charming young man told her about outdoor sport
in that country whose Lady Novelists had never
yet succeeded in inspiring her with one spark of
interest in its picturesque disorder. Not that
they wrote for the cosmopolitan Janes, but their
lyrical outpourings might well have set alight one
more enthusiasm in her life.

At last, her mind a confusion of horses, hounds,
foxes and their furs (there was something dire and
sinister about the last) hospitable houses, turf
fires, warm weather, men in red coats, horses called
"patent safetys" (how easy they sounded) and
hunts called "rasping," Jane, slightly light-
headed in the thought of an escape from Jessica
and the idea of improving her acquaintance with
Mr. Playfair, said: "I used to ride horseback in

South America. Do you think I would enjoy a
Fox-hunt? I don't see why I wouldn't enjoy a
good Fox-hunt as much as any one."

There was soon no room for doubt in Jane's
mind but that fox-hunting, and in Ireland, was
the one bliss left untasted in her life, the one thrill
untried. Listening to the whirl of plans for her
benefit and convenience, should she come for the
winter to Ireland, Jane said: "Why shouldn't I
stay with you? I could keep a man and all of my
horses some place else if you couldn't manage
them."

But Mr. Playfair demurred at this. In fact he
seemed faintly embarrassed. Jane wondered what
the difficulty was. What skeleton he was conceal-
ing when he said that he was afraid it would
hardly do as he lived alone since his sister had
married some years ago. Jane had so long got
the better of any false prudery in her own nature
that she could scarcely conceive a normally
conventional outlook in any one else.

"I tell you what though—rather an idea,"
George leaned towards Jane and then sat quickly
back in his chair, faintly frightened as she leaned
too eagerly towards him. "I tell you what we
might arrange. You might P.G. with Sylvester's
old cousins at Kilque."

"Do you live near Sylvester?" Jane asked.
She had not taken that in before. It added still
more to her enthusiasm for outdoor sport in Ire-

land. Here was yet another angle from which to
exhibit herself to Sylvester. "Don't let's say a
word to him about my coming over," some instinct
of caution urged her to say, "He'll just *die* of
surprise when he sees me. It'll be a wonderful,
wonderful joke."

"But if old Hester and Piggy know, I don't see
how Sylvester is to avoid knowing too," George
objected. "You know, he lives with them when
he's in Ireland."

"Oh well, maybe I could rent a little house of
my own," Jane suggested, "that is if you've
really decided you can't have me for a lodger
yourself."

"You know I'd love to have you," George
assured her warmly, "only I'm afraid it simply
wouldn't do. People are rather old-fashioned in
their ideas in Co. Westcommon. I am myself,"
he added bravely.

Jane was neither surprised nor abashed. She
was able to accept almost any situation without
violent emotion. When he had said good-bye
with excited repetitions of plans for the future
and untold regrets that his secretaryship to the
local agricultural show forced him to return
immediately to Ireland, Jane was sorry. She sat
and thought about him for a few minutes. But
soon her enthusiasm for Ireland and sport left
her like a fickle tide. For all in a moment she felt
very ill, unaccountably and terribly ill. Pain and

sickness took hold on her and she thought, as
Albert telephoned for her doctor, what a dismal
place Ireland would be in which to feel as horrible
as she was feeling now.

Jane was terrified of pain and sickness and her
fear was not without cause for she had very little
strength of mind or body with which to combat
either.

Now that nasty Albert arranged her bed and
filled it with hot water bottles and then set himself by her telephone to call up all the friends
with whom Miss Houpe-Boswell might conceivably
be lunching that she might be apprised of Jane's
unhappy situation.

The doctor came at last, and before Jessica
returned he had installed a nurse in the flat and
pronounced Jane to be suffering from severe
alcoholic poisoning.

Then followed for Jane a period of misery, pain
and depression such as she had never known before, and knew she would never know again, for
of this sickness she would surely die. And even
beyond pain Jane feared Death. That Death
should come for her was a terror for which she
was not able, and in her sad misery and dread
that she should die and be forever quenched, she
clung with the weak tenacity of a sea-anemone
to a rock, to Jessica, and to Jessica's serene as-
surances (delivered in the certainty of complete
conviction) that indeed and indeed [and [many

times indeed she would not and could not be permitted to die.

Albert too—on the nurse's hours off—would slip into her room and tell her how she did not look nearly as horrible as she said she felt, and how soon he was sure he would be fixing her a nice brandy and soda instead of a dreary barley water.

Albert and Jane's nurse did not get on at all well. She soon told Jessica that she knew his sort all right and had caught him helping himself to the face powder in the bathroom—the most expensive *Chanel* too, not the visitors' stuff in the green bowl.

Jessica, who disliked the nurse and her pink, healthy face and her crisp permanent wave, almost as much as the nurse disliked Albert, received the information with cold unconcern and went out and bought Albert a brocaded handbag from Mr. Selfridge to encourage him to think more of himself and give him confidence for the further annoying of the nurse.

There is no doubt but that in this sickness Jessica redoubled the strength of her hold upon Jane. For she was kind, strong and entertaining. She was determined, moreover, that Jane should recover as quickly as possible and genuinely concerned for the sickness and pain of which Jane never ceased to complain, lamenting herself in fever and in weakness of the sadness of her case.

It was many days before any of her young
friends were allowed to come and sit about in her
bedroom, drinking her gin and amusing her with
their nasty stories about each other. Before this
time came Jessica was her one and only support.
Had it not been for Jessica she would have died
of boredom and the fear of death would have
overwhelmed her. Eagerly Jane would turn to
Jessica as she stepped into Jane's room straight
from the world outside, saying: "My dear, the
heat of London——"'Sitting down square and cool
before Jane's dressing-table; taking off her hat;
(Jessica's hats were briefly and economically
correct both in colour and line); and telling Jane
of this and that with fire and with detail. Rakish
and charming Jessica could look too, with her
short dark hair flat and orderly on her head, and
the incredible perfection of one of her pale coats
and skirts almost producing angles from her
curves as she sat there with one knee crossed
over the other, a cigarette so clean and bright
and enjoyable between her red lips or between her
dark fingers.

She would tell Jane of an exhibition of pictures
she had seen and of the curious effects upon her
of the pictures, how and why they excited or bored
her; and her reactions to Art were curiously entertaining. Or she would tell her of a visit to the Zoo,
or of a party given by one of their friends—about
either she could be equally enthralling. If there

was no really good daily chapter in the current
scandal of the town she would invent a rude and
diverting one and tell it to Jane with every
circumstance of truthfulness.

"Thank God Nurse has gone out for a walk."

"Where to?"

"I don't know. Albert, you might bring me a
slice of lemon—You know I hate this kind of tonic
water. Where's Nurse gone, d'you know?"

"Down to John Barker's to buy remnants with
a lady-friend, Miss."

"How disgusting. How d'you know?"

"I heard her make the appointment by telephone
this morning."

"That woman's *for ever* using the telephone."

"Complained her egg wasn't fresh at breakfast-
time, too."

"Disgusting woman to eat breakfast this hot
weather. Is there any of the other tonic water
left, Albert?"

And in the stillness of Jane's room when the
door was shut, Jane's weak, absent voice said:

"Albert must go get his hair cut—the back of
his neck's like a tiger's bum—will you tell him,
Jessica?"

"Yes, my pet, I'll tell him. Look, here's a parcel
of books for you, Jane. Who sent them to you?"

"God knows. Sylvester, maybe."

"It certainly was never Sylvester who sent you
these." Jessica had snipped through the thick

white string with Jane's smallest crooked nail scissors and unfolded the paper in which the books were wrapped. She read their titles aloud:

"*The Wanderings of William.*"

"*The Girl who Gave.*"

"*Young Entry.*"

"*Joan whips-in.*"

"*Jane*, who could have sent you these books? All outdoor sport, my dear. And here's one just about girl friends—*Young Entry*; how rude! Why should they expect any one to know what they mean by their dreary huntin'-talk? Perhaps Sylvester sent them for a bit of fun. He knew I'd get a good laugh out of them, anyway."

"What are they about, anyway?" Jane asked weakly.

"I'm telling you. Girlish friendship and fox-hunting—now they're eating soda-bread—what's that? Oh, we're in Ireland I see. And never a silver cup but it's *engraved with a good horse's name*. What a revolting bit of camp. That's to show you that the hunting season is approaching. Disgusting—Here's a young man who *dons an overcoat of a rather wonderful brown colour*. Now he's stepping into his charging motor car—*Studying his bare brown hands on the wheel—he knows he'll want to kiss Prudence before he gets home to-night*—Really, Jane, Sylvester can't have sent you this. Now she's riding a hunt, I suppose— *This stops us, Old Girl! Prudence pulled the mare together and strove to consider.*—Oh, she's over it now *with a hoist and a flick of her strong quarters.* I thought she'd winkle out somehow. I wonder what it was? Oh, just a *mass* of stiff timber wreathed in barbed wire, I expect. It usually is. Let's see what the *Wanderings of William* has to say—such a nice simple title anyhow. Not suggestively sporting like *Young Entry*. Oh, it's *worse*, my dear. It's full of the lowing of hounds and every one stuffing themselves with buttermilk scones dripping with butter. Plenty of picturesque discomfort and cold bath water and these *incredible* Irish mountains *always* in the distance. Shall I read one aloud to you? It might be amusing for us. Which one shall I read?"

"No," said Jane, surprisingly, for she enjoyed nothing more than to hear Jessica read aloud from a book which was really abhorrent and despicable to her, her comments were as apt and unreasonable as the point of view from which she read was rude.

But Jane had given a good guess as to who the sender of this sporting library might be, and although she had not thought for weeks of his voice and charm of body, a weak flare of enthusiasm for his memory sprang faintly within her. She would never go to his Ireland but at least she would keep her brief romantic preoccupation with that country to herself.

She did not want to read the books in the least, but she wanted to write Mr. Playfair a letter of thanks which Jessica was not to see. It was some days before she could accomplish this, an invalid's life is such public property. And Jane's entire inability to write letters when in rude health made matters more complicated for her now.

"I'll write to Pipsy and thank her for those lovely roses," she said to Jessica one day, "bring me some paper and lend me your stylograph pen, Sweetie."

"Such *nonsense*, darling. They were filthy roses and I never lend any one my pen, you know."

"Well, I'll buy me a pen. I'll tell Nurse to buy it when she goes out."

"Well, she's gone out—Besides I know she'd buy one made of mauve condensed milk—Besides why *should* you excite yourself about Pipsy's roses. She's such a *tiresome* woman—besides the pen will lie about for ever reminding us of Nurse—We'll never have the strength of mind to throw it away. And if you start writing letters to Pipsy you'll have to write to every one who sent you things."

"Oh, Jessica, you're horrible." Jane was nearly in tears of weakness and misery. The impossibility of writing to Mr. Playfair swept her. She was swamped in her own sickness and inadequate strength of will. "Can't I ever write letters to my

friends? I'll say my friends have been very
wonderful to me."

"No, darling," said Jessica, firmly, "you can
give them all a nice party when you're better. Now
give me that book and I'll read to you."

"I wanna read it to myself," said Jane, defeated
and sulky.

"No. Give it to me," said Jessica. "Darling,
believe me, I know what's *good* for you. Thanks.
We hadn't got as far as this in it, had we? Well,
I hadn't. I'll read from where we were. Otherwise it's such a bore for me."

Nurse, for whom Jane cherished a sneaking
passion, although she ran her down consistently to
Jessica or Albert, proved much more helpful over
the letter-writing difficulty than Jane would have
thought possible. Indeed the matter cemented
between them that temporary bond which unites
a nurse and her patient against the world, a bond
that absence so quickly dissevers.

Nurse, of course, enjoyed an opportunity for
scoring off Jessica, and quickly gathered from
Jane's furtive and confidential demands for pen,
ink and notepaper, that here was a situation
demanding tact. And any situation which demands
tact is pretty sure to be productive of annoyance
for some one.

So: "Why buy a pen?" said Nurse, brightly.
"I'll lend you my 'Prosperity' and you can do a
little quiet letter-writing when Miss Houpe-

Boswell goes out to lunch. Now we'll just take
our medicine and not worry ourselves any more
about anything, shall we?"

Jane sighed her relief. How beneficient and pink
and understanding Nurse was—Lovely woman. All
would now be well. "What's your 'Prosperity'?"
she asked.

"Prosperity Pens? Oh, you buy one for 5/- and
you draw 2/6 up to £5000 for any you sell to
friends afterwards." Her voice was so bright and
confident that Jane wondered why she should go
on nursing with such a prosperous prospect
before her.

Nurse, who knew better than Jessica or Albert
how ill Jane had been, looked at her now as she
lay so well and comfortably arranged in bed, and
mending so nicely in health, with sympathy and
a vague disposition towards liking. "Pathetic little
thing," she thought. "All that money and bullied
to death by that *octopus*. I *am* sorry for her." And
when the time came she produced her Prosperity
pen with much good-will, and notepaper and
envelopes and stamps, and settled Jane comfortably to write her letter and arranged herself in a
strategic position from which she could prevent
Albert going into Jane's bedroom on any pretext
whatever, for she was rightly convinced that he
was an ally of Jessica's.

"Nurse," Jane called, "Nurse—Oh, I'm as
tired I could just *die*."

"Oh, we're not going to die *just* yet." Bright, capable, seraphic and clear-eyed, Nurse laid her down in comfort. She removed the Prosperity pen from the sheets and staunched its flow of ink. "Let me see. This is your letter, you'd like me to run out and post it, wouldn't you? I'll just pop down to the pillar box at the corner. I'll just pop this note-paper back in the drawing-room first. Explanations are so tiresome when one's not feeling quite the thing, aren't they? Bye-bye. Shan't be long."

From her happy invalid coma Jane was roused presently by Albert who came in with a sheaf of lilies sent by some one and presently told her that he *did* think it was a bit thick for Nurse to help herself to the best note-paper. Well, he just thought he'd mention it—at Miss Houpe Boswell's writing-table, too.

"Oh, she's a *horrible* girl," Jane murmured, weakly petulant. "Put those lilies where I can see them, Albert."

"They are rather lovely, aren't they, Madam? —had a crack at the *Cointreau* after lunch too, Madam."

"She's just *horrible*"—Jane murmured again, and turned her face into her pillow—that sanctuary of the sick—until Albert should take himself off. How well he fixed flowers!—How spiteful he was!

"Albert," she said, a sudden thought striking

her, "have you seen a parcel of books that came the other day lying about anywhere?"

"*Wanderings of William, The Girl who Gave, Young Entry* and *Joan Whips-in,* do you mean, Madam?"

"Yes."

"Miss Houpe-Boswell gave me the lot to dispose of, Madam. I happened to glance through one and I got kind of absorbed in it. It's a nice story. Light, you know, but quite entertaining. Why, I could hardly put the book down, Madam."

"What was it about?"

"Fox-hunting, racing, a little light love-making in an Irish setting. Well, there's something *about* Ireland, I don't know what it is; I was over there with a gentleman once and I *did* enjoy myself, Madam. Reading this book quite recalled old times, if I might say so."

"Well, you might bring one of them in here— just any one you think I'd like. And, look, Albert, there's a bottle of stuff I bought for growing my eyelashes, you might like to have it. In the left-hand cupboard—*left* hand . . . They told me it was wonderful and it cost the earth, but I got kind of disheartened with it."

"Oh, thank you, Madam. I've tried so many preparations for that, too. I've a friend who swears by pure castor oil, but it must be a *very* pure brand or there's a danger of its blinding one permanently. I'm sure this is excellent." Albert

removed the glass stopper of an ornate bottle and
sniffed. And as he sniffed his face fell. Castor oil,
he thought disappointedly. *How* they are done!
As he slipped the bottle into his coat pocket, he
could hear Nurse popping and rattling about on
her way back to the patient.

Nurse and Jane spent a very pleasant hour
reading *The Wanderings of William*. He wandered
in a pleasant country of mist and mountain, where
he encountered incredibly comical servants and
was exposed to the dangers and the glories of the
chase. What with hounds barking, and elusive but
strong-smelling foxes and the glory of big horses
jumping big out of their long strides—it was all
very peculiar—but a genuine element of truth and
excitement ran through its author's words to
Nurse and Jane, and they laughed aloud many
times before Jessica returned, rather truculent and
assertive from her lunch party.

Jane snatched the book away from Nurse and
concealed it in her bed for further entertainment.

"Had lots of fun, darling?" Jane asked solicit-
ously. For had she not successfully written her
letter to Mr. Playfair, and did she not wish to
continue reading those books he had sent which
whipped up in her anew her enthusiasm for his
sporting country. Let her keep Jessica in humour
then. A vague sense of the guilt of secrecy pervaded
and softened her manner towards her friend.

"No." Jessica sat down and glared at Nurse,

who was shaking one of her eternal medicine
bottles. "It was one of those 'amusing' places
Veronica is always discovering. The food was
worse than usual. *Must* we have these lilies in
here, Jane? So entirely Burne Jones, aren't they?
Or do you see yourself as a Rossetti child? Of
course if you *like* them, that's a different thing.
Who sent them to us?"

"I don't know, darling!" Jane closed her eyes
and their lids were like cheap white blotting paper
on which some one has newly spilt the Swan ink;
her face was white, too, and as thin and small as
a sixpence with Victoria on it. The scar that
made such an interesting wreck of her intended
prettiness seemed to-day to draw her face up and
down with a distincter cruelty. Jane's body lay
as flat and weak in bed as a sheet of paper on the
floor. Looking at her Jessica was truly overcome
in sudden pity and tenderness. She abandoned
her contest over the lilies, forgot her annoyance
with the dreary party—where she had not been a
success—and rang for Albert to bring her in the
gin and set her mind to making plans as to where
they should go when Jane was sufficiently recovered in health to leave London.

Jessica had a wide and exciting way of flinging
plans of travel about her. Usually Jane would
react enthusiastically, seeing herself now perhaps
in Ecuador, perhaps in New York, or again in the
utmost Outer Hebrides. In whatever place Jessica

contemplated a sojourn, that place she invested
with more than its native charm. For she had a
cultivated mind and could produce reasons for her
enthusiasm even to herself.

But to-day Jane lay in bed appalled at the idea
of a holiday in Soviet Russia, where Jessica
seemed to think she might recuperate quite
nicely. Quiet and unprotesting she lay there until
Jessica had enumerated all the possibilities of such
a trip, dwelling particularly on the prohibitive
price of vodka, a particular advantage since Jane
must keep away from drink for months to
come.

"No," said Jane at last. "Really, no, Jessica.
You mustn't ask me to go to Russia. Not this
year. Couldn't we ask just some of the girls and
some of the chaps and go to the Villa for sea-
bathing like we planned to do, Honey? Just like
we planned to do before I was sick."

"But *Darling*, have you *thought*? Have you
considered for a moment how difficult and awful
it will be for you lying about and watching every
one drinking delicious gin, while you sip barley
water and orange drinks? It wouldn't be possible
for you."

"I'd have to watch people drinking in Russia,
wouldn't I?"

"No, you wouldn't. Or only now and then.
Drink is far too expensive. And you're used to
seeing me have an odd drink. That's quite different

to every one lying about in the sun and putting
it away."

"Well, what the hell anyway? Do you think
I've no will power?"

"Well, I do give you credit for enough sense to
realise your own limitations."

"But I don't want to drink ever again. I'll
tell you the way I feel. I feel as if some one
had been slipping an anti-alcohol dope into
the barley water. Oh, Jessica, do we have to go
to Russia?"

"Oh, not if you dislike the idea so much," said
Jessica with sulky indulgence. "Just say where
you *do* want to go, and I'll take you there and
leave you there."

"I want to go to Ireland." The words were in
the back of Jane's head, in the back of her throat,
but a faint feeling of sickness and panic at Jessica's
certain derision of the idea kept them unspoken.
She was too weak. Jessica would be unkind and
argue her out of her young enthusiasm. It was
not such a very strong desire after all. It could
easily suffer and be changed and lost to her. So
she could only repeat weakly: "As long as it's
not Russia," for that was too much to endure
altogether. Presently, when she had more strength
of body and mind she would introduce the subject
of Ireland. But not now. She sweated slightly
to think of how horrible Jessica could be over the
idea. Horrible and discouraging. Atrophying its

possibilities with unanswerable ridicule. Was it possible to think of Jessica enduring or enjoying the life set forth so attractively by Mr. Playfair? Or by the authoress of the *Wanderings of William*? It was not. She would find the hideous ordered disorder of Soviet Russia infinitely preferable. In its relentless discomfort her soul would expand like the best elastic—or would afterwards when she was talking about it. In point of fact, Jessica was no better at enduring hardships, dirt, or exposure to infectious disease than Jane, who at least had the sense to whine about the prospect beforehand. If she couldn't have Ireland and the renewed acquaintance of Mr. Playfair, at least the sea and cushions in the sun were preferable to the unknown horrors and hardships of Russia.

For some days after this—days in which Jane still kept her bed but grew a little stronger every day in body and in spirit—Jane, Nurse and Albert continued to read with enjoyment the sporting and romantic novels sent by Mr. Playfair.

Albert insisted that Jane would enjoy the fox-hunting parts and picked them out for Nurse to read aloud. He was sometimes even able to explain what an enthusiastic authoress endeavoured to convey in her sporting jargon.

"When you were in Ireland, Albert, was everybody as crazy about a fox-hunt as these books say?"

"Well, I'd hardly say that, Madam. Some of

them hated it. The gentleman I was with did, but he came from Hampshire."

"And was the food as good as these books say?"

"Oh *no*. The food was very indifferent."

"And were there so many muddly little dawgs everywhere?"

"Yes, *everywhere*, Madam."

"And does everybody drink up when they go to a party?"

"Well, hardly what you or I would call knocking it back, Madam. Not constant at it, if you know what I mean."

"Are the beds good?"

"Well, generally speaking, no. They're horrible, Madam."

"And are the servants entertaining like these books say?"

"Well, they have their own idea of humour. I can't say it ever appealed to me. I had one great friend, but he was a telegraph boy——"

"And would you be crazy to visit Ireland again, Albert?"

"Oh, yes, Madam. I should. I should be highly delighted I must say."

"Well, I think the little dawgs sound cunning and these foxhounds too, they must be very, very thrilling. Oh, Albert, I'll say I'm crazy to go to Ireland."

Then Jane would read a bit of *Joan Whips-in*,

revelling in the picturesque confusion of the
heroine's ancestral home; in her compelling power
alike over dogs, horses and men, for all three loved
her after their kind, with devotion, obedience and
with fervour. Many were her adventures, out-
doors and in, before the hatchet-profiled hero
permanently gathered her unto his bosom.

The day came, of course, when Jessica discovered this secret romantic vice of Ireland. It
was well for Jane that she could not in any way
connect such sickly enthusiasm with the person
of Mr. Playfair, in which case her attack would
have been delivered with even more devastating
savagery.

It happened at the time that Jessica was reading aloud, for her own entertainment more than
for Jane's, from a thin black book written by a
young man of frail but bitter brilliance. But a
brilliance expressed in phrases of such tortured
simplicity that their comprehension demanded a
concentration of mind to which Jane was in any
case unequal, and had not at the moment the
strength of mind to affect. She yawned. She
fidgeted. She turned about and about in her bed
and she made up her face. And all the time, beneath her pillow, *The Girl Who Gave* lay caught
beneath her horse in a wet ditch—a bad horse
lent to the poor girl by the wife of the M.F.H.
who had observed her husband's preoccupation
with the generous heroine and had determined

that it should end. Even now, mounted on her
bay mare—*up to 14 stone and all quality*, she was
bouncing along, still two fields from the scene of
the accident (for the girl who gave showed them
all the way), but determined, although she was
a cowardly woman and hated leaping, to jump
on that girl should The Grey put her down. And
now he had. There had been *an evil strand of
barbed wire in the fence*, of course, and in it, much
to Jane's distress, the brute had awkwardly
tangled a forepaw. When Jane had been forced
to stuff the book under the bedclothes, horse and
rider were lying, inextricably confused, in the
ditch on the farther side, with the M.F.H.'s lawful
wife approaching every moment nearer to the
scene of the disaster. No wonder Jane was in
a perfect fidget to know what happened next.
She had her own experience of lawful wives, and
the wives of fox-hunters she felt sure were a
deadly and determined breed.

As the minutes passed the simple architectural
prose of Jessica's clever young man, delivered in
Jessica's cultivated reading voice, became more
than Jane could endure. She fished up *The Girl
Who Gave* from the depths of her bed and squinted
painfully down its pages from the shelter of her
sheet. So absorbed was she that she did not even
notice when Jessica's voice fell silent, nor when
Jessica loomed above her and snatched the book
from her hand.

"*Oh*, Jessica, I wasn't reading it. Don't be horrible to me."

"Darling, as if I would," Jessica replied in the small gentle voice which Jane knew now to be that which preceded some of her worst storms. "I'm only so sorry to have bored you with *Wind* if you had something that you'd rather I'd read to you. What is it? *The Girl Who Gave*—for a title that's a masterpiece of suggestive tact anyway. May I look inside?"

"Oh, Jessica, you wouldn't like it—Oh give it back to me—It's *my* book——" Jane wailed, baby-girlishly.

Jessica said: "Here you are, my dear. My stomach's not *quite* strong enough. I wonder why Albert hasn't brought in the drinks?" For it was six o'clock.

Instead of Albert, Nurse came crisply in, and Jessica's face darkened ominously.

"Hullo!" said Nurse brightly, seeing the book still in Jessica's hand. "How's *'the Girl'* getting on? I see Miss Houpe-Boswell has fallen for her too. And I've never seen you read anything but the brainiest book before, Miss Houpe-Boswell! But I do call that well written, you know, don't you? Mrs. Barker and I've been quite thrilled with it. I like more sexy books myself, I must say, but still it's rather marvellous."

"It looks *absorbing*." Jessica put it down on Jane's bed. "*Must* Albert *always* be late with the drinks? D'you mind ringing the bell for him, Nurse?"

"*Just* five minutes till I've made my patient comfy, please." Nurse fluttered busily between the washstand and the bed and made no movement towards ringing the bell.

"Do you mind?" Jessica repeated coldly.

"Well I do rather. I don't want that boy in here at the moment, you see, Miss Houpe-Boswell."

Terrified and fascinated, Jane looked from one to the other of them. Here was war. Either Jessica must give in about ringing the bell or else she must drink in the drawing-room and alone. In any case the situation was bound to produce a storm.

Leaden-white, with long shadows like pincers on each side of her nose, Jessica said: "Jane, d'you mind if Albert brings the drinks in here before Nurse begins her ministrations?" The shot would have been more telling if the ministrations had not already been begun. Nurse, her face scarlet with rage, pointed this out at once and Jane, being a coward as well as being sick, only whined: "Oh, I feel horrible. Oh, Jessica, you're horrible to me. Oh, Jessica, stop."

"Please don't excite the patient," Nurse said in a low cool voice, unassailably professional.

Jessica's temper was thoroughly roused now: "If you don't tell that bloody woman to get out of this room," she said, "I'll scream the place down."

"Do," said Nurse composedly, while Jane continued to cringe and whine in her bed.

"I'll throw her out."

"You'll be had up for assault," Nurse warned her, by now faintly apprehensive.

"That's happened to me before," Jessica informed her, "but I didn't mind much. I did a lot of damage first. Are you going out of this room or not?"

"I'm going to telephone to the doctor. In a case as *peculiar* as this one hardly knows what to do." Her rout dignified to a retreat by this shrewd blow, Nurse left the room.

"Jane—Tiny—I'm so *sorry* to have this upsetting you. Look, sweet, you mustn't cry any more. You shall read whatever book you like—of course you shall. It's that dreary woman I can't stand. You know what my nerves are and I've been out of my mind about you since you've been ill. The agony for me—you don't *know*. I tell you what, Tiniest, we'll burn all these bloody books, shall we? And go to Russia together and forget all the smallness and dismalness. Darling, you must *stop* howling now—I've quite forgiven you."

Then the doctor came. It was the hour he usually did come anyhow. Nurse had not really dared to telephone to him. But she came in looking sour and victorious behind him, and proceeded to soothe Jane while he proceeded to soothe Jessica and get her out of the room, because

he said he wanted to talk to her without Nurse.
He was an artful young doctor and in ten minutes
he had frightened Jessica badly about Jane, giving
her to understand that her reason if not now her
life was in some danger. If Jessica would refrain
from creating scenes of excitement about her,
all might still be well. If not——the doctor
paused.

"Has she any relations?" he asked, that quiet
insistent phrase of doctors.

"In America," Jessica felt slightly shaken by
all this. Fancy if Jane's motherly old mother came
along to take her in charge. Taking her away from
the powerful and loving Jessica—making Jessica
into an unnecessary girl-friend.

"Of course she might come over," the doctor
suggested.

Then how much Jessica wished that she'd said:
"A *paralytic* mother in America." So stationary.
One might have thought though that America
would have been enough to put him off the idea.
Now:

"I think we find this nurse rather a trying
woman," Jessica said, as much to take his mind
off Jane's mother as to vent her spleen against
Nurse.

"Do you? She's been very competent with
Mrs. Barker, I've found. And you won't have
her much longer, you know. I thought if she has
no serious set-back, Mrs. Barker might leave

town in about ten days. Somewhere quiet and
dull, you know. She simply *must* not drink—you
do understand that?"

"Yes. She'd thought of going to Russia."

"Well, she must stop thinking of going to Russia.
Russia's entirely out of the question."

And thus was Jessica's plan for roughing it in
the great open steppes overridden and put aside.
She said: "There's the villa at Cap d'Antibes.
But it's such a place for gin."

"Quite the wrong atmosphere. I thought of
Scotland."

"Jane hates the North. So do I."

"Well," the doctor looked at Jessica deliberately,
"you could always send her somewhere with
Nurse, you know, if you thought you'd be bored.
It might be best."

"Oh, no," said Jessica, "I wouldn't think of that
for a moment. We're sure to find somewhere."

She went into her bedroom then and locked the
door. She broke her soap-dish to pieces in her
hands. Her hands were bleeding from several
cuts when it was over but she felt much calmer.
It was the most satisfying china breaking she had
ever done. No mammoth crashing about it. Just
a passionate personal resolve towards destruction.
After she had bled over the broken pieces for some
time she felt that it was really in her power to
endure Nurse for a further ten days.

Albert tapped at her door.

"I've taken the drinks into Mrs. Barker's room,
Miss. Nurse has just popped down to the pillar
box. I thought you might like to know."

CHAPTER III

SYLVESTER was in Ireland. He was staying at
Kilque with his cousins Hester and Viola Brown.
Hester and Viola were sisters aged about thirty-
six and thirty-two.

Sylvester liked staying at Kilque, for he was
fond of Hester, and the observation of Viola,
whose pretty pet name was Piggy, afforded him
some amusement.

To-day Sylvester intended to employ the morning in literary effort. So, when breakfast was over,
he retired at about ten o'clock to the library, for
his mind felt fresh and well resolved towards
productive enterprise. Also the library at Kilque
was one of the few rooms known to him where
his brain could proceed undistracted on its way
through that blind sickness that so encompasses
original thought.

Just because he felt inclined towards work
Sylvester should the more have mistrusted his
mood. It was too bright and firm to last. Things
were bound to go wrong.

He opened the door of the library and stood
quietly inside it realising with pleasure the

quenched and musty atmosphere of the room. He had never known a less individual room— without character and without beauty of any sort. Here indeed a writer could be left unto himself undistracted. Here if anywhere.

Sylvester sat himself down at the writing table and read with some mild excitement the pages of his new novel which he had written the day before. They were not at all bad. Strange, when words found any life or fire that came so sulkily off one's pen, disgusting their writer with a mawkish paucity or a too dreadful intimacy with his poor self. For what he uttered to an audience through the medium of book or play, Sylvester knew to be dead to himself for ever. Although he was inclined to doubt the importance of these fatalities, still their occurrence saddened him.

However, all this was his still. His to destroy, or change or build upon. Let him see. How many words had he written yesterday now? Sylvester flipped the pages of an exercise book back until he came to the place where the ink showed very dark, the conclusion of an earlier effort. He tilted back his chair, for the sun came streaming enjoyably in behind him, certainly one of the most enjoyable benefits in life, and proceeded upon a calculation based on the number of words on one page and the number of pages covered in words. He had written about 725 words. If only, he thought, I could produce one thousand words a day I could

write a book in seventy-five days. How I wish I
could do that. Now at the rate of 725 words a day
it will take me ... but Sylvester, although he
was a successful author and playwright, was no
mathematician; besides, when he had almost
completed the sum, he could not cheat himself
out of the recollection that 725 was an unusually
large output for him for one day.

Gazing now upon his work he felt himself to be
but a thin-blooded and inadequate writer and
much doubted if his success would continue. At
least he had now filled three red exercise books.
He wondered if Hester had remembered to buy
him some more in the village as he had asked her
to do yesterday. He put down his pen with that
mixture of relief and annoyance with which a
writer momentarily abandons his uninspired efforts
to the necessity of the moment, and proceeded to
search for those books—the village virgins he called
them when new, or again, those unborn children
of my mind.

Almost immediately he found them lying, a neat
parcel of six, upon a window sill. The thoughtless-
ness of Hester! Could anything be more nicely
calculated to upset an author's mental excretory
processes than six new exercise books? All those
thousands—almost thousands—yes, certainly thousands—of bland and virgin pages waiting for him
with a frozen expectancy. And now he saw that
she had bought him a new sort. How incredibly

stupid she was. Why, these books were a different colour from the last. And a different shape. They probably contained a different number of pages, which would upset all his calculations over the numbers of words, pages and days. He would count and see. No, they had the same number of pages. But these were not the books with DON'TS on their backs. Very upsetting. Sylvester liked those DON'TS.

1. DON'T cross the street or roadway without looking to your right or left!
2. DON'T play games on a busy thoroughfare!
3. DON'T walk on the middle of the road, keep to the footpath!

SAFETY FIRST

He underlined SAFETY FIRST on the back of an old, a friendly, a well-filled exercise book, and looking out of the window, beheld the postman approaching. The wind of the morning sang in the wheels of his bicycle. Sylvester envied him his clean and simple life. At least he must see whether the postman had brought any letters for him. There might well be one requiring an immediate answer. It was a tiresome duty, but he must interrupt his writing and make sure. He opened the window, called the postman, and ascertained that there was no letter for him.

To counteract the faint shock of disappointment occasioned by a post devoid of human remembrance, even in the shape of bills, Sylvester desired the postman to give him the daily paper. He would see what he would see in that. He saw almost at once a photograph of Rotarian John Murnagh who spoke at yesterday's meeting of the Dublin branch of the Rotarian Club. Mildly disgusted, he turned to the racing news. This he always enjoyed, although he was no student of form, but he adored to read down a list of horses' names, and the pithy exactitude of the correspondents fascinated him.

Sylvester put the paper down at last and opened a virgin book at the first page. His mind was empty save for one thought which swam hither and over through it—a shell-less transparent shrimp in a pool as clear as gin. What a disgusting word "Cloy" is, he thought. Joy and Cloy. How terrible that they should ever have been coupled so indissolubly together by writers of hymns and other poets who should have known better. Who did it first? But now I am being fantastic, Sylvester thought. I must really write. Indeed, I must. He would have given much to recapture that rich vein in which he had written 725 words. Incredible industry. He looked towards the ceiling and instantly he wondered what rooms occurred above this room. He must stop and think for a moment, and brightly and readily his mind told him which and what they were. I must write a description of this room in which I sit, he thought then, but was lost for words in which to convey any adequate sense of its alienating ugliness or of its importance to him. He must write . . .

"Sylvester, have you finished reading the paper?" It was his cousin, Hester Brown, at the window.

"Do not be impish, Hester," Sylvester begged her. "I know now that it was by design you bought six exercise books instead of three. I do detest impish women. I told you I was working hard. Why should you think I would waste my time reading the paper?"

"Well, I saw you, Sylvester, as I was cleaning out my chicken coops."

"There you are," said Sylvester, coldly, pointing to the dreary paper. "Take it and go away."

"Do you know the time?" said Hester. Unperturbed by the preoccupied expression of authorship which Sylvester had now assumed, she climbed in through the window and sat on the window seat. "It is half-past eleven and Piggy has gone to see the dressmaker. Don't you think we might drink a glass of your sherry? It would be a help to us both."

"Oh, well, if Piggy has really gone to see her little woman round the corner." It was an understood thing that Piggy was from this morning sherry-drinking interdict. Sylvester was aware that the presence of Piggy disagreed badly with the progress of his work. Hester for a short time of space he found entirely tolerable. He was inclined to welcome Hester. But Piggy—no. A creature of pathetic and disgusting pretences.

Hester was a creature whole in herself. She sapped no strength from any one. Her many sad failures and unsuccessful ventures in life were her own. She leant on nobody. Hester was indeed a bold adventuress. A merchant adventuress. When she was still quite young she had adventured what money she had on schemes and enterprises so speculative and unsteady that now she had no money left and was in the unenviable position of an old sister living upon a younger—living but not leaning. True, an equal share in Kilque Hester had with Piggy. But of what value is an equal share or even entire possession of a small estate in the South of Ireland? Or of a house in any country with a mildly leaking roof and mildly defective drainage? Hester always said grandly: "When Piggy marries I will go away and find a job." But no one knew better than Hester that Piggy was growing every year more unlikely and more anxious to be married. Hester, whose early adventures had been connected disagreeably with the breeding of pedigree cattle, and of blood-stock, and with shares in South American railways, professed little interest in the amatory side of life. Sylvester took pains to point out to her how much, how insanely much, she had missed out of

the possibilities of life. "Even *one* lover, Hester,"
he would say, "even one dreary, ineffective, *tiny*
lover would have made *such* a difference to you."
But Hester who at the age of twenty-five had
been declared a bankrupt at the local court
sessions—quietly spending a morning becoming
bankrupt when her poor mother (for Hester was
old enough to have been born to one of those
nearly extinct creatures known as "Your *Poor*
Mother" if things went wrong) believed her to
be playing in a tennis tournament—Hester knew
only one thing of singular value in life, one thing
indispensable, and denied to her, and that was
money. She still had her schemes for making
money, and, small as they now were in comparison
with the grand days when she became a bankrupt,
alas, they were almost equally ineffective. A pity,
for, with the means to do so, Hester would have
made a royal entertainer of others and an artistic
dispenser of riches.

Now she sat and drank up Sylvester's sherry,
envying him his money but not his rich experience
in love, and Sylvester looking at her found a great
many things to pity about her. It was a pity that
her neck was so long and so thin, as full of sinews
as a turkey hen's and as fleshless. It was a pity
her nose was so long and so thin too, for that
unbalanced her face. It was a pity her hands
were so abandoned to outdoor and indoor work
for they were a lovely, severe shape and so

were her feet, long boned and unsolid as a
ghost's.

But Hester's eyes—there Sylvester could only
praise—for Hester had rare and lovely eyes, deep
sworn oaths of kindness and of beauty in her sad
disappointing face. Sharp and cold and ageing as
Hester was in face and in body, yet her eyes grew
more lovely as the bones of her temples sharpened
round them. They were full set, hazel eyes with
dark, strongly growing lashes and short arched
brows above, of a fine and restrained growth.
Admirable eyes, painted many times by the earlier
Italian masters who had a particular perception of
that full dropped shape, those heavy, angelic lids.

Sylvester stayed at Kilque for long periods of
time as a guest, not as a paying guest. But in
return for their hospitality he gave his cousins
rich presents, such as a combined wireless and
gramophone set. An almost racing car. Valuable
furs and quantities of caviare. He did not know—
how could he, for nobody told him?—that in his
absence the wireless was silent because the garage
in the village that charged batteries was rudely
and patiently suing them for £7 15s. 9d, or that
the car was almost never on the road since it
consumed petrol in such quantities that Hester
and Piggy very seldom felt rich enough to drive
her for more than six miles in six months. When
Sylvester was with them they would make supreme
efforts and wear their furs, play their wireless, and

drive their lovely motor about—for they were girls
of a peculiar and stubborn spirit, and the last
thing they wished Sylvester to realise was how
great a drain his visits and his presents were on
their resources.

It was true—and just too—that Piggy (whose
ready money it was, after all, which provided the
bacon for Sylvester's breakfast, the mutton for
his lunch and the money for the cartridges with
which Hester shot the frequent rabbit for his
dinner) should have the best value out of his
presents.

For Piggy had a girl-friend, rich enough even to
quench the thirst for petrol of Sylvester's car, and
it was Piggy's delight to lend this friend the car
whenever it suited the first shadow of her convenience. For Piggy loved her with a flaming
devotion that was her one true excitement in life.
Not only the car would she lend, but the wireless
too and often, to Hester's dumb complaint, when
its batteries were in good going order and would
have lasted for weeks longer without recharging.
The car, too, Hester well knew was presented as
often as not brimming over with petrol, although
seldom returned with more than a teaspoonful in
the tank. But love must show itself and Piggy's
was neither to be hidden nor discouraged. When
she worshipped she would give, it is love's silly
way.

Her friend Joan was beautiful, happy, married

(happy and faithful in marriage), had two charming children, an attractive husband, several good horses, a garden in which everything that was planted grew fast and well, many willing and obedient servants, good health, a good figure, a good eye for a horse, a good seat on a horse and an inexhaustible fund of conversation about horses. She had and was in short everything that a country and county lady need aspire to have or to be. Therefore Piggy counted herself lucky indeed that there should ever arise the occasion when she might practically demonstrate her love and her usefulness. And it was astonishing indeed how often such an occasion would arise. Therefore Sylvester's presents were of an incalculable spiritual benefit to Piggy.

Hester had a sort of value for Sylvester's presents too, but they were very much on the outer circle of her life. The car, for instance; she would have enjoyed selling that and having a Baby Austin to tat about in, but as she realised its peculiar value to Piggy she never opened the question. The only present of Sylvester's which she had succeeded in cashing was a fashionable diamond bracelet and the money which this brought in had all gone in one expensive night's poker. She was a gallant better but had no luck.

"Do you know, Sylvester," said Hester now, sipping her sherry and looking about her, "that Piggy is determined to do up this room."

"What!" exclaimed Sylvester in agony—"Cream walls and hunting prints—Mercy, Hester! You must put the idea out of her head at once."

"No, not hunting prints," Hester told him, "they are too expensive. But Joan has a scheme for doing up rooms by splashing different coloured distempers on the walls with mops and, unlike most of Joan's plans about her house, it's unfortunately cheap enough for Piggy to imitate."

"Well, let her start it in the bathroom. She will soon see how ugly it is as well as cheap."

"You know, I'm afraid nowhere but this room will do her for a start. You see, *Joan* came in here the other day and told her how shockingly Victorian it was."

"Ignorant women," Sylvester was very upset. "It's the most typical Edwardian room I've ever seen."

"Well, their subtleties aren't so tortured as yours, that's all. Anything that's not obviously old they think is despicable and Victorian. Anyhow they have decided it would look good distempered in flame and mauve splashes run in on a wet green ground with all the paintable furniture painted a lively green."

Sylvester looked at the rosewood writing desk where he sat, his temperate affection for it warming to a defensive rapture.

"If you want to know what *I* think, Hester," he

said, "I believe that that Joan wants to try
the effect of her disgusting idea on a house she
doesn't have to live in herself. She's always making use of Piggy in some way. Now she wants
to try the thing out in this room just in the same
way that I want Piggy to try it on the downstairs privy."

"No, you're wrong there, Sylvester. She has
done up a room already and quite pretty it looks.
But I must say she got a man down from Dublin to
throw the paint on the walls."

"*There*, what did I tell you? She wants to see if
it can be done as well by an inadequate amateur,
so she falls on Piggy and fills her with this dreary
amateur decorating enthusiasm—the poor silly
bawcock."

"Do not be Shakespearian, Chuck," Hester
reproved him. "I was only giving you warning
so that Piggy should not assault you unprepared.
And after all, if you don't like the library for
writing in, you can always go back to London to
finish your book."

"No, no." Sylvester was shocked at the idea.
London for plays, Kilque for books. "Besides,
Hester, if I go back to London there will be no
more morning sherry-drinking for you. And I
must stay too, to defend this room. I know you
would enjoy seeing Piggy and Joan splashing
about in their violent distempers. My feeling for
this room is nothing to you. You will step about

the difficulty acid and aloof like a Rose Macaulay heroine."

"Dear Sylvester," said Hester, "pray do not enrage yourself—but give me a little more sherry before I must return to my fluffy pets in the fowl run and leave you to your work."

"My work," Sylvester moaned, "you have made it impossible for me to work any more to-day. However, if you would really go away, I might try."

Left to himself again Sylvester did not commit the folly of immediately resuming his literary labours. That would have been the height of absurdity, under the circumstances a pernicious waste of energy. And if there was a thing that Sylvester was inclined to conserve it was energy. He looked around him and about him at this dear and valuable room, as he had already done once or twice in the course of the morning, but not with such protective passion.

Edwardian indeed it was. Piggy had told him before now, in the reverent little voice she kept for the dead, no matter how tried she had been by them in life: "This was *Mother's* favourite room."

Want of money and complete idleness had fortunately combined to prevent Piggy changing its furniture and decoration between 1919 when her mother died and 1933 when Sylvester sat and wrote. True, there were a few additions relative to the present age—a shelf full of unread books

from the Book Society—unread at all events by
Piggy, whose: "You know I *very* seldom read
novels" had been an indication that Sylvester
might withdraw his gift to Kilque of a year's
subscription to that much abused society. But
had Sylvester withdrawn it? No. Bright and
perverse, he had said: "No Novels? Very well.
I'll tell them to send you nothing but Travel and
Memoirs, shall I?" And to his intense annoyance
Piggy had eagerly accepted this suggested pre-
disposition towards intelligence on her part. She
saw herself at once enjoying a good mental plunge
through a tropical jungle; following with breathless
interest the career of a general; taking an intelligent
view of the meteoric flights of past brilliance. How
often since then had he heard her observe: "Well,
I read so *little* besides Memoirs and Travel. Sylvester knows what I like. He send along anything worth reading."

A cold row of seven-and-sixpenny (and
sometimes twelve-and-sixpenny) monuments to
Piggy's idle-minded stupidity, the books were
arranged in the library. Anyhow there was one
advantage attached to this—that of irritating
Joan. Piggy's sudden change of style in reading
matter had forced Joan to join the Book Society
herself, whereas previously she had borrowed
Piggy's books and despised the selectors' tastes all
for nothing. Sylvester had lately caught her
glancing peevishly towards that shelf of travel

and memoir, so made a particular point of asking
to see the last month's Travel or Memoir book
whenever he came to Kilque. Otherwise Piggy
might have changed it for one more suitable to
Joan's intelligence. In such small ways do we
gain satisfaction over those whom we dislike.
But these were not matters in which Sylvester
grudged the expenditure of a little careful energy.

Beyond the shelf of modern reading matter
there was little to distract from the pure style
of this Edwardian piece. Above an intricately
moulded mantelshelf a flight of fragile shelves held
quantities of valueless china. Small cups and
saucers with castles painted on them, or coats of
arms of towns and colleges. A cat and a detestable
terrier snarled eternal enmity at one another. A
china child sat in its china tub. There were many
more mild violations of good taste in the same key.

Pink convolvuli had been embroidered with
patient skill upon a strip of moss green velvet and
this was tacked to the edge of the mantelshelf.
Lower down a small and elegant fire-grate was
concealed by a fire-screen on which peacocks'
feathers were protected by glass and framed in
bamboo. And why not? Very pretty, thought
Sylvester, defensively.

The inspiration for the wallpaper was nearly
Morris in design. A conventional pattern of water-
lilies on a green ground. On faintly crackling
chintz curtains the bunches of lilies of the valley

had faded equally with the pink bows that tied them.

There were many photographs too in which Sylvester took a quiet delight. *Isabelle* 1903 was a particular favourite of his. There were also a couple of interesting groups of shooting parties. Here were men whose pale shooting breeches buttoned below the knee over black knitted stockings; men in deer-stalker hats and high single collars, their hands on the intelligent heads of black retriever dogs; many men in Norfolk jackets; many men wearing large smooth moustaches, either drooping or with a rakish twist up at the corners. Their calm, unfevered faces were very pleasant to Sylvester. They were part of his escape from the speed and the rudeness of every day in 1933. Of hunting groups too there was a fair selection. Gentlemen who sat thrown well back in their saddles and ladies who held their hunting crops upside down and wore curly-brimmed bowler hats and enormous bosoms and enormous buns of hair—for those were the days when woman abated not one of her crowning glories. Then there were the speed fiends— Sylvester had less sympathy with them. Uncle Thomas, for instance, a young man who wore queer breeches, stockings and shoes, and leaned gracefully upon the spreading handle-bars of his powerful bicycle, a large camera strapped to his back (its velvet pall no doubt stuffed away in

one of the pockets of his Norfolk jacket) for he
would go on bicycling tours in Brittany and other
places, taking excellent photographs as he went.
Sylvester considered him to have the features and
expression of a peevish Ariel. He would not dwell
upon his picture. Nor did he particularly care
about the First Motorists. As much as could be
seen of their faces above the collars of their Polar
clothing was wreathed in vulgar smiles of optimism
and self-satisfaction. No doubt Isabelle was his
favourite of them all. In a moment of idleness and
affection he had once swept all the photographs
off a bamboo table and placed hers upon it in single
glory on an embroidered mat. And in other
enjoyable moments he would put a small glass
vase beside it, and in the vase a pink rose.

But, except for this one piece of favouritism over
Isabelle, Sylvester was fairly impartial in his
affection for the furniture and decoration of this
room. Why particularise when so much was
perfect?

One slight bit of faking Sylvester had done, but
so long ago now it had grown in with the rest,
and that was the arrangement of Pampas grass
in a bottle-necked vase of red and white Japanese
ware. Dishonest, of course, but he thought, on
the whole, permissible. Yes, in the result he
considered himself justified. The whole room was
perfect. When tall mirrors become green and
spotted with age they look as bleak as faded

gentlewomen; one of these reflected his pampas
grass. If Sylvester sniffed for long enough he could
almost believe that a horrible cat had been in
here. But outside the windows there was a sense
of space. Bright water, he walked beside it yesterday . . . But Sylvester must write.

For forty-five minutes he wrote busily and ceased
only as the magnificent notes of the luncheon gong
boomed forth from the hall. With a sigh of happily
completed industry he whisked the pages backwards, pleased to see that they equalled in number
those filled with 725 words. He refused to depress
himself with the thought that to-day's pages were
largely occupied with dialogue and asterisks—
hollow stuff when it comes to the ruthless
exactitude of a typist's counting. How Sylvester
did dread those sickening moments when his neatly
typed manuscript was returned to him an obvious
15,000 words short of the required length. And
thinking of his Public who bought all this agony
of his soul for seven-and-six Sylvester would be
filled with bitter feelings. Sometimes, of course,
Sylvester thought of his Public very kindly—
times when he saw advertisements for his works
containing the words 35th thousand; 70th thousand. First Printing exhausted before publication. Then had his Public had but one back he
would have clapped him upon it crying: "Good
and perceptive Fellow." Sylvester deserved all
his success. He battled well and truly with his

temperament and his idleness and had at last
learned to give his Public what it wanted. He
hated those authors who played together at
writing books. He thought them rude and shallow.
Let authors play together, yes. But not at their
trade of writing books. He thought he would go
and wash his hands before lunch.

In the hall he encountered Piggy's fox terrier,
Tig. Now of all the dogs that lived Sylvester
considered Tig the least likeable. To Sylvester
he was disgusting. His tight white skin stretched
as firmly as that of a toy horse over his hard
plump body, his one black ear, and that round
black spot on his back were unutterably plebeian.
His back view was entirely coarse and his frequent
displays of unnatural lust displeasing. Then he
adored bounding about after a ball, such athletic
diversion was his only form of outdoor sport.
He was not a brave little dog. He was idle and
cowardly and stupid; and there was an eternal
black spawn of fleas under his coarse close-
growing white hair; and if anybody touched him
he would shudder with pleasure in an obscene and
unattractive way. He ran to and fro in the hall
now, brightly endeavouring to attract Sylvester's
attention, and covering its stone floor with the
neat wet pattern of his feet. He too, Sylvester
supposed, had been to see the village dressmaker.
He could hear Piggy putting her stick away in the
porch and whistling in a studied, out-door-girl

manner. No doubt she had seen him. Sylvester slipped gently into the lavatory.

The dining-room at Kilque was full of black oak —repellently Breton and covered with carved wheels. There were divinely comfortable chairs to sit in though, with red velvet seats faintly sunk to the shape of the human form. The sun came brightly flooding through a south window and lit the mauve Woolworth glass and discovered many layers of pale dust on the carved furniture. It struck cornelian light from the nasturtiums on the table too. There was a pleasant smell of curry in the room.

"Well, now," said Sylvester, sitting down with a plateful of curry and small peeled beans as dry as moss and a plateful of salad too. "Well, now," said he, with his spoon in the chutney, "and how is girlish Piggy?" For he felt in good heart and form for irritating Piggy. "I heard you whistling and rattling about in the hall just now, so I supposed you had been out for a healthy brisk walk. And had you?"

Piggy, who would at any time have preferred being teased to being ignored by Sylvester, admitted that she had. "I don't know about being very *brisk*," she added, "the poor old heart's a bit wonky you know, Sylvester."

She had a perfect vocabulary of words like "wonky," forgotten slang, and phrases like "the poor old heart." "How's the cold to-day?"

Never: "How is your cold to-day?" It required no great diligence to discover Piggy's impenetrable dreariness and affectation. Usually Sylvester would regard her from out a dark and disgusted silence, but now and then he would talk to her with savage playfulness or honeyed spite. And not always honeyed. And he could not bear to look at her. She inspired him with a definite hostility both mental and physical.

Piggy had enormous bright blue eyes as hard as glass paper weights with an eye painted at the back and magnified up through the glass until its size was a distortion of nature. She had long lashes too, and used them coyly. Fair dry hair, a pretty skin, an ugly figure, thick, unshaped and pre-posterous legs. Her name ought to have been Dora.

"Well, and where did you go on your brisk walk?" Sylvester pursued obstinately.

"Tig and I went down the avenue to see Mrs. Kenny." It was one of the higher benefits of Piggy's life that the local dressmaker should live in the gate lodge of Kilque. "Didn't we, Tig? Yes - and - I - met - a - big - black - cat - and - I - hunted - him - up - a - tree——" Her voice changed to a gruff mumble through pouted lips, and Syl-vester realised peevishly that she was giving speech to some lying boast of Tig's. For Tig was petrified of Mrs. Kenny's black tom cat. Sylvester had seen him routed by him many times. Nor was Tig ever the aggressor in these contests.

"And what progress had Mrs. Kenny made with your spring muslins, my dear? 'Tig' (Sylvester always spoke to and of Tig in inverted commas as it were, thus illustrating to himself his dislike of the dog and the dog's name), come here you nasty 'Tig.' Would you like a little curry? You would, I know. Well, you're not going to get any from me, so *go away*."

"Oh, Sylvester—teasing my poor little dog! And you *know* I don't like him to be fed at meal times." Piggy was indulgent. She laughed and filled a purple glass with water. "Really, Hester" (for she was longing to talk about her clothes, in spite of the "not much in my line" aura in which she tried to surround the subject), "Mrs. Kenny is too *maddening*. You know that black *Patou* dress Joan gave me, *rather* lovely, cut with a *terrible* deep V at the back and that marvellous swathed line?"

"You mean the black dress she wore at hunt balls three years ago? I thought it was too short even for you."

"She'd hardly have given it to me if it was useless, would she?" Piggy's voice rose instantly in defence of her friend.

"From what I know of Joan," Sylvester put in, "she certainly wouldn't have given it to you unless it was useless to her anyway. However, Joan's a lovely girl. I'm very *fond* of Joan. Go on, Piggy. What has happened to this pretty gown?

Can't Mrs. Kenny translate Mr. Patou's inspiration
into terms of the present day, or what?"

"Well, you know clothes aren't very much in
a Piggy's line, but I *did* think I'd hit on rather a
bright plan for raising the waist line six inches and
dropping the hem line eight inches at the same
time. Well, as far as I can see she's done precisely
the reverse. It's too awful. I can't tell you what
a mess she's made of it. I nearly went mad this
morning trying to get it pinned together even as
it was before again."

"She's probably given it a sly snip here and
there that she won't confess to," Sylvester suggested helpfully. He saw with a cruel enjoyment
a picture of Piggy, plump and cold in her underclothes, standing in Mrs. Kenny's dark and icy
parlour (dark geraniums and weeping ferns shut
out the daylight and equally prevented the eyes
of the curious from peeping in upon the privacies
of her trade) while, their minds in a fog which
would never be lifted, they sought to recapture the
infernal subtleties of Mr. Patou's three-year-old
inspiration. Their minds in a fog, their hands
cold, their mouths full of pins, to what strange
shapes had they tortured this hellish garment
before despair had settled in on them and they
sought to put it back as it was before and could not.

"The *stupidity* of it," Sylvester murmured.
"Why, do you see me struggling to turn a single-
breasted coat into a double breasted coat? No.

Because I know it can't be done. Next time Joan gives you a three-year-old gown, Piggy, accept facts, do not," he finished sententiously, "expect miracles."

"Sylvester, will you have stewed black-currants or baked apple?" Hester asked him.

"Baked apple, please. May I have some cream, please, Piggy? But was it Mrs. Kenny's fault, exactly?"

"Well, she might at least have done something about the dress before last week—she's had it since July and now it's the middle of September."

"And none too long to solve such a problem as it seems to be." Sylvester looked up from his pudding. "Were I you, Piggy—but where's the use of giving advice unsought?"

"Well, what were you going to say, Sylvester?" Piggy asked eagerly.

"I was going to suggest that in future, my dear, you should stick to green satin and *Weldon's Journal.*"

"Why green satin?"

"Why, I hardly know," said Sylvester, who had a vast contempt and dislike for green satin. "But I think you should find out whom Mrs. Kenny dared to sew for from July to September."

Sylvester had a profound regard for Mrs. Kenny —for her courage, resource and artfulness, particularly displayed in remaking Joan's clothes for Piggy. He often visited her when his walks took him past the gate lodge and they would discuss together the London fashions. He could tell her, speaking as one authority to another, of new materials and their sensuous names, and of new, exotic colours, filling her with a wild interest and an excited delight. And when he told her about the clothes worn by his leading ladies she would grow greedily intent on every word, sticking them in her memory like pins in a cushion, against the time when she would re-tell them for the confusion of clients who thought they knew too much, or for the delight of those with whom she was in sympathy. But no matter how good an opinion Sylvester privately had of Mrs. Kenny, he saw no reason why he should not sow a little discord between her and Piggy.

"I expect she was busily making a trousseau for Miss Maureen Joly, the Bank Manager's daughter," he said now. "I saw an account of her wedding in to-day's *Irish Times*."

"Just about what she *was* doing," Piggy spoke for once with real feeling and that vindictiveness of spirit which nearly all women display when they see or hear of the energies of their dressmaker being dissipated upon others. "I do think she ought to put me first," she said sourly, "after all, she does live in our gate lodge."

"I'd stop going to her if I were you."

"Oh, one can't quite do that, can one? Still, it is rather annoying—that appalling Maureen Joly."

Hester, who had sat through luncheon ruminating darkly, now said, "Piggy, do you want the car this afternoon?"

"No, I don't think so," Piggy answered in a faintly self-sacrificing voice. "Not if you want it, of course."

"Oh, it's of no importance," said Hester, and her project, whatever it had been, floated, floated away on a breath, a disregarded thing—"Sylvester, shall we have a game of croquet together presently?"

Instantly Piggy felt that, after all, she did not require the car. If nobody else was going to take it, it might spend an economical afternoon in its garage. But she did not say so. She was busily lighting a cigarette. And with Piggy, lighting a cigarette was an absolute ceremony full of studied gestures and deft observances. She was insufferably mannered and this was one of her tricks which particularly annoyed Sylvester. Piggy annoyed him very easily it is true.

"Heavens!" she glanced dramatically at her wrist-watch. "I must *fly*—Only just time to write to Joan before post time. I'd no idea it was so late."

"Oh, how insufferable she is," Sylvester said lazily, cruelly, and well before the door had shut on Piggy's fat backside so roundly moulded in purple tweed. He began to peel a pear. "Will you eat half this pear, Hester? It will never be so right as now. Tell me, how do you endure her?"

"People are not nearly so intolerable to me," said Hester, "as they are to you. At any rate," she added, "I do not stir about in my intolerance like you do. I never *provoke* people into being themselves, either. They are bad enough armoured in pretences, but when they are *themselves*——"

"But you indulge Piggy, my dear. No use indulging Piggy. And Piggy hasn't any self, any-how. Who is she imitating now? Joan—I suppose? I caught her talking very like Joan. Yes. The passion for Joan has certainly increased since I visited you last. And why?"

"Well," said Hester, "of course Joan has taken her up much more heavily since you gave us that lovely motor car."

"Do you tell me so? If I thought that I'd take it away from you to-morrow. But surely Joan has cars and cars of her own."

"No. They have only one car now—bad times you know. And Robin often wants to go shooting when Joan wants to get somewhere else."

"But after all you are equally guilty of lending the car to Joan, Hester. It's *your* car just as much as Piggy's."

"Yes, my dear, but——" and Hester stopped. "But," she would have said, "I live here at Piggy's expense. I have wasted my living. I have thirty-five pounds a year of my own. Since I wish passionately to live at Kilque and the idea of working for others is abhorrent to me, I must not go out of my way to sour Piggy. She is, on the whole, very good about her money. I do think it deplorable of her to lavish it on that grasping Joan, who has so much in any case, but at least I need not thwart her over it. How foolish and useless it would be."

"But what?" Sylvester asked.

"But life is very *difficult*." It was a phrase that Hester often used to get herself out of any conversational hitch. Very useful if one had said too much. Very useful if one was not going to say too much.

After this they went into the drawing-room to make coffee and drink it. Here they found Piggy sitting writing, writing pages—she who almost never wrote—with a sort of absorbed frenzy. Yet not so absorbed as to spoil the important effects: gathering up sheets: dropping them on the floor— "Beloved Joany" upwards: picking them up with a little start of embarrassment: sliding them under her blotting-paper.

The coffee was boiling over out of its glass container when they came in. Hester moved the lamp without any comment and Sylvester watched her making the coffee in that exact and formal way in which she did most things.

"Oh, I can't *possibly* drink it now," said Piggy, feverishly gathering the sheets of her letter together, reading them and numbering them and stuffing them into an envelope. "Shall I be in time for the post? I think I'll take the car; then if I miss it at Kilphelan I can go on to Hook."

Sylvester pursed his lips and turned his back to her. He almost laid back his ears. He looked like a hungry cat. Piggy rushed dramatically from the room.

"But if she's going on to Hook," his sour curiosity overcame his dislike to talking about Piggy, "why doesn't she go and see Joan? It's on the way."

"Oh, she never goes there unless she's expressly bidden. Or unless she has a magnificent excuse."

They both listened to the car—to her expensive roar in low gear, as Piggy came round the corner of the house and disappeared down the avenue.

"Disgusting," said Sylvester. "How I wish I'd given you a very small, cheap car that Joan would have detested."

"I almost wish you *had*," said Hester, opening a book and immediately losing consciousness of the moment in its perusal. Sylvester picked up his knitting, he was making himself a pair of mauve mittens against the rigours of the coming fishing season, and they both sat in silence while the sun coming in at the window almost extinguished the fire in the grate. Presently they would have their game of croquet.

"I'll tell you what I'll do," said Sylvester, looking up from his knitting at the end of forty-five minutes. "I'll sell that car I gave you. I'll have you taught to fly and I'll give you each a small aeroplane. With any reasonable luck Piggy and Joan will then perish together."

"How waspish you are," said Hester in her indifferent way.

"What was it you thought we might have done when you wanted the car at luncheon time?"

"I thought we might have gone down to the sea and gathered blackberries for jam."

"Oh, Hester, and you *know* how I enjoy that! Why didn't you insist on the car? How *weak* you are. And now you tell me about it just to upset me and spoil my afternoon." Sylvester disentangled his fingers from his knitting wool and put down his work with a sigh of displeasure. "I *do* adore knitting," he said, "but I must stop while I still want to go on, that's the great thing to remember. That's what keeps me constant to its charm. Shall we have our game of croquet?"

Hester mumbled and stirred over her book.

"Half-past three, my dear," Sylvester continued. "And when I've decided which pair of shoes I'm going to wear for our game, you must bestir yourself." Sylvester considered his feet for a while. "I think," he said then, "of all my lovely shoes this pair I am wearing is perhaps the prettiest." He went out into the hall where he discovered

Tig scraping his back sensuously beneath the sofa.
He chastised him with less unkindness than he
would have shown had Piggy been present and
gathering up a blue and yellow croquet ball and
two mallets from under the geraniums in the porch
he stepped delicately out into the afternoon.

The thin sweet fire of an autumn day, an autumn
afternoon, nearly gone, the brittle exactitude of
its hours profoundly excited Sylvester. In September he felt like King Lear. "Let me not be mad,
not mad, Sweet Heaven. Keep me in temper——"
Of course Lear was written in the autumn. Now
a little fire in a wild field is like an old Lecher's
heart. He saw a fire of weeds. He saw fields of
turnips, their leaves bright blue, frozen blue. And
by the sea hangs one who gathers samphire, dreadful trade. He saw the height, the dead cushions
of sea-pinks, the washing of blue air in against a
cliff, space and water—that disgusting Piggy!
This was one of his favourite sort of sea days.
Perhaps she would be back from the post in time
for them to go after all. But no. The proper hour
for sea-going was now past.

The croquet lawn at Kilque was a narrow slip
of grass at the back of the house. Dark plantains
grew on it. Weeping willows perpetually mourned
over it and beyond its level a slope fell away
abruptly to a river that hurried round a curve—a
curve that Sylvester found distastefully Teutonic
and picturesque—below. This river even had a

rocky bed and occasional waterfalls discharged
their waters heavily from varying heights, for the
bank opposite to Kilque was precipitous and
wooded. He preferred the other side of the house.
For one thing Piggy had not made a rock garden
there. He dropped the croquet balls on the grass,
where they rumbled on for a few feet and stopped,
so bright, solid and pleasing in the sunlight, and
laying one mallet beside them, used the other as
a crutch to support himself in the contemplation
of Piggy's garden.

Beneath the spreading shade of one of the weeping willow trees Piggy had in a sudden burst of
horticultural enthusiasm erected a dreary cairn
of stones. She had heaped a steep cone of earth
round the stem of the tree and stuck stones into
this after the manner of one who sticks almonds
in a trifle. Round this curious Phallic symbol
flat stones had been laid, a circular crazy pavement, from each side of which a short artery of
pavement led to two smaller symbols. Except
that the stones were not whitewashed it was much
the sort of crime that a lonely policeman with a
taste for gardening might have perpetrated in his
leisure moments. The only plant that flourished
there was the common periwinkle or *Vinca—*
Sylvester preferred to speak of plants by their
correct botanical names. Perhaps because he
secretly liked the Worts and Banes and Winkles
of their English names and preferred to keep this

liking to himself. He thought it an inexact and slightly mawkish preference.

When Sylvester had looked long enough at Piggy's garden to soak himself in a perfect rapture of abhorrence he then began to think it was more than time for Hester to come out and amuse him. After all he was a guest.

"Hester, Hester," he called, for the bow window of the drawing-room bulged above the croquet lawn, "Hester, Hester." Then he began to sing, for she loathed his singing:

Je suis descendu,
Boudonant
Boudon-ette
Dans le jardin
Qui fleurit
Je suis descendu
Boudonant—Boudonette——

How he and Hester had detested the French governess who had implanted these verses so unalterably in his memory; a hot-blooded girl—she had beaten them, had cherished a glorious passion for Hester's and Piggy's father and had (most sensibly he considered now) transferred her unsatisfied emotions to the postman, whom she loved happily for several months before her employer interrupted the idyll and returned her abruptly to her own country. Such a pity! The children's French was getting on so nicely. But one could not risk it, of course—Say *"Papillon,"* Sylvester. Of course you remember it perfectly well—Well, say as much as you do remember— And Piggy, plucking importunately at her mother's skirts: *I* can say it, mummy, *I* remember. Let *me* say *"Papillon"*—All right, darling. Begin— "Jolie Papillon" — And Piggy, reciting the verses with appropriate gestures, flapping her arms for wings and laying her fat rosy cheek on her folded hands, a last dreadful representation of sleepiness. Well, so much for memories of Childhood's Happy Hours.

Hester appeared. Her dark head with its curious strip of white hair was bare. She was wearing a magenta jersey, a sharp and grateful note of colour it was too, and at a little distance, her long neck gave her head the poise of a bird's. Her way of walking was like a bird's evening flight—straight and tired.

"Sylvester, *must* you sing?" she said. "Your singing destroys one."

"I always think I sing rather prettily—a tiny drawing-room voice, I know, but very sweet." He handed her a mallet and gave her her choice of either the blue or the yellow ball. She chose the yellow and they began to play.

The croquet lawn faced the west, so presently the afternoon sun filled it with warmth and light. With the house behind it, it was as draughtless as a box, a delicious hot box about which Hester and Sylvester moved slowly, directing the angular progressions of their croquet balls with quiet skill and unhurried venom, for in this game they were merciless antagonists to each other, foes who yielded never an inch of advantage, nor played the game for the game's sake, but venomously, despitefully and, if possible, dishonestly, each sought to inflict defeat on his opponent.

At last their game was over and Sylvester by the foulest means had won. Neither of them enjoyed losing so he set about conciliating Hester in her defeat. "You cheated more extravagantly than I did, that's all. That's why you won," Hester said coldly.

"Is it tea-time, dear?" Sylvester asked, "and tell me, why isn't that Piggy back? I hate a meal without Piggy to provoke."

"Not quite tea-time. And I must feed my chickens."

"Well, I'm going for a little walk."

Hester went round to the cold, shady side of the house and watched Sylvester depart down a side path that led away from the avenue and through the cold, grey stems of a plantation of beech trees—to a small wood where ash and alder grew and birch trees too. Here, near to some bright water, Sylvester had once planted a quantity of the Wanda Primula, which, finding their situation comfortable, grew there with hearty enthusiasm and in their season struck an in-

credible note of beauty. Sylvester had never seen
his Wanda in flower. He had once asked Hester
how she looked and when Hester told him in the
palest words she could find he had shuddered
faintly, saying: "Yes, I was afraid so. Almost
too good." But he still continued to visit the
place at other less vulgar seasons, cutting out
brambles, dealing harshly with nettles and spreading his Wanda farther among the rocks and birch
stems and along the bright low water of the stream.
There he had gone this afternoon with a sharp
trowel and a sharper billhook and the thickest
imaginable pair of gloves, for he hated nothing
so much as the thorns of briars, unless it was mud
under his nails.

Kilque was partly Hester's house as has been
said before. It was she who had painted the walls
yellow and the doors and windows and the avenue
gates that deep and happy shade of blue which
her neighbours considered such a futile exhibition
of bad taste. Hester, however, found it charming.
She had a passion for Kilque which she thought
must be like a little house in Bath. Why Bath?
Sylvester asked her once. Well, *near* Bath anyhow, Hester amended vaguely. But as she had
never been in or near Bath herself, Sylvester
could not quite follow the connection. Jane Austen
he supposed. Those flat windows in the small flat
Georgian face of it and the short flights of two
blank walls on either side, ending in tiny pillar-

box lodges. He wondered why she did not take down the dreadful glass porch that had been built before the door with its long-legged fanlight. But no doubt she wanted it for growing winter bulbs. He had seen it looking uncommonly pretty filled with purple and grey Woolworth tulips. He enjoyed with Hester a passion for purple flowers in the winter months.

Kilque was a complete miniature of a large house of its period with a tiny basement deep and dark, and a toy dog kennel of an attic. With money cleverly spent upon it, it could have been made the most charming little house in the world. But only Hester would have spent money on it and she had it not to spend. Piggy spent her money on clothes, on presents for Joan, on her silly life in general, but never on her house. And Hester resented this darkly and silently. She herself would buy bulbs, hardy shrubs and sometimes roses, but the profits of her chicken farming did not run to interior decoration. Sylvester considered the house was very well as it was and would not have given either of them a penny to change it. His horror would have been as great for Hester's decorative genius as for Piggy's splashings with distemper in his own particular Edwardian retreat.

Now Hester went down to the kitchen, which was as dark as possible, so dark that in the summer months the servants had to light a paraffin lamp by six o'clock to see what they were doing,

a lamp which, in the winter months, they seldom
extinguished for more than an hour and a half
during the day. Of course there was a certain
amount of that boastfulness in misery in which
servants are so inclined to indulge about this,
Hester considered. Still she would have liked to
have had a kitchen where one did not have to
peer about quite so much and where almost all
the available space was not occupied by a mammoth range, which had been installed in the year
1897 and had devoured coal with voracious greed
ever since. Hester seldom permitted herself to
dwell on the quantities of gold, which, in the form
of fuel, were yearly poured into its disgusting
maw. Sylvester, who hated cold bath water
more than anything else in the world, had insisted
on putting in an independent water heater which
stood beside the range like a bulky, sulky offspring
and was only lighted when Sylvester was staying
at Kilque.

Hester filled a bucket with dry chicken food.
The dust rose off it and settled quietly down in
the dusky dirty kitchen and on Hester's dark
bright hair. Neither of these things did she
observe, for she had a tranquil faculty of quelling
her powers of observation. Otherwise she would
not have found her life as entirely tolerable as
she did.

There was nobody in the kitchen. A long
beaming shaft of light struck in at the window and

rode down the gold confusion of dust to the table where it fell across a blue mug and plate, briefly invigorating their colour. There was a hot moist smell of washing and some one sang huskily in the still darker recesses of the scullery. Hester put on her blue chicken coat that hung from a nail behind the door, and picking up her buckets went out about her business. The kitchen was far from what she would have wished it to be, but still, had it belonged to her and not in any way to Piggy, she would have enjoyed it very much at some moments.

Hester felt pleased and contented as she fed her pugnacious cockerels and shapely modest pullets. Her fowl were Campines, small and silver and brown. As tiresome as all other breeds in their habits but pleasing to look at, a kind of wild-bird balance about them, a look as though they might almost use their wings for flight if really put to it. But this evening they were meek and biddable and easily herded into their small houses. Hester lit a cigarette before she gathered up the tin dishes, a rim of food upon them, and sat down on the roof of an empty coop. The air was thin and exciting. It sent a faint fever through her blood and set her thinking of knitting and winter bulbs and cinnamon. She was not displeased to see Sylvester come walking out of the wood and across the grass towards her. This autumn excitement demands a companion.

"Go on with your work, dear," Sylvester said, his eye on the lid of the chicken coop where Hester sat, the only visible seating accommodation anywhere near. "I will sit here and watch you. It must be almost tea time, so hurry up. These *disgusting* chickens——"He began to pick at the sole of his shoe with a little pointed stick, "*Must* they? I suppose they must."

"Tell me, Hester," he asked as they walked back towards the house, she carrying the buckets packed with empty clattering dishes, "when does the Pussy Willow kitten?"

"In March, I think."

"I thought as much! And the Alder puts forth her black buds in March too? I was afraid it might be so. Altogether too right and proper. I can't have such theatrical surroundings for Wanda. I must borrow a hatchet and chop them both down."

"No, Sylvester. I forbid it. Do leave them; I enjoy them, so *please*——"

"You are mawkish. I will put on a blue jersey to-morrow afternoon and chop them down with a bright axe."

"Pure affectation on your part."

"Well, *perhaps* it is——So Piggy's not back yet. How lovely! I thought I wanted her to be back for tea but I don't now. I forget how I was going to annoy her." Sylvester took off his Wanda-ing gloves, folded them together with the earthy sides

inwards and put them in his pocket. His hands,
Hester thought, looked as though they had been
nailed to a cross, they were so thin and drained of
blood—shells of hands not able to shutter out so
much as the last light of an old moon, should he
clap them over his eyes.

Sylvester set down his two small tools and wiped
his nose on a red handkerchief. "Winter draws on,
I think," he said, unfolding his gloves and putting
them on again. He picked up his tools and they
proceeded on their way along the bounds ditch of
the beech wood back towards the house.

To Hester there did not appear to be much sign
of the approach of winter. Certainly the summer
was ended. The last of the honeysuckle along the
ditch had died barren. The honeysuckle is so often
barren because the Hawkmoth is its only lover, as
Hester, in common with most other people, knew.
But she felt its sad case. Such a very pale desirous
flower, surely it was a pity. No distressing flowers
were left now, only the posed pairs of its leaves,
like grey china pigeons threaded on a string. She
thought: All the same I'm glad there are no red
berries. The contrast is too jolly and obvious.
I'm not sure that it is not rather an exquisite and
pleasing tragedy. She refrained from voicing these
meditations to Sylvester. She really did not wish
to do so in the least.

Sylvester walked along beside her, his delicate
nose lifted. Green wood was burning and green

wood burning is like burning honey. He perceived his happiness.

Hester and Sylvester still stood outside Kilque. Sylvester stooped to weed silky blades of grass out of the gravel. Hester waited beside him. The chickens were all gathered up and shut away, tidily, inviolably for the night. This was one of those pauses in the daytime—a moment like an island on which one stood, saying: Presently I will do such a thing. Presently I will go in to tea.

Sylvester straightened himself up and threw a handful of tiny uprooted grass tufts into a berberis bush.

"What do I hear?" he said. "I think I hear Piggy returning. I fear I do. Oh, Hester, and I thought we should certainly not see her till after tea at least. How unfair this is."

"Why? Did you think she would go to tea at Castlequarter without being specially invited? How little you know. She drove three miles past the gates to post her letter to Joan rather than do that."

"My *dear*——"

"It's because you don't understand. In a way I rather admire her curious technique of subservience. Anyhow this is not she," Hester peered up the short straight avenue at a girl who was trying with the awkward delay of entire inaptness to open the gates.

"It's the expensive motor I bought for you all right."

"Every car you hear gives you an opportunity of saying that."

"Hester, sweet, what an ungracious recipient you are."

"Look, Sylvester," Hester said. "These are strangers."

Full of strangers, the car approached. And in the curious horror engendered by the imminence of new acquaintances, Hester and Sylvester waited, the entirety of their afternoon now completely broken.

What could Piggy be doing with so many people?

"But this——" Sylvester spoke very faintly— "This is *not* true." With a sickness completely of the stomach he saw that Piggy's passengers were Jane, Jessica and Albert. Certainly this could not be true. As one who watches a bad play he saw Hester go forward to meet them. He heard Piggy's hysterical explanations of how she had run into their car at a cross roads; how their car was now "in pieces, my dear, just tiny *pieces*." This was Jane, her voice solemn and thankful; "and Jessica's leg too was in pieces, my dear, just tiny *pieces*." And Jessica, her dark face pallid and sweating with pain, was saying: "I've always wondered about real pain—and it is *frightening*—it's—*fascinating*——" Having thus brought off a bit of her own idea of herself in great stress and agony, she abandoned all such difficult mental posturing and sweated and screamed when they lifted her out of the car and carried her into the house.

Jane screamed too in sympathy and only Albert was intelligent and helpful, elated and braced to enthusiasm by this disaster.

Sylvester was useless, determinedly and utterly useless.

Piggy continued to take unto herself all blame for the accident—a terrible manifestation of the girl guide in her that would not be denied was stridently on the surface. Sylvester wondered whether this was not a skin of defence against her dramatically hospitable reception of the party at Kilque—the Cottage Hospital had been nearer to the scene of the mishap by nearly two miles, but then Piggy enjoyed overflowing with Irish hospitality, a tradition of wasteful jollity behind her.

Sylvester had time enough to wonder about the entire situation, for after he had unwillingly (and indeed the sight of pain filled him with a quite unaffected nausea) helped to carry that horrifying monster of suffering upstairs and deposited it upon Piggy's bed, he fled from them all and from their futile efforts towards the alleviation of pain —the aspirin tablets and the brandy, so silly and impotent—to the cold Edwardian seclusion of the library.

From here he presently observed the arrival of the doctor, and with his disappearance into the house the fog of pain that had lain over Sylvester's brain was parted. He was able at last to think quite freely and potently of his immense dislike and disgust of and towards Jane and Jessica and of his horror that they should have invaded Kilque in this unforeseen manner—an invasion which—he must face it—looked like being prolonged into a considerable stay.

"Well, I must go, that's all," Sylvester decided roughly. Then looking about him, from Uncle Thomas leaning upon the handle-bars of his bicycle to that English Edwardian rose in her splendid isolation upon her bamboo table, he knew that it was not expedient for him to go. On the contrary he must stay here, for only here could he write. And Jane and Jessica must be turned away immediately if possible.

God, it was incredible that they should be here at Kilque. And Jessica wearing dark grey flannel trousers and a wine coloured high-necked jersey—well, *well*—Sylvester took another look at the Edwardian rose just to reassure himself. But perhaps in these days the Jessicas too had their photographs taken with muslin folded above their bosoms and adhering apparently by faith alone. No, there were no Jessicas in this room, or if there were they had not learnt yet to discuss themselves or to devour the Janes.

It was six o'clock now—a lean hour with dinner dim in the distance and tea an unrealised moment of the past. Bitterly though Sylvester resented this intrusion, a rising curiosity pricked him as to how and why and when Jane and Jessica and Albert had done anything so incredibly unlike themselves as to come to Ireland. For Jessica and Albert he could find no reason for this departure from a precedent of Cap d'Antibes, sun, water, and a mass of gin; and for Jane the only reason he saw offended him to a weary disgust and to an unwilling admiration of her application in life. Really she was indefeatable.

"But, tell me, Jane, what *brought* you here?" Sylvester, kept in temper and even slightly sweetened by dinner, sought an answer from Jane through which he might pin down the soft and wriggling body of her reason.

They were sitting in the drawing-room after dinner. The faint chill of a room which is heated by fire alone was present behind them. Corners of this room, Sylvester was pleasantly aware, were cold, quite cold, and the flowers in these outer places would not dye the air with their fainting scent as these last roses were doing. Piggy had chopped them off by their heads and put them in a glass plate and put the glass plate too near the fire—so let them die, pleasing him in their deaths.

"Pray tell me, Jane. You have plenty of time.

Hester, impeded as she is by Piggy, will scarcely
have finished her plans for your comfort and
Jessica's and Albert's until long past her natural
bed-time."

"Oh, Sylvester, aren't we just being a very
terrible bother?"

"No, darling. Not at all. It's not your fault
that Piggy ran into you and smashed your car
and Jessica's leg and then brought you here and
left Hester and myself to deal with the situation,
is it? But I do want to know *why* you came to
Ireland."

Jane's scarred face was like a broken sixpence
or some lighter foreign coin. Her blonde, colourless head lay upon a blonde, colourless cushion.
Her brown dress fastened up to her chin and its
sleeves came down over her narrow meaningless
hands. Its skirt covered her pretty silly feet. Sylvester could almost look upon her as a Thing
again.

"But her leg is not really smashed, Sylvester,"
she said, unhappily, harking back to one of the
earlier mischances he had mentioned; "only the
ligaments torn. Six weeks the doctor says and
she will be all right."

"In a fortnight, I heard him say, she would be
fit for the road."

"He told her six weeks," said Jane firmly,
"that was the one thing which consoled the poor
girl when he said it was not broken."

"Why should that console her? Is she so excited by Ireland?"

"Well, yes; well, no. Oh, Sylvester, the time I had persuading her to come over here. I was mad to come here."

"Indeed?" said Sylvester—a prim encouragement.

"I was very, very sick—you know that, Sylvester?"

"Well, I heard. I was over here at the time."

"God, I was sick—*frightening* it was. Such *Pain*. But when I grew ever so little better Albert used to read out to me in some books we had about *Ireland*. Oh, they *were* good. Laugh? Well, I'll say I laughed! And then the bits of description were very, very lovely and sweet."

"Yes, yes. But why did Albert read them to you?"

"Well, you see, Jessica said they made her feel kind of vomity and she gave them to Albert to throw out, but Albert saw they were all of them about Ireland, and so Albert for the sake of old association with his telegraph boy kept them to read. And so one day when I asked Albert to find me something light to read after Jessica had been reading to me quite a while, he found me one of these books and I got real thrilled about the story. It made me just wild about Ireland. Have you never read *I'm going a-hunting, sir, she said?*

Oh, it's just ever such a lovely book. Or *The Courtship of Shawn O'Grady?* Or—"

"No," said Sylvester sourly. "I neither read nor do I write about Ireland."

"My dear, I should have thought the funny quaint people here would have given you a mass of copy. But perhaps it's just that I'm a real observant girl, I notice their little ways and all that. I think they're *fascinating.*"

The unreality of Jane sitting there under the lamp at Kilque voicing her dreary reactions to a land or a dream which Sylvester kept to himself, unpraised and something less than enjoyed, shocked him again to a full sense of the enormity of this invasion. He looked at Jane for a long rude moment and then gave his attention to reading the *Nation.*

In her chair Jane sat still and tired, for once she saw herself in no particular posture or situation. She was indeed very weary, weary of her trip with Jessica, who for two days had discussed the Split Atom under every conceivable circumstance of discomfort and with a cold searching precision that needed no soft inducement towards speech.

Elaborate as the detour had been which was to bring them into the country in which Mr. Playfair lived, Jane had not succeeded in fulfilling her purpose of a passing call. Instead the cold discussion of the Split Atom had, over a disgusting lunch of mutton chops (both fat and sinewy),

changed into lowering silence and progressed into
one of those public rages where one whispered
instead of screaming.

"Go and see the man if you *must* ... No. I'd
rather walk round this *filthy* little town. Oh, I
don't *mind*, my dear ... After all, if this is what
you came over to Ireland for, the sooner you face
the thing the better. . . . Well, I know it is. If
only you could be aware of what you are *doing* ...
Unconscious people terrify me, terrify me and
disgust me ... Do try and know your own lusts
and know what you're *doing*—put it on a plate and
face it. Of course I know the man quite well. He
was at Sylvester's party the night before you
succumbed to alcoholic poisoning and you were
being pretty animal-girl with him as well as I
remember. . . . No, don't let's discuss the thing—
it's a side of life I'm *not* very interested in."

Then she had screamed, screamed in a whisper
that Jane was not to go and see George, and named
Jane's emotions one by one with horrid revealing
words. There she had sat, power over Jane in her
hands, power in her dark loving, in every way
mistress of the situation. She yielded then and
flung power from her as nothing. She had won
nothing: said nothing. There she sat lighting a
cigarette, drinking gin and tonic in the wan light-
ness of the hotel parlour, her face dark in the light-
ness that was no light. And Jane whimpering and
defeated sat opposite to her. Behind Jane's head

there hung a shocking picture of Jesus and the sacred bleeding heart of Jesus. In the curious lighting of the room, Jane's painted mouth was precisely the same colour as that heart, painted as big as a bullock's heart and as red as Jane's mouth.

Jane stirred in her chair at Kilque and stirred again to consciousness the thought of Jessica upstairs, moribund under morphia and with all the ligaments in her leg torn and bruised and twisted. In *pieces* and the car in *pieces*. She shivered with pleasure in the contemplation of the situation and drew her hands up inside the sleeves of her brown dress and folded her feet away beneath her. An idol lost from heathen China she sat there in Hester's plum-coloured room.

Sylvester, looking up from the *Nation*, perceived that she was having a moment of quietness and wondered whether now he would surprise a version of the truth from her.

"Jane, how did you and Albert persuade Jessica to come here?"

"Well, I told her how lovely it would be, Sylvester; how in Ireland she could wear grey flannel trousers all of the time, or maybe even shorts, and that is what really decided her."

"And what really decided *you*, sweet?"

"A man called George Playfair," Jane replied, so surprisingly that Sylvester was silenced for a minute or what seemed sixty times as long.

"What? Not the George that you met at my party?" he asked stupidly, "the night Jessica threw a bottle at you and you told me a string of dreary lies over the telephone?"

"Yes, the night I was so drunk. That night. And indeed they were not lies."

"*Must* we have all that again?" Sylvester observed an ominous pitiful look pulling Jane's eyes even farther down her face than they were held by the thread of her scarred mouth. He knew what this foretold. For Jane, an enjoyable ten minutes detailing the scourge and the terror of girlish friendship with a savage Jessica; and for him, a sad disgust and a weary pity because he believed nearly all she told him and understood the horrifying difficulty of any real escape. He would turn her mind back to George—poor George. What had she meant by accusing him of her present whereabouts? Sylvester suffered no hurt to his vanity in accepting as without question Jane's declared reason for coming to Ireland. Indeed he had not much vanity of any kind. A malign and all-embracing sense of curiosity at least turns its possessors' interests outwards rather than inwards.

"Well, tell me more——" Sylvester spoke in a voice of persuasive interest, and no one was better aware than himself of its poultice-like power of drawing confidences. He had indeed known moments when the least imaginative of women had been driven by it to the tortured fabrication of secrets and difficulties—simply that they might confide—for some of these moments he had a rare value.

"Tell me more, Jane," he repeated, "about George."

"I mean to marry him," Jane said, although she had not thought of this until Sylvester's voice had laid upon her the necessity of providing him with some definite mental excitement; she knew now, in so far as she ever knew any truth about herself, that she meant what she had just said.

"You'll never marry him," Sylvester said. *"You'll never escape from Jessica."* He would know, he must know, whether he could surprise any genuine terror in her; any horror; any realisation of her bound life. Sylvester leant forward in his chair, his sharp unkind fingers, perceptive and unsympathetic, were joined together, fine and cold as picked fish bones.

But there was in Jane for once no smallest quickening to his interest. She turned her face away and tears of despair ran down her cheeks. For once she made no drama of her distress, but snivelled and whimpered: *"Oh,* Sylvester, you're horrible to me, *say* you were only being horrible, Sylvester."

Sylvester, along a different set of perceptions, was aware that this was the first time to-day he had heard Jane use that horrible word. Something else had taken the place—what was it? Oh yes— *fascinating*.

But in the meantime here was Jane with the truth in her for once. Why had he sought for it? He disliked the truth. It was apt to bind sympathetic natures like his own upon the wheel of their friend's necessity. Could he have changed Jane back now into the object she had been but so short a time ago he would gladly have done so. Simply an object of art in her brown gown, with a white broken face and hidden hands and feet, her false voice and false garrulous mind and her joyless body that had passed through all loves and known not one. That was what he would have wished her to remain. Now he had surprised a moment's fear and a moment's truth in her and he could not ignore her sad necessity, poor tiresome girl.

"Jane," he said, "stop crying, Sweetie. Listen to me, Jane, while I discuss this matter. Are you crying? Are you listening, then? Well, I myself will help you to marry George. I don't mind whether he feels inclined to marry you or not. He *shall* marry you. Between us we will secure him, Jane. And thus we will sicken and madden first Jessica, then my cousin Piggy, who has a maundering old passion for George, then George's sister Joan whom I dislike intensely and absolutely. But you must promise me to delight and gladden

George's life, for I have the strongest regard and affection for him."

"*Oh*, Sylvester——"

"Don't interrupt me, Sweetie—what was I saying? Yes, between us we must woo him, Sweetie, for I know him to have no—or almost no—experience in Love. And that is why I think that you, your life having been such as it has, are one of the few women who might hope to make a success of marriage with George. You're not in love with him?" Sylvester paused anxiously.

"Oh, *no*, Sylvester——"

"No, I didn't really think you were. You don't know why you want to marry him—just marriage, not an affair—do you?"

"I can't tell you, really. But it's all in one of those books he sent me, *The Girl Who Gave*, I think. But I'm not certain, I must ask Albert."

Piggy's vile dog pushed the door roughly open at this moment and laid himself before the fire with an almost insulting air of propriety.

"Oh, what a *horrible* dawg——" Jane darted out a foot and dealt him a shrewd kick. She tucked her foot back again beneath her brown gown; her foot was bound to a high-heeled brown sandal and each of its toenails was painted like bright synthetic coal. Her foot had been like a fierce darting lizard and she had known at once that Piggy's dog was unworthy of any gentle thought.

Sylvester approved this quick unsentimentality, but he thought it augured badly for her relationship with George. For to George a Dog was a Dog, just as a White man was a White man, and the Virginity of unmarried women as unquestioned as the Honesty of his friends at cards.

Hester came in and stood for a minute warming her hands at the fire. Hester was like a quick living bough, Sylvester decided, watching her, the bough of a plum tree, leafless, and without flowers, but strong with life. Why did he think of plum trees? Because she was wearing a plum-coloured velvet coat, perhaps, some such dreary association of ideas. But his mind was truly in February. He watched her put a small knotted log firmly and tidily in the fire and heard her saying to Jane, in her distinct, unembarrassed voice:

"No, indeed it has been no trouble. Your man is such a helpful creature. But I want to tell you, as my sister is rather stupid I think over things like this—that if you're going to make a long stay with us you will have to pay us something, we can't really afford to keep you otherwise. My sister's hospitality sometimes gets the better of her sense of proportion."

"Oh, *yes*! I'm so very very happy you've suggested this plan. I wanted to propose it when the doctor said my darling friend might be laid up quite a while, but I was frightened to, really— your sister was so kind and difficult, you know.

Now tell me, do you think six guineas a week? Do you think you get out on that? Six guineas for each of us I mean, of course. Please do say if we would be robbing you."

"No. I should make on that," Hester said. "But after all," she added, "one does not have P.G.'s for fun. I've always wanted to, but Piggy's been so difficult about it. Do you know, I think it might be almost *better* if we kept the fact that you *are* P.G.'s between you and me and Sylvester." How artfully she included him in her confidence, "and didn't tell Piggy anything about it. You can make the cheque out to me. And if you wouldn't mind letting me have an advance for the first week to-morrow morning it would be definitely convenient."

Hester was going to make certain of eighteen guineas at any rate and Sylvester admired her for it. There was no knowing when Piggy might not overcome her reluctance to accept money in exchange for the legendary hospitality of Kilque.

Hester was saying: 'Of course we can't give you unlimited drink on that," and Jane delayed not a moment to proclaim her own willingness to drink water and the undoubted benefits which Jessica would derive from an unstinted flow of milk.

"It's not quite as bad as that," Hester reassured her, "more—a glass of sherry before dinner—*just*

before dinner—not cocktails from six o'clock onwards."

"I think, Hester, you might let them have
another *tiny* glass of sherry with their soup and
still not be a loser." It was beyond Sylvester to
resist this small shaft of comprehending insolence.

Hester dropped a heavy, unexpressive eyelid in
Sylvester's direction. Her other eye continued to
express hospitality on a businesslike footing towards Jane.

Presently she took Jane up to bed and Sylvester
was left alone. He thought he would go out and
take the shortest of short walks upon the croquet
lawn. But almost before he had opened the window
and leant out into the evening he had changed
his mind. The night was not his. He would not
walk here under the rainy moon, or discover any
bleak daytime familiarity with the changed trees.
He would not see this river lest a Teutonic vulgar-
ity of reflected moonlight should alter for him the
loud sweetness of its flowing. He heard a small
terrible screaming near on his left hand, but he
had not seen the white owl go by on dumb tilted
wings, and for this he was thankful. For he was
afraid.

He shut the window upon the romantical sharp
bark of a fox and turned round again to Hester's
warm, sweet room. There was a bloom on its
tired prune-like colourings and its pale brown walls
were as blonde as a skin. For one moment as he

turned back to it from the night without, the whole room lived and was. The flower's scent turned faintly animal. The chaste citron quality, thin and passionless, of autumn flowers was changed in them to this lusty breath. The dark oily gleaming of Hester's Waterford glass, to-night it looked as familiar to the hand as glass in daily use. All china pieces in this room, too, must now be smooth and luxurious to touch. Sylvester would not lay his hand upon one single piece for he knew it must be so. But—God help me—I am turned all whimsey now, he thought, and he guarded the fire and put out the light for it was more than bedtime.

He met Hester on the turn of the staircase. They each carried a lighted candle and their shadows flew about them as the draught flattened the flames of their candles like little flags.

Excitement seemed to him to be burning through Hester, her thin body had taken on a new quality of rapture. Her purple coat was dyed in the stain of true romance. (In one of its pockets no doubt was the cheque for eighteen guineas.) Her full eyes looked about in all directions but never at him. She was like an eager, ageing woman who has always seen Love pass her by and now sees Love stop to look her way with clear intention.

Sylvester said: "Hester, do you look like this when you receive my expensive presents, or only when you have stolen eighteen pounds from Piggy?"

Hester said: "Don't be absurd, Sylvester.
Good-night, my dear. You'll try to endure them,
won't you? I know it is terrible for you."

He saw her hurrying down the last of the stairs,
her shadow jumping malignly behind her, a little
stuffed monkey on the wall, and heard her shut
the drawing-room door. No doubt she would be
doing a little honeyed calculation within there, sitting before her small bow-fronted bureau with its
shallow softly-sliding drawers. Many, many plans
and calculations Hester must have made sitting
there upon her powdering chair that had no back.
Plans that failed into dreary abortive conclusions,
calculations too unsoundly rooted to bring the
success towards which they seemed so surely
directed.

But to-night she would sit in excited peace, the
steady gold light of her candle in that warm place
illuminating for her a cheque for eighteen pounds,
a cheque stolen from Piggy, and, with luck, the
forerunner of many more such cheques. He
wondered if she would gamble this away too as
she had done her other monies. He supposed she
would, putting it after quite meticulous calculation
into some really absurd enterprise, unsound as it
was unlucky. Then there she would be again,
cast back upon her embittering necessary depend-
ence on Piggy and with yet another dishonest
idiocy scored up against her.

Hester's complete personal integrity, the untroubled wholeness of her self-esteem in the face of the constant discovery and humiliating discussion of her financial mistakes and small dishonesties was quite fascinating to Sylvester.

He had before now heard Piggy demanding from Hester the change due to her from a ten-shilling note. And heard Hester lie and quibble and wrangle to keep one-and-ninepence her own and unexplained in her account. He had heard her defeated in her lie and seen her yield up the disputed sum and still retain possession of her own cynically calm view of the matter. It was a state of mind which he found entirely admirable in her. A detachment of spirit in which personal vanity had an even lesser part than personal morality. Both to her were the shadows of shadows, dull, unreal ghosts, unworthy the harbour of her conduct.

CHAPTER IV

THIS afternoon Piggy was going to see her lovely girl-friend, Joan.

She did not wish to arrive too early, nor yet did she wish to waste a moment's intercourse.

Joan wrote letters after luncheon; the post left Castlequarter at three o'clock. To synchronise her arrival with the outgoing post, to appear as the fever of letter-writing subsided and before the activities of the afternoon began, Piggy exercised

the most artful calculation. It was so important to
the success of the hours to arrive at the proper
moment. This she felt rather than knew by any
conscious statement to herself. It was awkward to
be surprised waiting at the gate of Castlequarter,
as she had once been found by Robin, Joan's
husband, for the appearance of a bicycling servant
with the post. Piggy, who could neither lie nor
tell the truth, found such a moment cruelly embarrassing.

For half an hour before she retired to her bedroom to dress her body for the occasion, Piggy
wandered nervously about the house, a faint, cold
sweat of excitement on her, a sickness and a
restlessness until at last she could with decency
withdraw and attire herself.

Then again the situation was encompassed by
difficulties. How To Look One's Best In Old
Clothes was a question that fevered Piggy to her
very soul. The passion that was on her to look her
very best on these lovely days was set about miserably by the knowledge that her appearance at
Castlequarter in any clothes not in rags would be
met by a cold scrutiny, and Joan's faint ridiculing
voice would examine the matter, saying: "All
dressed up to-day, Piggy?" or, "Why are you so
grand to-day, Piggy?" or, "I *did* mean to take the
children ratting in the manure heaps this afternoon,
but it seems a bit severe on your nice new clothes."
And nothing would be left for Piggy but an em-

barrassed wriggle and an incoherent explanation of
the positive antiquity of her clothing.

To-day Piggy dressed herself up in as faithful an
imitation of Joan's outdoor clothes as her own
passionate concentration and Mrs. Kenny's skill
had been able to accomplish. True this rough
tweed skirt was new, but, instructed by her love,
she had torn and darned a good three-cornered
hole, she had left her dog's wet footprints to dry
upon it too and hoped its unfamiliarity would so
pass unnoticed. A plain silk shirt with a bright
sleeveless pullover pulled over, a dirty fawn-
coloured cardigan and a beret worn at the least
becoming of all its possible angles, and Piggy was
dressed and ready. No. She still had to powder
her face with a heavy ochre powder that must
soon turn to yellow dough in the creases of her nose.
And she must clean up her mouth with a greasy,
white lipstick that tasted of scented lard. Yes—and
fill her case from a package of cheap Turkish
cigarettes. Then she was dressed and ready—all
but her chamois gloves with string sewn in the
palms. Although she never rode they had been
Joan's gift and preserved with holy care for the
last two years.

Piggy left the house with an air of secretive
importance. To complete the moment some one
should have asked her where she was going, pre-
ferably some one whom she could have left in a
mild state of interest, possibly of envy of her where-

abouts on this afternoon. However, she saw no one but Sylvester, who was killing flies at one of the hall windows with a very grim expression on his face.

As she passed, Sylvester said: "Aren't you taking your pretty dog?"

"Oh, I don't think so—not to-day, old man——" Piggy bent over him in denial. "We were ever so naughty last time we went to see the Little White Ladies at Castlequarter." She giggled and simpered. For the life of her she could not have avoided somehow letting Sylvester know where she was going. Sylvester, who was not popular at Castlequarter, for his sour absurdities alarmed his cousin Robin and disgusted Robin's wife Joan, said:

"Going to Castlequarter, are you? Well, I think I'll come with you. I want to see Robin."

The whole of Piggy's mind went white and sick at this unwelcome suggestion. "Yes, yes, do come," she staggered about in her mind to find some reason, any reason, to prevent his coming. At last she produced it. "The only thing is—I know Robin and George were going to Kellsfoot moat to stink out the badger earths and if they do that, aren't they certain to go to see Tommy Knox? They always do."

"Oh, it's all right, Anxious Piggy. You don't really think I wanted to come with you, do you?"

Piggy was too relieved to hear he did not intend his suggestion to be taken seriously to be offended at the manner of his withdrawal. In any case it would have been difficult to tell from Sylvester's voice whether he was being insulting or reassuring, it was so gentle and uncertain. She hurried out of the house before he could again change his mind.

She arranged herself in the car, for she drove like a lady, sitting up very straight with two cushions behind her back, and embarked on the full tide of change that carried her out from the familiar Piggy of Kilque to the romantic Piggy of Castlequarter. As she drove, chameleon-minded, from one house to the other she was happy, very happy indeed, for had she not matter enough to entertain Joan for every moment of every hour she should spend with her.

She proceeded to compose a mental *précis* that nothing be lost. Smashed motor cars. (Difficult to explain that one had not lost one's head. One must not, however, avoid all responsibility for the accident.) Well, anyhow—smashed motor car. Smashed leg; all the doctor said; all the friend said; all Hester said; all Piggy thought. Million-airess friend; clothes, hideous scar, American voice. Over-dressed. Painted. Nails. Toe-nails. Sandals. Sylvester. Hester. Bedrooms. Food. Albert.

A rich conversational seam indeed with side pockets innumerable for excavation. Piggy saw curiosity and interest growing each moment more sharp and vivid with such a tale unfolding. She saw herself providing these curious strangers as an exotic dish for her friend's delight. It was within her power to delight Joan. Providence was kind to Piggy at any rate, if in such kindness a little harsh to Jessica who lay to-day in severe pain, poor girl.

Unknowing of the day through which she drove Piggy hurried, in uneven spurts and with much horn blaring at cross roads on towards Castle-quarter and the telling of her tale. Piggy had spent her whole life like this, without actually *living* for one moment of her thirty-two years. What she would look like, what she had looked like, what she would tell, how much success her story had met with—always the future or the past tense of living. Her extravagant generosity ran so much ahead of her means that she never had one actual moment's joy of its bestowal. She did nothing actually, seeing always the ceremony of doing a thing, the picture of herself doing a thing, or the thing perhaps done, but having no present joy of any act. All her life was made as she had made her rock garden, with ceaseless rather grand chatter and an extravagant and ignorant ordering of plants that never began to think of growing. Then: "I must make a viola garden because my name is Viola." But even the vulgar violas grew bleakly and obstinately for their namesake. And every year she would say: "I don't know *why*, but the roses weren't very good this year," while the six dreary monthly roses round the sundial would rattle their starved, unpruned growths in the east wind which always blew where they were planted. Piggy would do tremendous things with a rose-grower's catalogue and a pencil, putting a mark against all the new, expensive names of roses which she had heard Joan mention, but as far as Kilque was concerned, all the catalogued excellence remained unproved.

In all Piggy's self there was no lonely place—not one thing that belonged to Piggy—not one thing that a word of encouragement could not at once elicit. She had never known a single-minded effort or experienced a sincere desire—not even for marriage, although here she came as near sincerity as she would ever go. In all her romantics for Joan she was least sincere in that on this she most believed her life was founded, and so deceived herself with the most energy, persuading herself of Joan's necessity towards her and bolstering up her own belief in this in a hundred ways—in the giving of little gifts and in the giving of rich, expensive gifts; in this like nothing so much as an amorous and impotent old man, buying a rich jewel for a teasing young Miss to see her lovely gratitude for a moment. Piggy's adoration had known several periods of intensity. There was the first, the briefest interlude in childhood's happy hours.

Joan came to stay at Kilque. She was a long thin romantic creature who ran and played and laughed, told stories marvellously, climbed trees like a monkey, ate biscuits in bed and said she liked the feel of the crumbs. Such romantic originality! And Piggy? She was fat and six. She watched and worshipped. Joan would paint pictures, too. She would paint in a book with drawings printed ready for colouring. One day she said:

"I think I must put a bit more calf on this leg." Piggy, ignorant of anatomical terms, said:

"Why? Why? Joan? Why should it look any more like a leg if you draw a calf out of it?"

"Silly!" Joan said kindly. "Your calf is the fat part of your leg." She put her leg on the schoolroom table and showed Piggy what a calf was. Piggy's heart thumped.

Again, Piggy would sit like an envious and worshipful little toad upon the third branch of the Spanish chestnut in the garden while Joan was far gone among the topmost branches, among other stars.

Joan went away. Her visit was ended. Her clothes were packed and gone. Piggy's nurse was clearing out the back of a drawer where Joan's belongings had been. She threw a worn and wasted piece of Joan's dark green hair ribbon into the waste-paper basket.

Piggy saw this happen. She flung herself upon the basket and tore the ribbon out. She rushed from the house with it and in the morning sunlight she swore eternal Love and Loyalty. Hat in hand,

and across her heart she swore it in the hot kitchen garden at eleven in the morning.

Joan was gone for many years. She lived with an aunt in England. She went abroad to finish her education. She returned to Westcommon to live with her brother George Playfair and she married without delay the most proper, rich, charming and eligible young man in the country.

A flame of romance had transfigured Joan's return to Westcommon. She was young and pretty, incredibly girlish and incredibly well-dressed. She rode bravely and charmingly. She was mad with enthusiasm for all outdoor sport, asking no more of life than the excitement of the chase, happy to lie for hours on her stomach with her head down a fox's earth while her favourite terrier stayed bravely below ground. Happy to dance, happy to tear lovely dresses in rough and noisy play. Happy to kiss the older men who had known her as a child (kiss them prettily and publicly) and to feel they all thought: "Ah, she's little more now—*just a lovely child.*" Happy indeed to be young, lovely, girlish, successful, adored by her brother, adored and applauded by her friends, photographed madly by every press camera at every race-meeting in Ireland, worshipped and imitated by unsuccessful girls to whom she was always kind when she could spare a moment, but not so kind as to involve herself at all in their dreary lives. A lovely stranger who was yet of the country (and those who are not

so bred can have no idea how necessary a factor this
is to success in Westcommon) it was right and
fitting that she should become Mrs. Robin Nuthatch, wife of an M.F.H. and very efficient mistress
of his country.

Marriage did little to impede her in the course of
her representation of the Girl Eternal in Irish life.
Indeed the birth of her twin sons did more than
anything to confirm her in her pose of the complete
wonder-child. Perhaps now at the age of twenty-
eight she had to pause sometimes a little longer to
hear the "Joan, you are a *baby*," which had once
followed so quickly on almost everything she said.
That, or: "Now isn't that the *purest* bit of *Joan!*"
There were even occasions when it was necessary
for her to re-introduce (wide-eyed) her babyism or
mispronounce once more that word in Joan language. But with Piggy she never had to wait or
repeat. The homage almost preceded the event.
Piggy adored and served and could be relied on to
repeat everything Joan said which Joan would have
chosen to have repeated. Piggy, one of the many
unsuccessful girl-worshippers of other days, was
now the homely girl-friend of the star. And how
happy it made her. Happy to love and serve,
beside herself with pleasure to be photographed
with her idol at a horse-show or race-meeting; to
be made use of flagrantly; to be asked with much
fuss and ceremony to any dreary party at Castlequarter; ("Piggy, darling, you *must* come and help

me, you'll be the *only* person I can have a good
laugh with over these ghastly people"), and fiercely,
determinedly impervious to the unkinder moments
when Joan had lovely parties of the young and the
rich and the amusing to which parties Piggy was
not invited. ("I wonder if you'd quite enjoy it,
Piggy? I'm afraid not, so don't come unless you
like, but do come if you think you would.")

And poor Piggy would make the obvious reluctant refusal and retire to Kilque full of brittle
excuses and complicated reasons for her absence
from the jollities at Castlequarter. At such moments Hester found her pitiful and tolerable and
Piggy, realising in some unconscious gland this
pity, would manifest her resentment to it in a sour,
unhappy sulkiness or in a hysterical fit of dark
unhappy temper.

Castlequarter was a happy house if ever there
was one. A rich and happy house whose owners
could afford to take their pleasures as the more
serious side of their lives and did so in the natural
course of events.

Piggy stepped out of her car into the sunlight
which beat upon the steps up to the hall door.
She was an imitative alien to the serious circumstance which they set about their pleasures, yet
here her life drew its colour and its shape. Here
burned the flame of her life and should it fail her
she died indeed.

The hall was cool and airy with the bright scent

of flowers. A sofa and two chintz-covered chairs
made a square within which were an empty fire-
place and an open window, a window looking out
on grass and trees, bright water and the pleasant
fall of hills.

Piggy was almost though not quite conscious of
her enjoyment of the atmosphere of this room. At
least she knew that she desired it to remain forever
unchanged; its cream distemper and vigorous
sporting prints the same, the table where Robin's
hunting caps sat, their greasy lining smelling of
stale hair oil and the black used leather of hunting
crops she wished to remain the sporting same
for ever.

"Piggy! Piggy!" a high childish voice called
and hearing it Piggy's heart made a tiny rush and
all in a short piercing moment her sense of adequacy
left her and with it her sense of equality with Joan.
She was in a mid-air of excitement, and abandoned
by all her resourceful jokes, conscious only that she
was wearing new clothes and that in a moment she
would be with Joan, defenceless with Joan.

"Piggy! Piggy!"

"Where are you?"

"In the schoolroom——"

"Coming——"

In the schoolroom, full of dingy furniture and
bright expensive toys, Joan was sitting on the floor
plucking handfuls of hair out of an unhappy terrier.

"Stay quiet, you little brute——" she screamed

at it. Its toe-nails rustled and clattered on the newspaper spread below it. The sunlight fell on Joan, on her gold hair and active dirty hands, a fan-shaped wedge of sunlight on the floor. Her little dog, who was in no pain whatever, looked up at Joan whom she loved to distraction and growled at Piggy, which she knew to be a popular move.

"Sally—naughty-*girl*! You mustn't be rude to Piggy—She does hate you, Piggy, doesn't she? Precious one, stay where you are one moment more, then you shall bite fat Piggy, I promise you——"

Piggy knelt on the floor and gave a little clumsy assistance to the matter in hand. Joan continued her dog's toilet to its end quite undistracted by Piggy's arrival.

"Joan," Piggy said at last, "have you heard about our visitors at Kilque?"

"At Kilque—No. Who?"

"People Sylvester knew in London."

"What, like that appalling man he once brought over who came out hunting in a bottle-green coat and corduroy breeches? Robin said he ought to have had a fevver in his hat."

"No; these are two women."

"*Women?*"

"Yes. I think they're *too* awful. But the unlucky thing was I ran into their car at Kilfane Cross last night and one of them broke her leg, or almost, and really I just had to bring them all three back to Kilque."

"Three of them?"

"One man—a sort of lady's maid as far as I can make out."

The drama was gone from the tale. The drama had sickened and died. There was no more life in the tale. Joan was almost bored. She was not interested. Piggy said, with a desperate attempt to excite interest:

"One of the women is a terrifically rich American, terrifically painted and terrifically overdressed with a terrific American accent (that's not the one who broke her leg) and she wants to hunt."

"Oh——" Joan suddenly woke to life, "are they going to be here long?"

"Well, the doctor thinks it will be a month before the one with the broken leg can be moved."

"Only cub-hunting then. Has she brought any clothes with her?"

"I don't think so. The other one was wearing grey flannel trousers."

"Well, if you see an opportunity to sell her those old field boots of mine, Piggy—you know, my brown Balmorals I hate so much—you might do something about it."

"I will. I'll try." Joan's passion—or perhaps it was too cold and reasoned a thing to be described as a passion—for selling her clothes to her friends and the friends of her friends was a matter in which Piggy frequently found herself an ardent mediatrix.

"Darling, you look so *lovely*, now! Such an

exquisite girl! Mother's *beautiful*—Good-little-dog!
Bite Piggy, darling—*Piggy*, you're terrified of her—
you know she doesn't hurt you."

The little dog, thus encouraged, barked hysteric-
ally and in the confusion really did inflict a sharp
nip on Piggy's fat and tender ankle. Piggy yelped
shrill and Joan laughed till she was nearly ill.
"You're such a *child*," Piggy said successfully and
she would gladly have endured worse pain for an
opportunity to make this remark, invariably calculated to put Joan in the best of tempers.

They collected the newspaper, the dog's hair,
the combs and the chalk and put them in a wooden
box. Then Joan said:

"I promised the children I'd go and tear up the
old badger earth in the church wood with them—
but aren't you wearing rather *grand* clothes for
that sort of thing, Piggy?"

"Oh, no," Piggy's explanations all left her.

"Oh, I thought you were all dressed up. Isn't
that a new skirt? I call it frightfully smart. I
suppose it's a Mrs. Kenny masterpiece."

"Oh, it's not *new*." Piggy repudiated the im-
putation feverishly.

"I live in *any* old rags," Joan said. She brushed
dog's hair off an odd tweed skirt that had once cost
a mass of money and surveyed its exquisite line
and requisite state of decay with an indulgent eye.

They left the house, carefully shutting the wire
netting gate across the door, the gate that kept

outdoor dogs outdoor dogs, and gave indoor dogs
so rooted a sense of social superiority. The September sun still shone. A wind blowing from the
kennels brought on its way the faintest bouquet of
boiling. A ghostlike horse moved stiffly in the
field below the kennels. The smell on the air did
not startle its weak dream of living, nor did the
faint bell-music of the hounds' voices, nor the
sudden harsh uproar nor the harsh admonition that
rated it to stillness.

Joan said: "I must ride Edward's pony up to
the wood, she wants a good beating, she plays up
with him."

They walked round the house and through an
archway into the stableyard. The yard was
stirring with busy boys and full of the muted
sounds of horses in their boxes. Here was excitement blunted in daily use, yet in daily usage still
romantic.

A boy saddled a small fat Welsh pony with a
back as wide as a table, she stood in wheaten straw
up to her belly, and Joan made her invariable
remark about her children's ponies as this one was
led out into the yard: "miniature weight-carrying
hunter, isn't she?"

Piggy nodded agreement. On the subject of
horses—even of Welsh ponies—she was entirely
mute and entirely self-conscious. Never forgotten
to her was a dreadful moment, years past, when,
having viewed in a trance of dumb ignorance blood

horse after high-class blood horse, she had stopped
in the last box in the yard and made her one unlucky observation: "Now this horse really does
look like galloping," she had said. And they had
answered, briefly and coldly: "Yes. That's the
carriage horse—mother still hates motors so."

Piggy's nerve had never quite recovered from
the unhappy shock of that moment. However, she
would collect now and then some one else's opinion
or observation about a particular horse and
produced it fairly convincingly as her own.

Joan mounted her child's pony. She was very
proud of her long thin legs and their pretty knees.
She was serious and intent on chastising Edward's
pony, for she had very sensible theories on the
subject of children being able to be the bullies of
their ponies.

Piggy leaned upon the iron railings of the field
in front of the house and watched Joan bending
Edward's pony in figures of eight, beating her
occasionally and riding her back and forwards past
the gate through which yesterday she had run out,
grazing Edward's fat leg upon the gate post.
Gazing thus upon Joan a blessed sense of being
possessed, bullied and fulfilled flowed happily
through Piggy's being. She was whole and at one
with herself. She was found again. She knew she
would now be able to talk with Joan.

Presently she walked beside her as they proceeded through a hot and narrow glen above which

hung the woods where Joan's children expected their mother. Joan and Piggy talked about books.

"Have you read *Boys*?" Joan asked.

"Yes."

"What did you think of it?"

"I thought it was *marvellous*. Have you read *Wind*? You know I hardly ever read novels, but I thought it was awfully good."

"Yes, indeed I have."

"Didn't you adore it?"

"Yes, I thought it was incredibly good."

"And have you read *Night Bird*?"

"No, I haven't read that. Is it good?"

"*Marvellous*."

It gave them a great sensation of quiet intelligence, this literary conversation. And they had not yet used up all their phrases of critical praise or condemnation—for instance there was still: "Well written," also "unnecessary."

There was a narrow stream of water in the very depth of that hot glen. Joan's pony stepped through the water with careful precision. Piggy hopped with clumsy exactness from stepping stone to stepping stone and fell silent as she toiled up the steep other side. Flies buzzed about the hot blackberries, Joan's pony walked strong as a bull before her. "Hold on to the stirrup leather," Joan said, "and she'll pull you up—Awfully good for you to walk, fat Piggy," but her laugh was quite fond and sweet. Piggy sweated along happily enough.

"*Gwen* wants to come and stay," Joan twisted round in her saddle to give Piggy this piece of information. They were in the dark woods now, in a sheltered green ride.

"Oh *no*, how boring for you——"

"Oh, poor old Gwen——" Joan's indulgence condemned Piggy's tone towards Gwen immediately. "She's not a bad old thing, but Robin is so tiresome about her."

"Robin *hates* her."

"Well, it's so stupid of him to hate her because she's really getting quite interested in Edward and you know she's his godmother. She might really do something about him in her will if Robin doesn't antagonise her."

"Robin does dislike her, doesn't he?"

"Yes. But you're about the only one of my girl friends that Robin *does* like."

Lovely and brief the flame that these words lighted for Piggy.

"Darling, what makes you say that?"

But she never heard. For Joan was much too idle to continue to invent friendly sentiments for Robin—who, indeed, found Piggy perhaps the most tiresome of all Joan's uninteresting friends.

However, these kind words sent Piggy's emotions reeling in a warm vertigo of pleasure. To her the assurance of a person's liking was far more real and necessary than the liking itself. So to be assured by Joan that Robin found her so entirely tolerable translated her day to an extreme point of pleasure.

"Dear old Robin," she said, "he's terribly sweet."

"Yes, he's a sweet creature," Joan agreed, placid in her assurance of Robin being her sweet creature and mildly aware that she was quieting a faint feeling of unease for those occasions when Robin said: "*Must* you ask Piggy? You know I can never think of anything to say to her," and she answered: "Yes, darling, I know she's a prize bore, but poor Piggy—one must be kind to her. Besides I rather thought of borrowing her car to go racing on Thursday. It's a long way and you know the lights of the Fiat are pretty shaky."

And now Piggy walked beside her through the wood, her heart uplifted to an almost intolerable emotion which had no end or purpose but to serve.

The wood was as dark as though green rain were falling within it. Clouds of pale flies were almost luminous, and in the black earth of its rides one stepped soft-footed. There seemed no sign of autumn within here—the death of years was upon the wood, whitening the smelly elders' hollowness, slowly encompassing the teeming life of a wood, but this one year's lovely failing was not apparent.

In a peculiarly dreary corner, smelling sour of

nettles and unwholesome fungii and darkened by
the monstrous shadows of ivy tods squatting
obscenely on little trees, Joan's sons were busily en-
gaged digging out an old badger earth, into which
they vainly encouraged a sweet but cowardly
terrier.

"She's no good, mummy," Edward, the more
decided of the twins explained. "Cowardly bitch,
she won't face a badger I don't think. I'd like to
kill her."

Sweet John, the other twin, came backwards out
of the earth like a very plump caterpillar, he had a
long briar in his hand and examined its point
carefully for hairs. "I thought I felt something,"
he explained, not that he really hoped anybody
would believe him, but one might as well cause a
little excitement as not. "Oh, *Piggy*," he exclaimed
in delight, and flung himself upon her, for he really
did adore Piggy and saw nothing to despise in her
simple slavery to his own and Edward's pleasures.

He blushed now with delight and said: "Lindy
is a good dog, isn't she? I *think* I'll call her
Venture."

"She's not. She's a 'orrible bitch, isn't she,
mummy?" Edward kicked at Lindy—that miser-
able nursery dog.

Joan was grave and stern with him over this, for
the right sort of boy does not kick his dog, however
cowardly and horrible it may be.

Edward encouraged Piggy to thrust her head

into the earth and when she was obediently grovelling blind upon her stomach he and John pinched her behind simultaneously. The colossal success of this joke reduced them to a state bordering on hysteria. They rolled upon the ground together screaming with laughter. Joan too thought the joke pretty good and Piggy, though slightly ruffled and sharply pinched, was obliged to admit that she found it all most entertaining.

After this a little serious digging took place. Suitably encouraged by Joan, the nursery dog overcame her nerves and went to ground in the bravest manner imaginable. The little boys were delighted. They lay with their ears on the ground. They thrust stones and small branches into every possible exit for a hundred yards round the earth. They swore to hearing peculiar rumblings beneath their feet in one direction and to hearing their brave dog throw her tongue in another. It was all very exciting. At last she came out (and not before Piggy had begun to long for tea), her morale restored, and her popularity for the moment reasserted. They set forth for the house once more.

Edward mounted his pony with slightly nervous courage, for she had rather frightened him the day before. Joan and Piggy carried the spades and John trailed along behind them, wearily dragging his feet and knocking his boots together and asking tiresome questions all the way.

Robin Nuthatch and George Playfair were sitting on the steps when the party returned.

The children disappeared with the alacrity and obedience of hunger towards the schoolroom and Joan and Piggy and Robin and George, all four of them mildly tired and hungry too, sat down to tea in the hall.

Feathers on the chintz, a light sky outside, too few buns, medlar jelly and weak scalding Chinese tea, meant Castlequarter from five o'clock till six to Piggy. There was the embarrassment of not being talked to and the consciousness of an eager audience if one had a funny story to tell about Joan or about the little boys, for the Nuthatch family had a really passionate interest and enjoyment in the Nuthatch family and the Nuthatch jokes. To-day Piggy was bound to have a bit of success for not only could she tell of how John and Edward had pinched her black and blue, but also how Joan had made her little dog bite her severely.

Robin Nuthatch had a red head and a rosy face. He was brave and stupid (though not in all ways stupid) and adorably kind. He loved Joan with an unswerving devotion. He loved his children and his hounds. He loved fox-hunting and good horses —a perfect Masefield saga might be written of his likes and dislikes. He would come out true to the Masefield type nine times out of ten, but the tenth time he would surprise Mr. Masefield considerably.

He had great perspicacity and politeness in his

dealings with rogues, and great patience in his dealings with honest but trivially minded men, such as formed his hunt committee, or the Select Vestry of which he was a member. His aunts all adored him—narky, humorous old Irish ladies who left him pieces of Waterford glass when they died and all the money they had saved out of the jointures his estate had paid with such uncomplaining regularity. Piggy at times enjoyed and at times suffered darkly from an unknown vicarious passion for Robin. Through Joan she loved him and would flare up wildly in his defence if he was criticised by word or implication in her hearing. Stupid, helpless defences with tears behind them and pretences and a terrifying unconsciousness. And criticism of Robin was no less frequent than criticism of any other Master of Hounds in any other country.

In Piggy's attitude towards George Playfair there was a veiled unshaped coyness, a chattering combative state of unease; for she had never, never forgotten how once—in a moment of extraordinary expansion Joan had said: "You know George really *likes* you, Piggy. He asked me if I'd never noticed your eyelashes." The excitement of this was forever in Piggy's mind when she was with George. For years it had been a definite rock on which to pitch her faith in her own attraction for men. Although the matter did not come quite within the region of material speculation, still

George's continued celibacy was an undoubted goad for girlish fancies. And when he joined in Pig-baiting, one of the stock Sunday afternoon amusements at Castlequarter, Piggy was excited to an unnatural brilliance of repartee and to a defence of her person both violent and shrill. Indeed not infrequently she would provoke John and Edward to a frenzy of ragging on the lawn in which the other members of the family could hardly forbear to join—for of all things they adored a good rough and tumble on the grass.

Now Robin said, in the dreary gentle voice which was so unexpected in him:

"But Piggy, I heard an incredible story about you to-day——"

"About *me*?" Piggy blushed into instant life.

"Very odd story—wasn't it, George?"

"Very queer story. Very surprising, I must say, Piggy. I wouldn't have believed it of you."

"Oh, you are *unkind*. What d'you *mean*? Joan, aren't they beastly?"

"I don't know what you're all talking about."— Joan at least knew that no one was talking about her—"Robin, I put my hand on Gayboy's leg after lunch and there's a lot of heat in that joint still."

"Is there, darling? I'm afraid you'll never keep him going this season."

"Oh, but I *must*. You know how I love him. I've had him long before I had you——"

"Darling!"

"But I want to know if this is true about Piggy?"

Dear George bringing the talk back to Piggy again. She bridled with pleasure.

"But I don't know what you *mean*," she said. "What *have* I done now?" She implied a life full of girlish misadventure.

"Oh, don't be dense, Piggy. I suppose they mean those unfortunate people you ran into yesterday——" Joan thought it was time for all this nonsense to come to an end. "It is true, isn't it? You broke one woman's leg and you have a party of Americans at Kilque. I should make them P.G.'s if I were you. Why should you feed them?"

"Well, they're friends of Sylvester's." Piggy was wounded and stuffy. Poor Piggy.

The little boys created a diversion here by coming in for their after tea-time hour with their parents. Such a diversion that Joan did not notice her brother go a dusky red and see a light of interest quicken through him, which would have excited her curiosity if not her disapproval had she observed it.

Edward and John, assuming the slightly laboured politeness of children at this hour, answered questions as to their day's employment with an evasive skill which many of their elders might have envied. Then they played the gramophone, an entertainment to which they were extremely partial since it was an electrically

controlled instrument and its complicated switches
enthralled them.

Under cover of a noisy tune George said to Piggy:
"Tell me more about these people you ran into,
Piggy. I met some American friends of Sylvester's
in London. I rather liked her."

"I don't think it could have been this one."
Although Piggy had not taken in the full portent of
George's mixed tenses, she found herself out of
accord with him. Accord is such a very evanescent
thing and so unbearably dependent on personal
vanity.

"This woman strikes me as just being *every* thing
you wouldn't like."

"Oh?"

"Yes. Over dressed. Painted up to the eyes.
Reeks of scent. Blood-red nails."

"Has she a scar on her mouth?"

"Blood red nails and a scar on her mouth—
Piggy, what are you talking about?" Robin came
and sat on her other side on the sofa. George on
her left hand and Robin on her right, and Joan
playing with her children's toys in the most
absorbed manner while they played noisy opera
on the gramophone. Piggy was going to adore
every minute of this.

"Has she?" George repeated insistently.

"Yes. Poor girl. Such a *pity*!"

"Oh, do you think so? Why?"

"*Well*"—Piggy was not going to discuss these

pre-natal disasters with two men at a time—"It is rather disfiguring, isn't it?"

"What are you both talking about?" Robin wanted to know.

"People I know who've come to stay with Piggy." George got up and went over to play with his nephews. He was all upset and excited.

Piggy explained all over again for Robin's benefit. She took pains to describe Jane, as she appeared to her and was rather upset to find Robin on the whole more interested than disgusted in her recital.

Joan—who had been listening all the time she sat on the floor playing at "Shops" and eating the pink dusty sweets out of a glass bottle—said:

"Oh, bring the dreary woman to lunch on Sunday. She sounds simply disgusting, but she might buy my balmorals and we can always have a good laugh at her afterwards."

"Make Sylvester come too," Robin said. "He hasn't seen the young hounds yet."

"My dear, *do* you imagine Sylvester wants to look at your Entry?"

George said: "No, Joan, you're wrong. Sylvester likes looking at hounds."

"Sylvester does? What absolute nonsense. You know he *hates* it."

"You're wrong——"

"I'm not——"

"You are——"

"Oh, don't be *tiresome*, George. Robin, did I
tell you *Gwen* was coming to stay?"

"Oh, Joan, you promised me you wouldn't have
her again this year."

"I can't help it. She's staying with Alice Drumderry and she wants to come to us for two nights
on the way home."

"How *awful!*"

"I don't really mind. I want to see what the
new bedroom looks like with some one sleeping
in it. Piggy, have you done anything about
distempering the library? I thought it might be a
plan to buy a bottle of gold leaf from Woolworth
and see if that would look well splashed in with
the rest."

"Oh, I think it would look *lovely;* that's a very
'Joan' idea."

"Disgusting! Revolting!" George and Robin
said.

"Mummy, mummy, when is Cousin Gwen coming
to stay?"

"On Monday, darling. Come here, Edward,"
Joan gathered to her knee the twin whom she
wished to make a favourable impression on Cousin
Gwen. "You love Cousin Gwen, Edward? Edward? You love Cousin Gwen, Edward?"

"Don't put ideas into his head about that dreary
woman," Robin said.

"If Gwen was one of your relations you wouldn't
be so beastly about her."

"Thank God she's not."

"Thank God she's not," Edward echoed—rather a disarming young parrot.

Robin sent him back to the gramophone before Joan could rebuke him and give him the opportunity of retorting—"*Daddy* said——" He said to Joan with unnecessary sentiment perhaps: "I'll be good about Gwen. Sweet, I *promise*——" And Piggy endured one of those terrible poisoning moments when she knew herself to be outside love for ever. Blindly aware that this thing was never for her.

Later on Robin gave her a glass of sherry. The children went to bed. It was almost time for people to dress for dinner. It was almost time for her to go away. They said: "Don't go, Piggy. Why not stay to dinner?" But she had sense enough to go. Joan saying good-bye in a faint preoccupied way, then suddenly catching herself up into a cold sweetness. George and Robin coming out to the car, saying it was almost a frost, saying:

"Will she start, Piggy?"

Saying:

"She's a great car, Piggy."

"Good-bye, Piggy. Lunch on Sunday."

"Make Sylvester come."

Piggy smiling and nodding and reviving her engine, drove away into the evening. The sky was as grey as a battleship and wild duck were flighting slowly across it to secret lonely waters.

CHAPTER V

ALBERT brought Jane her morning glass of orange juice. Then he went limping round the room, tidying up her clothes.

"Albert," she said, for she woke more easily and completely at Kilque than she did in London, "why are you so lame? You've been wearing those brown and white shoes again, I know."

"Well, yes, Madam, I have. I went for a little stroll in them last night."

"I think it's ever so stupid of you, I must say——"

Albert, rapidly folding her underclothes, defended himself with vigour, almost with passion.

"What I say is, Madam, you mustn't let your feet go, must you? Well, it's the same as letting your figure go, that's the way I look at it—once it's gone it's gone—the same as letting your feet go."

Jane agreed with him absently. There was no use arguing with Albert. He scarcely felt himself to be looking his best until he had attained a state of physical suffering of some kind.

Jane was tired—a little tired. She usually was, but to-day her excuse was greater than usual for she had spent such a day yesterday looking after Jessica. And to-day, she supposed, would be much the same, perhaps worse, for as her acuter pains abated, Jessica's instability would increase.

"Albert, have you heard how Miss Houpe-Boswell is this morning?" she asked.

"No, Madam."

Jane sighed and subsided. Presently she would know.

Presently she was in Jessica's room—Piggy's room where Jessica slept. Jessica was feeling stronger to-day—that false strength succeeding pain. She had just been washed and tidied up by Hester and a nurse who was fetched twice a day from the Cottage Hospital. Really she was in no pain whatever and quite ready to be maddened by her surroundings or by any one who came near her.

Jane said: "Darling, darling, *how* are you?"

Jessica, whose eyes had been hollowed out by pain in the most romantic manner—she looked like a youngish actor manager—lit a cigarette before replying. Then she said:

"I've defeated this pain, I think. I'm glad I have. Suffering's pretty sordid really. Of course I only fell asleep a moment before I was called this morning. *Pretty* embittering——"

"But, Sweetie, Sylvester and I went in to see you last thing——"

"Yes, I heard you," Jessica closed her eyes. "I was in a sort of trance—imagining *Black*. If you can really vividly *see* Black in your mind, you know, you destroy all pain."

Sylvester came in on his way to the bathroom.

He wore a lovely black dressing-gown spotted like a leopard. He wore it with extreme grace and carefulness for he enjoyed making the most of those moments when he looked his very best.

"Hullo, Lovely," he said to Jessica, "can I have a cigarette? You look, oh, so well and girlish this morning, I'm glad to see."

Jessica frowned and fidgeted with the signet ring on her little finger.

"—If you can imagine *black*," she went on to Jane, "a really deadly unpolished *black*, you've won."

She flung herself back on her pillows in silence, waiting for Sylvester to ask her what she meant by this curious remark.

Sylvester said: "This is really the *oddest* room for you to be in, isn't it, Jessica?"

"Horrifying. *Fascinating*," she agreed. At least he was going to talk about Jessica. "How can I get well in a room full of signed photographs from girl friends?"

"All this futile past romance," Sylvester murmured, looking about him at the many many photographs framed and unframed with which Piggy larded every available inch of space in her bedroom. All shades of a Past that was no Past. "It's nauseating and stifling," he murmured almost to himself. There was a photograph of an Australian soldier: "With love from 'Aussie' Reade." And there had in reality been as little for Piggy in that as in the present expensive shadowy likeness of Joan and her twins. Tiny black wood-cuts of elves in a vast white mount, windflowers, a simpering virgin, muslin curtains and artificial silk cushions quilted by machinery, all these girlfriends and their mementoes, all part of Piggy and Piggy's life. Terrible. Terrible to Sylvester.

He was quite pale when he looked back at Jessica, and almost grateful to her for being Jessica, not Piggy in Piggy's bed.

"It is rather disgusting," he said. He gathered himself up to go onwards to the bathroom.

"Come back and talk to me this morning," Jessica said.

"My dear Jessica, I'm supposed to be really working," he told her with the faintest show of pomp, really only to lend weight to his excuse for not returning. Jessica must understand and forgive work. However, she said:

"Book or Play? Oh, that *reminds* me. I read the script of Jeremy's play and it really is *frighteningly* good."

A shade passed through Sylvester. Jeremy's plays were better than his, he knew. Jessica knew it too. She adored upsetting authors. "Jeremy was awfully amused by your last book," she went on. "He was enthralled by the bit about the girl who had hiccups. He says he told you about Lindy Carter having hiccups."

"He *never* did." Sylvester was betrayed into a heated moment. The incredible idiocy of people who must seize on one stupid incident in his book and then say they invented it for him. What if they had? It was all too dreary and shameful. But why mind?

"—I've *bought* your book, darling," Jessica was saying.

And this touched Sylvester. He always felt a momentary tenderness towards any one who had really put down seven-and-six and taken up a book of his in exchange.

"Oh, darling, and did you hate it?" he asked.

"No, darling," Jessica yawned faintly. "I haven't *read* it yet."

Sylvester's book had been published six months ago. Its success was almost quite over. Yet by the time he reached the bathroom he was still minding Jessica's twice barbed arrows. It was so *silly* to mind. But intentional malice is always upsetting. Somehow, beyond all the malice he was aware of a sterilising sense of Jeremy's plays being so much, much better than his own.

Jessica was a hateful woman. He would like to inflict some more physical pain upon her. Sylvester was increasingly resolved in his plan to free Jane from her possession. Then he would bestow freedom on that poor thing, Jane, and inflict a crushing blow upon Jessica. Two good things to do.

In Jessica's room Jane was wondering drearily what to do about the next few hours. Jessica was well enough to-day to want to read to her. How

much Jane wished that it could be one of Albert's
duties to listen to Jessica reading aloud. Really,
as far as an audience went, two cows in a field
would have been quite as attentive and intelligent
as Jane. And compared to her Albert was a bright
and receptive listener. But Jessica had a thing
about reading to Jane. She derived from it an
obscure sadistic pleasure. And this morning after
so much pain she had no intention of denying herself anything.

So she read and read to Jane, saying at intervals:
"I do think that is *so* right," or ,,Pretty rude,
don't you think so?" just in case Jane should be
thinking quietly about something else, some dreary
triviality such as the design of a new evening gown,
and from such a state of absent coma Jessica's
remarks would jolt her roughly enough.

The day outside was bright with the piercing
excitement of an autumn morning. There was as
though a ringing through the day, endless circles
of sound such as come from a glass finger-bowl
flipped by a thumb nail. Jane, sitting fidgeting on
the window-seat of Jessica's room, was outside the
day, but she ought to have belonged—it was unfair. She was a sad, weak creature but there was a
shivered possibility within her, a quality that was
not alien to the day—alien as Jessica was alien,
lying there in her rich dressing-gown, reading on
and on in her educated, affected voice.

"There's the doctor——"

A car stopped at the door; yes, its engine was switched off, but Jessica, paying no attention either to this or to Jane's interruption, read on to the end of a long, involved sentence. Then she said:

"He won't be long. There's really nothing for him to do."

Hester's voice came calling up the stairs:

"Jane, Jane—*Could* you come down a moment?"

Jessica's face went dead. "How *very* unnecessary," she said. But Jane was gone, flying out of the room on long, light feet—escaping. It was a flight.

Jessica sat up in bed listening. She heard voices in the hall—a man's voice that was not Sylvester's or the doctor's voice. Odd. Very odd. Maddening. To be anchored by pain, her leg strapped in a wooden box—her helpless state overcame Jessica. She called:

"Jane! Jane!"

She was weaker than she thought. Such pain as she moved, scarcely stirred, in bed. They should not leave her alone. It was monstrous.

"*Jane!*"

She called again. They were laughing in the hall. They had not heard her. By God, she would ring the bell. A sharp jangling on that little brass bell would startle Jane back to her. Back she'd come. Flying back. Jessica stretched out her hand for the bell. But the bell was not beside her. Away and far off upon the dressing table the bell was sitting beside that mammoth photograph of a silly woman and two gross little boys with knees like elephant's feet.

The voices in the hall were silent. There was an emptiness of silence in the house. In a minute she heard them again out on the grass in front of the house and Jane's voice light and brittle saying: *"Fascinating"*—saying: "Oh, you're horrible——"

Jessica moved herself again in bed, straining all her power to see out of the window, desolate and angry and now in some pain she called again and again. But Jane did not hear.

Piggy, who was seldom up and dressed before eleven in the morning, heard, and came bustling in, full of goodwill, her face freshly powdered, her hair newly released from its rows of curlers, her mauve kimono tightly folded about her body.

"Aren't we comfy?" she said. "Can a Piggy be any help?"

Piggy in her day had ardently attended quite three Red Cross lectures before her enthusiasm for nursing left her. She shifted Jessica's leg and fastened it up in its box again, and tidied everything on the bed deftly out of reach in quite a professional way. Then she sat down, longing to have a little talk about herself. Jessica ground the teeth of her mind together and closed her eyes.

Piggy was saying: "So, like most other people, you probably think I'm very lazy just because I don't get up before eleven; but I find going through life one can do ever so many quiet little jobs without any one knowing anything about them."

"Yes."

"For instance, last Thursday I tidied out the medicine cupboard. So I knew at once when the doctor came to look at your leg that there were no bandages in it and only three aspirins left in the bottle."

"Oh."

"And yet people will tell you I am lazy——" Piggy went fidgeting round the room, peering at her photographs as though she had never seen them before and longing for Jessica to ask her questions about them. At last she could contain herself no longer, so, picking up the photograph of Joan and the twins, she said in a voice full of feeling, which she vainly imagined to be entirely casual, "Don't you think that's *rather* a lovely face?"

After this Jessica could no longer with decent politeness keep her eyes shut. Neither could she simply say No. Or, Oh. Neither would she say, Yes. She said instead:

"It depends on what you mean by lovely."

"Most people think she's rather wonderful," Piggy proceeded, undeterred by Jessica's lack of interest and determined that she should hear all a Piggy could tell of the Beauty and importance of a Piggy's friend. There was a burning enthusiasm in her to tell of Joan, a testament that would not be denied.

"——Of course you've probably seen masses of photographs of her in the *Tatler*," Piggy wound up a lingering description of Joan's beauty. "She's in it almost every week—Hates it simply—She and I are always dodging the camera at race meetings."

"Oh. Are you a keen racing woman?" *Anything* to get away from this dreary girl-friend, Jessica thought.

"Oh, it's not really much in a Piggy's line, you know, but I do try to take an interest for Joan's sake. She so loves me to go to horse shows and race meetings with her."

"Oh, yes."

"Of course, with the poor old heart so wonky, I can't hunt, which *is* sad. Of course, as you probably know, Joan is the most brilliant woman to hounds in Ireland. No two opinions about it. She's a real *Crasher*."

"How lovely."

Piggy drew a deep breath. She was about to make her favourite remark about Joan——

"——And in spite of all this, you know, her beauty and her success and what I call 'being Joan,' if you know what I mean, all the time at heart she's *just a lovely child*. Just the youngest, most unspoilt *child*, that's what Joan is."

"How too *frightening*."

"Oh, you mustn't be frightened of her," Piggy

answered with literal reassurance. "She's sometimes a little silent with people she doesn't know,
and the silly asses think she's rude, but she's not—
she's simply *shy*."

"Oh, yes."

"I'm longing for you to meet her," Piggy proceeded heartily. "Did Jane—you know we've
decided to drop Mrs. and Miss, it's so formal,
isn't it?—did Jane tell you Joan had asked me to
bring her over to lunch at Castlequarter on Sunday?"

"No, Miss Browne, she did not."

"Oh, you *mustn't* call me Miss Browne."

"But I don't know what your Christian name is."

"My real name is Viola but everybody calls me
Piggy."

"Piggy? Of course. How fascinating!"

"I used to call myself Piggy when I was a little
girl——"

"How quaint and whimsey of you——"

"——And somehow the name has stuck to me
ever since. I must have been a quaint, funny
child as you say. I don't believe anybody *quite*
understood me."

"I daresay not."

"I was rather a lonely little sprite, I think, and
you know—you *mustn't* laugh at me—I *really*
believed in fairies. I'm not sure there aren't
moments when I still do. Do you?"

At this moment Albert popped his head round

the door and Jessica, breathing a sigh of nearly rapturous relief, murmured: "Sometimes—*Almost* —Albert, you promised I should have that drink by half-past eleven and now it's twenty-nine minutes past. Pretty good!"

"Ever such a time I had, Miss, went round every pub in the village and did one of them keep your tonic water? Not likely. And then I had *such* a fall off the housemaid's bicycle on the way back."

"How *savage.*"

"Yes, Miss, and such a saddle, most uncomfortable——" As he talked Albert put back on the bed all the objects Piggy had cleared off it and arranged a cocktail shaker and two green glasses on the table beside Jessica.

"We shall have to send to Dublin for our tonic water, I'm afraid, Miss. I just made this cocktail out of what I *could* get in the village. I know you prefer your gin and tonic but what can one do?"

"Never mind, Albert. I'm sure this is lovely. Where's Mrs. Barker? Do you know? Tell her there's a cocktail in here—a tiny drink won't hurt her."

"Well, I passed her some way from the house, Miss. She was walking with a gentleman and some little dogs."

"With who? With Mr. Browne?"

"Oh no, Miss. *Not* Mr. Browne. I rather think it was the gentleman who lunched in the flat the day Mrs. Barker was first taken ill."

Then followed a silence, a silence in which Jessica's face darkened.

"Have a drink," she said to Piggy, sharply, bitterly.

"Well, just the smallest one—Oh, stop! Please! *Masses!*" Piggy was all girlish excitement before her glass was half full. But Albert treated her protests with indulgent inattention.

"Cigarette?" Jessica's voice was her own again, almost. But she broke a match as she struck it, and there was a stiff tremor about her hand as she lit their cigarettes.

Piggy sat on the edge of the bed, sipping away at her delicious cocktail. Presently she felt so young and gay, flooded with a mildly amorous light-heartedness. She longed to tell Jessica what a girl she had been. It was always simpler to boast of the past than the present. She could remember as if it was yesterday every detail of the affair with "Aussie" Reade, and then there was George's famous speech about her eyelashes. Piggy was simply bursting with girlish confidences.

But not for the first time Jessica's stony profile, all secrecy enclosed within its terrific reticence, saved her from Piggy, saved her from an hour's disgust of Piggy. Even Piggy could find no voice in which to boast of her past. She drank up her cocktail and wandered over to the window.

"Why, *George* is here——" Her whole face changed. She became for the moment a confident

and happy person. She was transfigured in her
assurance that George had come to Kilque to see
her, was even now demanding her presence, her
protection from that painted foreigner Jane—one
who could neither speak nor understand his language, one who must be to him anathema. She
must fly to his succour. How lovely that only she
could help him. Just the least, least bit drunk
and immeasurably elated Piggy clasped her
kimono tightly about her and rushed from Jessica's
room.

Jessica was left alone with the gin

In Sylvester's wood Jane and George were sitting
and talking. Hester had suggested that there they
might find Sylvester. So she often protected his
working hours from himself and withheld from
them the interruptions he might have welcomed,
for he was very fond of a gossip with George.

Now George was talking most. He had re-
discovered Jane and he was mad to talk to her.
That was the thing about Jane. Although she
might say no more than: "Fascinating!" "Frightening!" "Are you being horrible to me?" she
enclosed within herself a sense of the undiscover-
able—a completely false sense, but that did not
matter, for it was always round a corner. There
was in Jane for those who loved her the illusion
of an unknown place, obscured from them—
forever obscured from them because indeed it was

not in her. She was not reticent by nature, but she could not communicate, and for her this was a most fortunate disability. The mirage of lovely secrecy was in her, never discovered for it was never there.

"It's grand to see you again," said George for the third time, "I never really thought you'd come over here. And if Piggy hadn't run into your car I wouldn't have seen you anyhow. I do think you were a tiny bit unkind not to let me know you were coming—I do think you were."

Jane said: "Oh no, I'm never unkind." She was a masked creature sitting there beside him in this small wood—faint and unreal and hidden from him entirely, as apart from him as she was from this glade of birch trees, as distant from all his life. George was encompassed and excited by this sense of her absurd unreality to him. He must talk to her. One could not risk boring her.

"——We'd rather a good morning yesterday. Two litters in Carlough Hill—cubs going in all *directions*. Very little scent with all that bracken, of course, but these hounds of old Robin's are champions to hunt."

"How fascinating!"

"Well, they're a grand pack of hounds to look at and they're great hounds to hunt a fox——"

"How delicious——"

"D'you know, I think they must have been

hunting three hours when they marked a fox in a rabbit hole the edge of the wood—scratched him out themselves and ate him."

"Fascinating—but *just* a little horrible."

"Oh, terribly good for hounds to eat a fox like that. When they're really savage for him."

"*No?*" Jane spoke the word "no" on a peculiarly beautiful and questioning note.

"Have you a cigarette?" she said. "Oh, Gold Flake. No, I'd love a Gold Flake." She lit her cigarette in a curious unaware way as though her mind really was not working, and said to George: "Yes. Tell me more."

He said: "Are you coming to lunch with my sister on Sunday?"

"I don't *know*—are we?" Jane knew nothing.

"Yes, you must come—promise you will. I'll tell Piggy she's not to come without you."

"The poor sweet—she's ever such a kind girl."

"Who? Piggy? Yes, poor Piggy—but you will come, won't you? Sylvester must bring you."

"The poor sweet! He's ever such a sweet man."

"Yes, he's a dear. But you haven't told me yet if you're coming to lunch on Sunday."

"Who? Me?—Oh, but I shall have to stop with Jessica——" Jane turned round at last and looked at him. "I couldn't leave the poor sweet like that, could I?"

"Of course you could. You must. I'll tell Sylvester he's got to make you. You'd like to see the hounds, I know. They're a lovely pack of hounds. And you'd like Joan; Joan's a lovely girl."

"I'd like very much to come along. I will if Jessica's better, I promise you." Jane did not promise lightly as though it did not matter. There was a careful solemnity in her undertaking.

This question of luncheon on Sunday had become now a thing of moment. George had put himself and herself into the question. It was a matter of importance now, Jane hoped she did not find herself wondering whether it was all going to be too tiresome and difficult and better left alone. It was all so intangible, so hard to get hold of. She had told Sylvester that she intended to escape from Jessica and to marry George. But that was purely fantastic. All in a moment she saw Jessica as Jessica was—Jessica strong, enthralling, amusing, bullying. Her own life for ever controlled by Jessica, forever given over to her ruling. How could she take herself back from Jessica? How could she do anything about it? She, so weak, so idle and so untruthful. She with nothing, nothing but a sad desire to escape and no trust in herself, or anybody else, no trust even that she would want to-morrow what was to-day desire. A sweet, a poor sweet or a dreary poor sweet—that was all she thought of any man. Jane had an almost unprecedented moment of realisation about herself. It terrified

her. She stood up and threw away the end of her
cigarette (she hated Gold Flake really). Had the
truth been in her now she would have cried out,
"You dreary man! You smoke Gold Flake
cigarettes which I loathe and you ask me to lunch
on Sunday, and neither you nor any other will
ever help me to escape from Jessica and from all
my weakness and terror."

But, luckily, the truth was not in Jane, for such
an outcry would have dismayed George exceedingly
and put him as a means of escape forever outside
her life. She stood there still with grief in a green
shadow, pale in the shadow of a tree, and looking
on her thus George's heart, a heart full of kindness,
full of charity and love and pity, was stirred
within him beyond all these things to an over-
powering excitement. Beyond all that was kind,
self-denying and reticent in his life he was moved.
Yet all these qualities were his still, defending,
fencing him always from any intimacy with Jane.
His whole character, brave, ascetic and outdoor,
was surely too stupid, too strong, too unknowing
of its own austerity and unaware of its own
possibilities for living to admit any romantical
illusion such as the love of Jane.

But George had never known light love. He was
earnest and full of a lovely enthusiasm, he knew
only two kinds of loving and this, betraying him
to so strange a thing as Jane, was to him in its
future comprehensible only as a lovely and

permanent security. Where he loved he would marry, and then all would be well.

As there was in Jane that blank wall of defence against a too comprehensive familiarity so George's blind and obstinate chivalry would protect him to the last from the knowledge of any evil he might prefer to ignore. Fortunately they knew very little about each other as they stood there together in the arrowy light of Sylvester's wood. And still more fortunately their several armours would, if they were lucky, forever protect them from one another.

George's dogs came screaming up the wood. They were hunting a rabbit, caught and held away unto themselves by their natural lust for the chase. Lovely they were in their endeavour, extreme and helpless in their desire as fire in a wind. Such speed they showed, such agony to kill, and they were but small and loving dogs when the blood lust was still in them. Their hunt was of divine importance to George. He pursued them up the wood and brought Jane with him, Jane running and laughing and screaming, suddenly awakened through him to a new excitement. It was not silly. It was an actual and thrilling lust, this hunting of a wild creature for its life and in its escape there was a vivid shaft of disappointment. What was this, this new and sudden life that had come to her? She neither knew nor asked. For a moment life had been as a lust—

"savage, extreme, rude, cruel, not to trust," and Jane had been as one with it, all her pretences at living gone from her. She looked to George now as the reasonable interpreter of such excitements. He would answer all questions. He would never laugh or in any way wound a girl. From being but a dreary poor sweet and a possible way of escape, he was endowed with a sudden significance. He was the quickened counterpart of all those unreal outdoor men she had read about with such excitement. And she herself, an ignorant poor thing, so unfit to compete with those quantities of able-bodied and lovely sporting girls whom she might now reasonably expect to come to life all round her. Since one type had been so faithfully reproduced, why not the rest? And she so weak, such a creature of unrealities and such a one for her comforts, how could she compete? Were it not better to avoid all rude and savage scenes and retire from the contest quietly with Albert and Jessica, before one became further involved?

George was calling his dogs to him and speaking to them in love and tender commendation as they appeared. They walked back towards the house, Jane saying:

"Sylvester doesn't seem to be here——" her mind on George and his sweetness to those dirty little dogs.

"You talk to your dawgs as if they were *women*," she said. He did not hear her. And for once she was speaking a thought aloud, not simply uttering a remark to provoke a comment.

They saw Piggy coming fluttering and rustling towards them. She was out of breath and rather embarrassed by her nasty Tig's advances towards George's dogs.

"*Oh—Tig,* stop it!—Hester told me you'd gone down to the river. I've been all *over* the place looking for you. Good-morning, Jane. *Tig,* will you *stop*—Kick him, George."

"He won't do *that* little dawg any harm," said Jane with brief accuracy. They proceeded on their way back to the house, Piggy talking away with rattling confidence, for had not George come to see her? And had she not at last contrived to interrupt his enforced *tête-à-tête* with Jane? Hester had been so inconceivably stupid about it. Poor George. But Joan and she would have a good laugh over his hour with a girl so obviously terrifying to him as Jane must be. Alone in a wood with her too! They must rag George and find out what he talked to her about.

Sylvester looked out of his window to see the three of them standing there upon the gravel. A resolution came upon him. He would encourage Jane and madden Piggy and gossip to George. For the last hour his mind had been bound away in a productive effort in which his conscious brain seemed to have neither part nor lot. Do I write books with my hands and feet? he wondered.

Now this striven effort ended he was in a state of calm almost physically pleasurable. He opened his window and came out to sit on its hot stone sill.

"Let's have a delicious glass of sherry," he said. He caught hold of Jane and set her gently beside him. George who knew the cupboard where Sylvester kept his sherry, climbed in through the window to find it. Then he sat on the window seat, leaning out beside Sylvester and Jane, to talk to them. His head and shoulders in the sunshine, his head bowed from the bright heat. Jane leant against Sylvester's shoulder and kissed his cheek lightly and easily. She was a thin sweet thing and no sentimentalist. How hot the sun was. The sleeve of her pale woollen dress was almost scorching hot.

Alone on the gravel Piggy stood. They had not given her a glass of sherry. They had not given her a cigarette. There was no room for her upon the window sill. Whatever she said now or did she was purposeful and not careless. Her resolve to rescue George had been taken from her by Sylvester, but she was not quick to realise a change in any situation. So:

"Albert has been hunting for you everywhere," she said, "Miss Houpe-Boswell—I'm still shy of calling her Jessica—was in such a state. I tried to look after her, but a Piggy's rather helpless, really."

"Must I go?" Jane asked Sylvester. Piggy

still stood on the gravel like a bulky purple rock.

"Certainly not. I never heard anything so monstrous. You must stay here, my dear, and continue to entrance George and me. I shouldn't wonder if you had great success with George."

"*Don't* go away," George said.

"Jane and I are coming to lunch with you on Sunday, aren't we, George?"

"Yes, that's right. She's *promised* to come."

"Only if Jessica——"

"You and I are going together, sweetie. Will your delicious motor car be ready to take us?"

"Albert can go to town and find out."

And Piggy stood beside them. Alone, burningly alone, terribly apart and unwanted. Fat, stupid Piggy, almost in tears—not quite but very nearly. She was the unpopular child, the child who cannot belong. She was poor Piggy who had no success at parties. This was typical of so many moments in Piggy's life, sickening, frightening moments in which she was impotent and alone and a terror of life and of her own stupidity was as a web spun about her, stifling her mouth and blinding her eyes. She would crash out through this web with loud and hopeless words, saying now:

"Did you enjoy the dance at Knockfin, George?"

And he did not hear, nobody heard except Sylvester, who looked at her, faintly, silently

jeering at her. Her tongue felt dry inside her
mouth. She could not speak again. George's bright
dark head in the sunshine destroyed and fascinated
her. He was leaning far out of the window to pick
up one of his dogs—a mass of affectation and
sentiment. "My tiny sweet," he said to her, "my
sweet one. Beautiful one——"

Piggy, with Sylvester's eye upon her said, again,
"Did you enjoy the dance at Knockfin?" Harshly
and desperately she said it, and this time he heard
her.

"Oh, I'm sorry, what did you say?" He had
not quite heard her. Christ, to have to say it
again.

"Did you enjoy the dance at Knockfin?" Her
voice was striving small as gnat's now.

"I did, I think. I think I behaved rather badly.
Joan told everybody I was drunk. Did she tell
you I was drunk?"

Adorable George who asked one a private lovely
question, setting a poor Piggy back once more
upon her little monument of conceit. One could
giggle. One could sidle closer. But before she
could think of an answer Sylvester had begun to
tell them a story—Sylvester with his ice-cold face
and quiet hands was saying: "Do you *know*—
very embarrassing it *was*—Mm. I was pretty
tiddly too—*ever* so malicious, sweetie—just attack
and retreat, my dear—don't let's—it'll spoil everything—we didn't in the end. I'm rather regretting

it now—The atmosphere was a *little* tense the next morning—rather a drawing aside of skirts as we boys say. Personally I think these week-end parties destroy *everything*——"

Oh, he was rude and cold and unashamed. And they laughed with him as they would never laugh with Piggy. But remember, Joan hated him. Joan did not find him amusing. Remember, Joan would find Jane Barker a sad bore. She would not indulge her as George and Sylvester were indulging her. She would talk to Piggy and not to Jane. What would Jane find to say at luncheon on Sunday? Obviously she would find nothing to say whatever. Piggy would have it all her own way there. Sweet Joan would talk to Piggy and lift her thin arching eyebrows towards Robin as he tried to talk to Jane far off at the other end of the table. They would share an amused pity for Robin doing a host's best towards this manicured, painted, overdressed Alien.

"Sylvester, you must come out some morning soon. Come out on Thursday to the Park. I'll have old Barney there for you."

"Nonsense, dear, it's much too early, why should I?" Sylvester seldom wasted words on unnecessary gratitude but George obstinately ignored his refusal.

"Oh, yes. You are idle. Come out, and you'd better both come." He looked vaguely at Jane, and then said with more determination, "I'll

have a horse there for you that you really will
enjoy."

"Oh, it's ever so long since I rode horseback,
and I have no clothes," Jane's panic was too faint
to be real. She had not sufficient imagination to
panic, that was it.

Here was Piggy's opportunity. She said in her
best Little Madam Tact voice:

"Oh, *clothes*. Well, I know Joan has a pair of
Newmarket boots because a girl was trying very
hard to buy them off her the other day. She might
let you have them. I should think they'd fit you.
You've rather small feet, haven't you? Of course
for her height her feet are wee, but these boots are
just, *just* on the small side for her."

"Don't pay the smallest attention to Piggy,"
Sylvester said, "and *whatever* you do, don't be
bullied into buying any of Joan's old clothes. If
you *must* be a sporting girl and go hunting at five
o'clock in the morning, borrow Jessica's flannel
trousers—you'll feel ever such a little man in
them."

"Oh, Sylvester, you're horrible."

"Not at all. George can lend you a pair of those
fascinating knee guards and you'll be *quite* all right.
How you girls do fuss and go on about your clothes.
Now I shall look so simple and *chic* in my shep-
herd's plaid breeches—quite Period Pieces in their
way. They belonged to my grandfather who was a
marquis and they button up on the outside of my

legs, but *I* don't mind. Just dainty simplicity, darlings, I'm always the same."

"Seriously then, you will come? You will really, won't you, Sylvester?" George was so pleased.

"Oh, I *suppose* so. I do hate being dragged about and forced into decisions—why can't people let me alone?"

Piggy was busily whispering: "You mustn't mind what Sylvester says about it. They're lovely boots and *such* a bargain."

Jane, who really missed the thrill of bargains owing to her extreme wealth, stared blankly back at Piggy with nothing at all behind her eyes. She was still leaning against Sylvester, who supported her affectionately, and once she smiled.

"Have a sip of sherry, dear," Sylvester said, and then, "I think it's absolutely lovely the way you've given up drinking."

"I'll end by having a real bad bout, I know I shall." Jane was dimly accurate about herself.

Hester came down the path from her eternal chickens. She nodded to them all and stood in her dark doorway—the door as dark as a night behind her. There she stood in her purple coat like a magenta tulip, the sun burned out her clear lines, they were printed for a moment against that false darkness, a moment while she stood there, saying:

"It's lunch time—stay to lunch, George. Please do."

"Why is luncheon early to-day?" Sylvester demanded fussily.

"Because I thought we might go to the sea after lunch. I want to go to Corah Bay and gather blackberries and lobsters and shrimps. Will you come, George? That'll be lovely." Hester disappeared from them into the house.

"There's a sort of power about her," Sylvester thought. "The money, I suppose. *Fascinating*."

"We'll all go," said George, looking only at Jane. And his voice was hoarse and drowsy like a summer bee. "I know a lovely place where you can hook lobsters out of the rocks on the end of a wire. I'll only show it to you——" So he tempted her.

A faint shadow came on Jane's face. Between happiness and Jane its curtain fell.

"I guess I'd better stop with Jessica." She stood away from Sylvester and all her peace fell from her. Her scar was only a pitiful ugly twist. She looked frightened and helpless and unwilling. Sylvester looked at George and saw the complaint in his eyes. This, he thought, is progressing almost too well. I must check things a little. She will give way to him too rapidly and George is one of these virile old-fashioned men whose love thrives best on opposition. Look how it endured for Blanche, entirely because she was another's. He said:

"Yes, Jane, I think definitely you ought to stay with your darling friend this afternoon."

"Yes, I think Sylvester is so right. I suppose

you *must* stay with her." Piggy could not refrain herself from this little speech, it was unfortunate for her and proved the ruin of her day for not only did Sylvester turn upon her like a female adder, saying softly, "Oh, I wasn't serious *really*. If Jane doesn't go none of us will——" but Jessica, who had for the last twenty minutes been straining all her powers of hearing from her bed above them, happened to catch this among other fragments of the discourse and her determination that Jane should at all costs spend the afternoon with her was sadly shaken by the notion of displeasing Piggy by encouraging her to accompany the sea-party. Anyhow, whatever Jane did or did not do, Jessica was fully determined she should suffer for it. And how better make her suffer than from the high altar of her own chosen martyrdom. It was an entrancing eminence from which to inflict spiritual punishment upon one's friends. Jessica, anxious to begin, rang her little bell sharply.

"Oh, there you are, darling," she said weakly as Jane came in. "I do hope you've had a lovely, *lovely* morning. Who was your outdoor friend?"

"Oh," said cowardly Jane, "just a tiresome boy I met in town. You know, darling, I've told you about him—Sylvester's friend—George Playfair."

"Oh yes? The one we came to Ireland to find? Well, I hope he'll come up to expectations, my dear. He sounded deliciously hearty to me. Are his pockets full of dog biscuit? They ought to be.

Otherwise he's hardly the Right Sort. You must find out. Just listen. You'll hear them rattling from time to time."

"Oh, Jessica, you're horrible——"

"I'm not horrible, my dear. I only want to make *quite* sure you know what you're doing—involving yourself like this with a frightful boring man with his pockets full of dog biscuits——"

"Oh, Jessica, must you go on and on and on about his pockets? I tell you they're *not*. And I don't ever want to see him again, and I'd leave this place to-morrow if the doctor would let you be moved or the car was mended. I'll get an ambulance and have you taken away in it now if you like."

"Oh my Christ, the *selfishness*. The terrifying *selfishness* of people like you, Jane. Don't you realise what pain *is*. Don't you realise the sort of Black Agony in which one only wants to be left *alone*—left in any corner that's dark enough and lonely enough to hide the *shame* of the way pain can *break* one——"

"Sweetie, I'm sorry, I'm so *sorry*. Oh, girlie, I'm dumb, I know, and tough and all that, but I'm crazy about you—just crazy, Jessica. I wouldn't hurt you for the world."

Jane was easily defeated in any emotional contest. All her opponent's point of view became instantly and agonisingly her own. It was given to her as a present, and fitted well into the hollow

place in her mind where her own opinion might,
had she owned such a thing, have belonged. The
vague wants and sad alarms that rode her living
fell from her—weak, unreasoning and no support.

"Oh, I don't *want* to go to the sea," she whined
now. "Say you want me to stay with you, Jessica,
and then I needn't go. They all bore me so. We
could have a lovely afternoon with you reading to
me, Sweetie. Just you reading out loud——"

Jessica was giving her all this to say, compelling
her to say it. Jessica with her wide cool hand
holding Jane's hands—Jane's helpless, painted
hands—giving her these words to say, making her
feel a sort of dreadful truthfulness in saying them.

"No." Jessica put Jane's hands down, strongly
and gently giving them up. "You must go, darling.
Go, because I want you to—will you?—Oh, that
frightful Miss Piggy Browne—I know you'll annoy
her if you go. My dear, *such* a fidgety, oversexed
woman—she came *bouncing* in here this morning.
Really, she's preposterous. I can never tell you
what a time I had with her. Obviously she has
the most absurd passion for that constipated
looking woman on the dressing-table and of
course she would tell me all about it. No *restraint*,
darling. Frightening. Finally Albert came in and
rescued me. My dear, he's awfully lame, isn't he?
If I could get hold of those brown and white shoes
I'd burn them. If he can't trot about and fetch
things he'll be so useless to us."

"I'll say I'll have to buy him a new pair," Jane was feeling unfit for argument about Albert's feet.

"Well, it's a pure waste of money, I think. He always tells one a size too small, he's so absurdly vain.—Here he is now with my food. Look—lamer than ever. Albert, we're so tired and bored watching you hobbling about like that. You may think it's ever so pathetic, but to us it's just *disgusting*."

Albert said nothing. He arranged Jessica's tray and limped out of the room, looking incredibly sour.

"Jane, you know you must *speak* to him," Jessica began to gobble up her luncheon. "I'm in no sort of state to argue with servants or I'd tell him he can't wear a tie like that. Didn't you *see* it—black with *jade* green spots. He just *can't*."

"I suppose he thinks he's on a sort of a holiday," Jane apologised for Albert. She hated scolding him at any time for he almost always got the better of the argument and made her feel silly. Therefore she tried not to admit his faults even to herself. "I suppose he thinks he can wear more amusing clothes here than he can in London."

"Well, when he comes in to wait at dinner in his pale grey flannel suit, co-respondent shoes and that girlish blue jumper I hope you'll still think he's ever such a funny joke. Seriously, Jane, I think it's disgusting."

"Yes, he's a horrible boy. I'll speak to him. Shall I go down to lunch now, Sweetie?"

"Yes, Sweetie. Your face is looking a tiny bit untidy, isn't it? Look Jane, if you go through a town will you try to buy some Tonic Water. Perhaps you could go round by that town we had lunch in before the smash. They had it there. What are you looking for? Lipstick? No, it's in the other drawer—the *other* drawer. Albert couldn't find any in the village. He's so stupid, really. He had no ideas beyond getting it from Dublin. So tiresome. You might ask that Hester Browne about it if you remember. Don't go down for a moment, darling—I adore looking at faces when they've just been painted up—so divinely artificial."

Silly Jane sitting on a hard chair with her hands in her lap, as quiet and strange as a soapstone idol, a lovely idol with a flawed face, that was what Sylvester saw when he put his head round the door of Jessica's room and said:

"Jane, aren't you ever coming down to lunch? Hester wants to know if you'll have it sent up to you here."

"Oh, no," said Jane—again on that round sweet note. "I'm just coming down." She slipped off her chair and looked towards Jessica for leave to go.

Jessica nodded absently. "Come and see me before you start on this delicious excursion," she said.

"Oh, yes," and Jane went, flying out of the room again. She could not go fast enough.

Sylvester paused and looked at Jessica in a peculiarly unpleasant way.

"Well?" she said. She caught just the end of that look. But why had he waited? What did he want to say to her? Strong in her recent assertion of power, Jessica looked back at him with insolence —defensive insolence it was.

"Oh—nothing." He was less contemptuous than absent-minded. No, he was not even absent-minded. He was simply not thinking of Jessica. It was a mistake on Sylvester's part, he knew, and Jane would in due course suffer for it. But, really, Jessica disgusted him so very much and then she'd been so rude this morning about his book. He went out of her room, all his thoughts obviously before him—not one left behind with Jessica.

Jessica stirred about in Piggy's bed. She felt a little sick with anger. But the consciousness of her power was still undimmed in her. She could do as she pleased. Jane should stay with her after all. Perhaps it would be best. She pushed back her tray and picked up a book—*Atoms*, it was called. But she could not read with the strength and concentration of which she was usually capable. Pain had slackened a little her usual grasp upon herself, or the exquisite relief of having no pain to bear. One or other reason betrayed her. The meaning of what she was reading swelled out of her comprehension and retreated then beyond the distance of possible consideration. Meanings heaved and swam before her eyes. She closed her eyes to think, to avoid the unconsciousness of mental action which so disgusted her, and thought became an unanswerable repetition, an endless smooth thing of beads. She was defeated and she slept.

"Of course," Sylvester said when Jane came down to tell him that Jessica slept still, "she *did* eat an enormous meal. There's no doubt she's very greedy."

"Oh, Sylvester, the car will waken her when it starts, right under her window."

"Well, does it really matter? You can go off in that motor and if she does wake it will be too late for her to stop you."

"Oh, Sylvester, don't be horrible. She wanted me to go, the poor sweet."

"She's quite capable of changing her mind if she wakes up."

"Yes, I know that. Sylvester, bring a coat for me, will you? I'll just pop off now in George's car."

"Do take that tiresome Piggy with you, Jane. I can't bear sitting there in front with her. If she goes with you, Hester and I can have an enthralling time by ourselves. Piggy!"

"Oh, Sylvester, *must* you shout like that? You'll surely waken Jessica."

They found Piggy already established in the front seat of George's car so they put her in the back to look after the dogs. "For Jane, you know," Sylvester told her, "is always sick in the back of a car without losing a moment."

"We can sit three in front," said Piggy, who did not feel too well herself in the back, but was determined to drive in George's car and be his protector from Jane.

"Oh, no, fat Piggy. You pop into the back and look after the dogs. You'll be all right."

"Oh, Sylvester, you are a beastly bully!" But Piggy allowed herself to be hustled into the back of the car all the same. A little fuss of any sort was always welcome to her if the fuss happened to be in any way connected with Piggy.

At last George's motor started and they drove away. Hardly had they gone half-way down the avenue when Sylvester heard the sharp ringing of Jessica's little bell.

"Albert can hobble upstairs and answer *that*," Sylvester said with a certain amount of sour triumph.

"Really, Sylvester," Hester was making plans with baskets in the hall, "how you have the courage to interfere in other people's lives to the extent you do quite defeats me."

"Don't be narky, darling Hester. I feel before long you'll be saying something about Lame Dogs and Stiles and that I could *not* endure."

"No dear, of course not. What about a coat for Jane?"

"Oh, yes. I'd forgotten that, with all my other plans for her welfare. And she's such a weak poor

girl. One must really think more of others and less
of oneself, mustn't one?"

"One should indeed. Are you going to get the
car out of the garage or am I?"

"Oh, you do—you know I'm *terrified* of her—"

Presently they took the road. Hester drove.
She was a safe and speedy driver. Sylvester threw
himself back at his ease and admired, not for the
first time, the richness of his gift to his cousins.
"What is this for?" he would ask. "Oh, yes,
visiting cards. Very nice. So like a brougham.
And this is for face powder. Piggy *would* keep it
full of powder. How nauseating it smells. And
this is for cigarette ash—Oh, Hester, give me a
cigarette."

"I will, if you'll stop counting up the luxurious
fittings of this motor car."

"All right, darling. Give me a cigarette, anyhow, then I can sit quietly and indulge my vulgar
passion for scenery."

After a pause, Sylvester said, "No. You know,
on the whole I prefer mountains on the way home.
They look more unreal then, don't they? Don't
you think so, Hester?"

"I agree with you."

"Yes. I like mountains best when I can see their
bones. They are inclined to look too plump and
wholesome in the afternoon."

"Which road are you going, Hester? Through
Waterford?"

"Yes. To tell you the truth, Sylvester, there is a tiny chest of drawers in an old junk shop which I'm itching to see again. I didn't like to look at it too long when I first saw it, I *did* want it so much. But, really, at the moment I feel it would be quite an investment."

"How lovely it is for you to have money to invest again. Where had you thought of putting the chest of drawers when you have bought it?"

"In my bedroom for a wash-stand."

"Very pretty it will look, no doubt."

"No doubt. I've always hated my present wash-stand."

They drove on in silence for a time after this, an enormous flat silver river curling its way slowly along below them. Quite large boats with immense sunburnt brown sails plied occasionally up or down its tidal waters and beds of ice blue reeds followed its turnings with precise exactitude. Sylvester thought it the most lovely river he knew, and, when on any distant height, he always looked out for its glass-like course. He enjoyed all the mercantile business conducted on its quays of Waterford too. A very wide roadway divided the quay and its shipping from the great lonely heights of the warehouses—great houses that looked as barren and secret as empty mills, like the mountains they were better in the evening. Or were they? With the sunlight on the river and the ships and the road all these dark doorways and flat windows were dramatic with a sense of hidden space and darkness.

Hester stopped the car opposite a furtive sort of archway and they proceeded on their feet through it to her junk shop.

Sylvester would never know what it meant to Hester, this visiting of a junk shop with money in her bag. He thought he had never seen her look so full of life, so near to happiness as to be almost in peril as she did this afternoon. Something of this he had seen in the morning when she had stood in the doorway of her house making her dispositions for the afternoon in her voice of a bird—a sweet, hoarse bird—but it was more apparent now. She might have been some rich old merchant on a nice little venture, his coat of puce brocade disappearing round dark corners, loosestrife bright in a patch of sun that travelled steeply down between the houses.

He followed her into a dark furniture shop and through the usual welter of incredible bedroom suites until they stood at last before her treasure. It was a small, bow-fronted chest of drawers, pretty enough like many another of its sort, but to Hester unique because she had wanted it so badly. She looked at it with a hungering, evasive eye, and asked the girl who appeared to show her some pieces of glass from the top of a high and distant shelf.

"It's dreadfully sweet," she said to Sylvester,

when the girl had gone to fetch a step-ladder. "If I can get it for two pound ten, I really think I *am* robbing him." She ran her finger along its dusty edge, pleased at the touch. "Such nice feet," she said, "and the right handles. Oh, it's a darling."

"Yes, it's adorable," Sylvester agreed. Her hardly restrained ardour astonished but did not appall him. What Hester must have suffered in all her lean years if she really harboured within her this lust for pieces, for pieces for Kilque. He could imagine her coming in here to buy odd bits of china, flawed, incomplete and valueless, with the hoarded shillings and sixpences of which she had cheated Piggy. In a way how lovely for her, but how embittering too when she saw this or that entrancing bargain from which she must restrain her hand. And now such great, if unstable, riches were hers, it was both wise and prescient of her to spend like this on carefully chosen bits and pieces. These she would have when her lodgers were gone and her deceit discovered.

"What else will you buy, Hester?" Sylvester asked. He sat on the edge of a sharp washstand and observed her minute examination of the chest of drawers for worm.

"I was thinking of buying myself a really superb bed," Hester said. "It would so comfort my declining years."

"Yes, it would be nice," Sylvester agreed.

"The beds at Kilque are *not* very good. In fact, Hester, I often feel just one long headache when I wake in the morning."

"I wonder you never thought of buying yourself a new one. We should not have been in the least hurt."

"No. I'm not a moneyed woman."

Hester's glass appeared now, but she did not buy it. She ascertained that the chest of drawers could be bought for three pounds, left a bid of two pounds ten, and said she would call back in the evening to see whether her bid had been accepted by the proprietor who was not at the moment to be found. As they were picking their way out of the shop Sylvester spied an enchanting glass goblet with a design of tiny corn-flowers cut round its rim, discovered it could be purchased for twelve-and-sixpence, and immediately desired the girl to wrap it in paper and have it ready for him in the evening.

"I have not got twelve-and-sixpence on me at the moment," he said, "but I will pay for it some time."

Hester picked up the goblet. It pleased her too. She hesitated a moment and then said with an effort as though she overcame some slight distaste: "Do you really like it? If you do I will give it to you." She paid the girl twelve-and-sixpence and they walked out of the shop.

Sylvester was terribly pleased. He wondered

when Hester had last given a present to any one, and dared say she had almost never done such a thing, certainly she had never before given him one. None of those spotted silk handkerchiefs, laboriously marked, that came to him from Kilque at Christmastime, had anything to do with Hester, he was quite sure. A pure bit of Piggy. He said now: "Thank you, Sweet Hester. You are a kind girl". They had a delicious drink then before proceeding on towards the picnic.

It must be allowed that all roads near the sea have a faintly exciting character. Just as the approach to any new state of being is pregnant with untried possibility so the way to the sea excites an expectation of beauty, of which in the event one is so often disappointed. But many sad falls of heart induced by a leaden sky and wretched sea had never entirely armed Sylvester against his desire for the sea as it should be. Nor had countless hideous experiences taught him how terrible picnics can be. In any case he had never yet found a picnic with Hester in control really unendurable. They were her talent, and a talent which she exercised seldom and briefly, many times curbing Sylvester's outdoor designs on doubtful days, many times saving him from squalor, cold and disappointment.

But to-day she had ordained a picnic and how right she was. As the roads to the sea grew each moment narrower and sandier, no dreadful tempest blew in their faces, no cloud vilely muffled the sun.

The purple loosestrife in the ditches was more vivid
than her coat in colour, the gold ragweed and late
pale flowers were quiet in the heat as though hands
sheltered them from the least wind blowing. Little
sheep moved cosily on little hills, knoll-like as hills
in a picture book. Heavy as grapes the blackberries awaited their harvesters. Probably the
tide would even be right for shrimping and those
greater game, the lobsters, come forth from safety
impregnable to their unknown, dreadful endings.
Hester had chosen out the day and all things
would be propitious.

Suddenly with the road's twinings the sea was
before them. Sylvester felt a sudden brief connection between himself and a dreadful little boy
in a white sailor suit who had been taught to cry
out: "Hurrah! Hurrah! for the sea!" by the aunt
who was so like her daughter Piggy. "Hurrah!
Sylvester—Hurrah for the sea!" It was comforting
to remember that a day had come when the little
boy had gone purple in the face and sulkily refused
to cheer and scream as his little cousin Piggy so
obediently did upon her first sight of Corah Bay.
The tie of imperishable faint delight between oneself and these moments did not endure beyond such
gross publicity.

The car stopped in a pebbly clearing. Between
rocks and sandy grass and sand, there was no more
than room to turn. But Hester managed tidily
enough.

"Can't I help you with your baskets, dear?" Sylvester stood in the sunshine—the smell of the sea at least defeating the smell of the car for him. The rich and rotten smell of seaweed, the everlasting smell of the tides.

"Not at all!" Hester, too, stepped out into the sunshine. "These two little boys will carry the baskets. They will also collect wood for the fire"; she summoned to her two wraith-like little boys who chanced to be upon the rocks at the moment, and obediently on their bare feet they ran to and fro at her behest. In such masterful ways Hester would often cope with a vexing situation. Presently, no doubt, the little boys would gather blackberries. Sylvester hoped so. He rather disliked gathering blackberries, carrying baskets or picking up sticks. Hester would deliver him from such small evils. He saw Piggy approaching.

"Oh, Hester, there's nasty Piggy! Shall I tell her you want sticks gathered for the fire?"

"Oh, do leave her alone, Sylvester."

"Poor Piggy—she looks so fat and jolly!"

Indeed she did. Her dress was tucked into her knickers and she was full of the animal spirits that beset some young women at the seaside. Piggy would look perfect, Sylvester thought, as he turned his back disgustedly upon her, in a red bathing dress with short sleeves, frills and anchors all over it. It should be worn with black stockings and a round mob cap of checked rubber. No, he thought then. Piggy belongs to a slightly later date in the world's history. She belongs to the Age of Underclothes. She should have had an affair with a vulgar man in the Great War. Then the "hot" books frothed and bubbled with underclothes. Well-shaped legs in black silk stockings stuck out of them in all directions. Sickening the way they wrote and talked about women's underclothes then. Sylvester's mind was in quite a fury of disgust at it all. And for him Piggy typified all this. She had called this moment into being for him. She belonged to the age of underclothes if ever any one did.

"The others are shrimping, Sylvester," Piggy said, panting up to him at last. "You can have my net if you like."

"Thank you, kind Piggy. But why should I take your net? Surely Hester has brought a net for me."

But Hester had not brought a net for Sylvester. He was forced to accept Piggy's reiterated offer and so fell in with her plan that he should shrimp with Jane while she and George (for there were only two shrimping nets among the party) should repair to the farther rocks and hook out lobsters. This was all crystal clear to Sylvester as soon as he saw George smoking a cigarette and watching with indulgence Jane's not very skilful efforts at shrimping.

For a moment Sylvester thought he would give

Piggy's net to George immediately and so thwart all her stupid plans. Then looking at Jane and looking back at Piggy he had a far better idea. Let George be forced to spend a dreary hour with Piggy for his companion, and there was no doubt he would return to Jane more than ever enamoured of her company. Therefore he said: "Jane, I see that you are not a very artful shrimper. I will instruct you"—he sat down to take off his shoes and stockings—"while George and Piggy are lobster hooking. It's a much coarser sport and one I don't enjoy nearly so much as shrimping."

"How fussy and pompous you are," said George, who had not the least wish to oblige either Piggy or Sylvester in the matter.

"Oh, go on, George. Don't be so idle. Piggy's *longing* to catch a lobster. I tell you what I *will* do," Sylvester said, standing delicately upon the rocks on his incredibly ghostly feet and turning up the legs of his trousers, "I'll have a good sea-romp with you after tea. We'll throw Piggy over the cliff if you like,"—Piggy squealed with delight at this importance—"but we must be kind and tender to Jane and not forget how weak she is, poor girl."

"Well, come on, Piggy," George said. Obviously Sylvester wanted him to take Piggy away. How cruelly rude he was to her. George's kind heart was often touched for Piggy's sake. For this reason he would spend many and many a dreary hour in her company. Alone with him she was more than ever silent and awkward and tiresome. Although she would scheme and angle quite skilfully for such a moment as the present, when it came it left her dumb and dismayed.

Jane was absorbed in her shrimping. She did not see or hear the others go. For once, all the arguments about who should stay with Jane had fought out their way unknown to her. When she looked up and saw that George had gone, Sylvester perceived, or thought he perceived, a faint sense of loss about her. She stood in water in a rocky pool where the water came half-way up to her knees. Her brown woollen dress was belted up above her knees—she had not tucked it into her knickers in Piggy's sea-side way. Her legs were as unsolid in the pale seawater as the darting shrimps' bodies were. So were her hands and arms. She had put her hair back behind her ears, her absurd painted face looked like a school-child's made up for theatricals. The scarred side of her face was away from Sylvester—he saw her in profile, against a rock covered in pale gold weed. She held the shrimps' thorny bodies in her fist for a moment as she took them out of her net, feeling for each the delight in a new capture, and then stuffed them into a jam-pot which stood on a ledge well above the water for safety, muttering to herself as she did so.

"You must not talk to yourself like that," Sylvester said, stepping carefully into the pool.

"It is a very unsteady thing to do. Look, Jane, you are no good at shrimping. I will show you. I am a perfect demon in the art."

Delicious hot rock pools; fatted and idle shrimps easily netted, horned and rasping in one's hand in their brief transference from net to bottle; the white jade of water where rock pools were the colour of flesh, the colour of the palm of your hand; the flight of sea birds, and Jane's gentle rhyming movements—these pleasures were Sylvester's to-day; these along with paths of light in the sea and the sea's hyacinth channels.

Jane's unquestioning obstinate pleasure in shrimping pleased him so much. He said to her once: "Wouldn't you like to go and hook out lobsters with George now?" And she shook her head, pursuing her own game with silent intensity.

"Hell, I'll say we gottalotta shrimps now," she said at last like a gangster, and sat down to dry her legs in the sunshine. Sylvester continued to explore the pools with furtive exactitude till Hester came down to say it was tea-time.

"Oh," Jane looked up at her suddenly, her face was not bland and silly. It was enchanted in delight. "I've had such a *wonderful* time." It was as though she could not realise so much delight. She was ardent in her acceptance.

"Simple pleasures, dear," Sylvester said sourly. He stood upon one foot, drying the other on his silk handkerchief. The faintest rapture terrified him. But Jane said no more. In fact nobody said anything either rude, witty or silly for quite a long time. Piggy was quiet at tea-time, having exhausted herself in previous efforts at conversation with George upon their isolated rocks, where, by the way, they had not captured even one lobster. Sylvester was determined to enjoy being hungry and ate an enormous quantity of food. Beyond saying: "Well, silent Piggy, and have you nothing to tell us of your adventures on the rocks?" he even left Piggy alone. George helped Hester to look after every one, and what with buttering bread and carrying the kettle to and fro between the fire and the teapot, he had very little leisure to do anything more than eat his own tea and take an occasional good stare at Jane. He seemed uneasy about something and fidgeted sadly after tea, instead of smoking a quiet cigarette like any one else. He would look from the incoming tide to Jane and back again. At last he asked her to come for a walk with him.

"To tell you the truth," he said as they set out, "you may think me a frightful fool——"

"Oh, *no*——" said Jane, a shadow stepping by his side.

"But the fact *is*," George went on with a rush, "I didn't go to the real lobster places with Piggy before tea. I—I kept them for you."

"Oh, *no!* How lovely of you."

Sylvester was gathering blackberries. Hester

had insisted and he had given in. "You will enjoy it, Sylvester," she had said, and really he was enjoying it. His enjoyment would not last for long, he knew, but at the moment it was rather pleasant to gather blackberries in a clean blue cup, the scoured sands and sea on your right hand and the smallest field in the world on your left. A field of old dark grass eaten down to the very sod. Then Sylvester saw a mushroom. And of all the things he did enjoy, perhaps the excitement of gathering mushrooms appealed to him most. Even in shrimping there was not quite that pure fever of selfishness, that sneaking poaching way one crept up on a mushroom unseen by a fellow picker, crept up and pounced as on a secret prey. Sylvester really yearned to gather mushrooms, but true to the precept of contradicting any urgent and immediate desire, he continued still in his blackberry picking. Terrified as he was that Piggy might also have observed that this was a mushroom field and start picking before him, he continued to gather blackberries, faithfully filling his shining blue cup and emptying it into the basket Hester had left between them.

At long, long last Hester admitted that, together with those her little boys and Piggy should have by now amassed, she really had enough blackberries for one day.

"I should hope so, indeed," Sylvester gazed down into the basket where the heaped black-

berries gleamed oily as water in a deep well, black
and shapely as packets of glass-headed pins. There
was a sensation of almost priggish satisfaction in
having helped to gather and store them away like
this; a dormouse feeling of preparation for the
severities of the winter—or did dormice hibernate
like little bears? Anyhow, Sylvester felt like an
autumn dormouse.

Presently, when he saw Hester walking below
him on the wet sands and Piggy—full of industry
and noble thoughts—filling a bag with sand (no
doubt for Joan's carnations), he set himself, with
the furtive adventurousness of a tinker stealing out
at dawn to milk the farmer's cows, about gathering
up his mushrooms.

Tiny mushrooms they were and not very many
of them, but the romance and adventure of their
gathering was his alone. No vulgar striving with
Piggy getting the better of him, for she was a
violent and quick-sighted mushroomer. This
lonely vigilant quartering of the fields was much
more to his mind and competition out of the
question, Sylvester could spend as many minutes
as he chose in the careful lifting of small, earthy
mushrooms, grass marked and creased in their
births. And in the capture of lovelier prizes,
sweating cold through their thick whiteness, there
was an almost piratical sensation of pleasure. A
Raiding.

When he had scoured all the immediate fields

and collected from them a quantity of mushrooms
sufficient to satisfy three not very greedy people
for breakfast, Sylvester placed his prizes carefully
on top of the blackberries and descended to the
beach where he wished to walk a while with Hester.
It was nearly seven and the air was growing chill,
smooth but chill as though the wind blew off wet
oyster shells, that was the colour of the sky and
the sand and the flying sea-birds. Sylvester's face
felt as cold as a bone. He and Hester walked
swiftly for a mile in that intoxication for walking
that overcomes some people by the sea. Then they
turned and came back to the cars where George
and Jane and Piggy were waiting for them with
their backs to the grey sea and its embittered
insistent complaining. It was changed with the
evening. Unkind, no longer for them.

Jane was wrapped up in the coat Sylvester had
so nearly forgotten. She looked very tired but she
was not cross. They had captured two nice lobsters,
she and George. Now it was the right time to go
home. They all got into Piggy's and Hester's car
this time, for George's way home parted almost
immediately from theirs. Piggy drove and Hester
sat with her, while Sylvester and Jane arranged
themselves at the back among the shrimps, the
blackberries, the lobsters and the mushrooms.

"You will be quite cosy," Hester said, nodding
at them. She had determinedly told Piggy to drive
and sat herself down beside her in the front, for

she saw all too clearly that Piggy was in that condition of mind known in the nursery as "a state," there was no telling but that a few well-chosen barbs from Sylvester might not precipitate her into sudden dreadful tears. If Piggy drove she would have something to do, a great armour from the unkindness of life, and if Sylvester sat in the back he would have something to do other than thinking of taunts and rudenesses for Piggy, for he would be busily thinking that he was going to feel sick, or worse, that Jane was going to be sick which would be hideous and upsetting to a degree.

Jane was not sick, she went to sleep. Sylvester did not feel sick, as really he never did, it was only a sort of vision he had of his condition, a vision which frequently saved him from long drives in the backs of other people's cars. He was quiet in himself, realising why Hester had put him in the back. He felt faintly penitent and sympathetic towards the emotional Piggy who, he had to own it, had endured a wretched afternoon entirely due to him. From the start he had set about wrecking Piggy's afternoon, and indeed he had contrived to do so well enough. But since there is no use helping, altering or enduring Piggy, Sylvester considered the matter, why deny oneself the enjoyable infliction of a little careful cruelty. One's pleasure in it far exceeds her pain, for she is much too stupid to realise how unkind one is being. And

in any case, thought Sylvester (who loathed all
mawkish penitence) while Piggy is Piggy, she is
very lucky to be tolerated by anybody. How
Hester endures her as she does is beyond belief.

"Oh, Hester, must you go back through Waterford?" Piggy was complaining peevishly.

"Oh please, Piggy, do you mind? I so frightfully want to call at Morgan's" (Morgan's was her
junk shop).

"We're going to be terribly late and I've a
simply splitting headache, but, of course, I'll go
if you like. It's only five miles longer."

Hester said nothing. Presently they came to a
cross-roads and Piggy, after an obvious hesitation,
took the one that led to Waterford. She sighed
exhausted sighs and drooped over the wheel a good
deal, but Hester still said nothing. When they got
to Waterford she was out of the car and back
again in the space of three minutes looking com-
posed and victorious.

"Two pounds ten," she said to Sylvester, "and
he'll deliver it to-morrow. It looked nicer than
ever."

"What a pleasant day you've had," Sylvester's
eyes were at rest on the wide quiet river, no business
now among the shipping, no winking little lights
as yet, all was steel-coloured and sepia in the
evening, and the warehouses unimaginably dark
against the sky, unreal, cut out in black cloth.
"Chests of drawers for your bedroom. Mushrooms

for breakfast to-morrow, and shrimps. Lobsters and blackberry tart for luncheon. I suppose I may have my goblet to drink out of at dinner to-night? I'm sure Albert will wash it for me."

"Have you been buying furniture?" Piggy asked sharply. It was this governess-like attitude of Piggy's towards Hester's money that Sylvester found particularly intolerable. The more so because he knew it behoved Piggy to keep a sharp eye on Hester's deceitful ways with money. But Hester was unruffled.

"Yes, an adorable chest of drawers Sylvester bought for me to-day," she said.

"At Morgan's? Oh, I'm sure it's the one Joan has been trying to make Robin buy for ages. They wanted six pounds for it."

"That is probably the one. We bought it for two pounds ten."

"Oh well, it will be all right. I'm sure Joan will give you four pounds for it. She bid Morgan that."

"If you dare to sell my lovely present to Joan, Hester, I'll be annoyed and offended," Sylvester put in huffily.

"Well, we'll see," was all Hester said. She was not going to become involved in any argument.

They continued on their way home. The mountains had cast from them that daytime wholesomeness which Hester deplored. They leant apart and leaned together now in an old, evil dream. The mountains were sick in the evening, ageing women fighting for beauty. There was no kindness in them or any calm. Their lines were striving together in the near darkness. Lovely in their striving and their failing. A gold river crawled through the evening dragging out its way, a pale, cheesy gold between its unstirring reeds. What about a drowned swan? Sylvester wondered, being in a mood to pile sadness on to sadness. Could anything imaginable be more defeated of its beauty? Had any one ever seen a drowned swan? Sylvester had—a wild swan shot and fallen in water, water lipping at its dead feathers. Shivering, he recalled it to mind with other sad disasters suitable to his mood and the hour, and answered them: "For I impair not Beauty being mute."

Looking at Jane he wondered whether she too would not in time be to him only a sad disaster, fit to remember on such an evening as this. Was she not one of those fatal creatures always over-looked to their undoing? In the wild sadness of the hour Sylvester almost thought she was. He was ravished in the thought of her never lasting happiness. Looking still upon her sleeping, white rhododendrons were in his mind—their papery, pallid throats spotted green as orchids. No poly-anthus flower has such single grace in each of its repetitions. Aloof, almost bleak, not rich, and again and again lovely.

Poor sleeping Jane, no doubt she thought she had found a harbour and a safety, while George, simple creature, romance and adventure had come to George. Sylvester wondered how they would both cope with events and situations so unusual to their lives. And Jessica? What, what indeed would Jessica do when the danger and urgency of this matter were fully known to her? Her reactions, Sylvester suspected, would quite certainly be horrible.

CHAPTER VI

A WEEK since that sea-day and Sylvester sat within the armoured seclusion of his writing hours and thought of all that had befallen in the time. The dramas and the complications of life really were getting beyond him. As Hester had so rightly said, How did one discover within oneself the temerity to interfere? After all he had not interfered very much. He had simply allowed matters to take their course. And the course of matters, once they are set going, is past all imagination unknowable.

For instance, had Sylvester intended this wreckage, this really catastrophic tragedy into which the wretched Piggy had now been plunged? No, he had not. It appalled him.

It had all started on Sunday. That Sunday luncheon of Joan's, a function which Sylvester usually went out of his way to avoid. But he had become involved. He had promised George. He

had said he could not go—raising Piggy's spirits at
breakfast time that he might damp them at twelve
o'clock. Finally, one o'clock had found him standing in the hall of Kilque fitting a purple flower into
the buttonhole of his grey flannel suit, all ready
for the party. There had been a conversation with
Jessica first:

"Jessica, I think you're a particularly clever
woman. D'you mind my saying so?"

And Jessica darkly glowing, leaning towards him
from her armchair, her hurt foot out before her,
her fine strong hands gripping the arms of her
chair, saying:

"I'm not sure that I know what you mean;
do be *exact*." Jessica with her devastating power
to suck effort and vitality from another, to insist
on getting what she wanted, her power to obtain
mental sustenance from flattery. "Do be exact,"
do enlarge upon your praises. Well, that was what
Sylvester wanted to do after all.

"Oh, I don't know. Can one quite explain these
things one has about people? I suppose I meant
your ability to have a kind of chart of life, to know
where you're going, what you're doing, what you
want——"

"For instance?"

"Oh, I don't know. Can one quite take an
instance? Well, for one instance, this line you've
taken with Jane——"

"*Yes.*"

"I mean, letting her pursue her dreary way through this outdoor moment she's having. Not *interfering*. I think it's pretty brilliant of you, really."

"Oh, my dear, is it? I *think* it's obvious. My God, she'll be so *bored* so *soon*. But I didn't realise you saw all this."

"It's rather my nasty trade, isn't it, Sweet? Dramas and motives and all that."

"Yes, but one doesn't think of you like that." Jessica rather pleased him with this unthoughtful word of truth. Well, he had given her a grand line to pursue. No doubt Jane would now be compelled to attend this enthralling entertainment.

Jane came down and joined him in the hall. She was effectively dressed for a luncheon party at the Berkeley. She looked lovely really, if incredibly wrong for a Sunday luncheon at Castlequarter. There was still that surprised air of escape about her, although Jessica had been all in a moment changed, insisting on her going.

Piggy was looking at Jane, highly contented. Piggy in her indefinite tweed and new felt hat exactly like the last, thinking: "What a laugh Joan and I will have. How *can* she wear a hat like that? and those absolutely London shoes—well, *I* wouldn't wear them in London. And she has a new colour on her nails. What *do* they look like? Joan will have a fit when she sees her. Joan will have something to say to George. I'll tell her all

about yesterday. After lunch. Perhaps I'll get
her upstairs alone. We might escape. I really
feel she *ought* to know George was so very nearly
silly yesterday. Of course one knows with George
it means nothing, nothing at all. He'll probably
be *terrified* of her to-day. Probably he won't appear
at lunch at all."

But Piggy would never tell Joan of that terrible
feeling of contracted pain which had been hers
yesterday, as if Unkindness put a small icy hand
on her heart and squeezed her heart and Piggy
was left without anything at all. A helpless,
hysterical Piggy with nothing in the world to keep
her whole and safe ... To-day she was strong
again in old conceits and new hopes.

"Must we have sacks and sacks of sand in the
car?" Sylvester asked fretfully.

"Oh no. I don't know why they left it
there." Piggy was quite eager to get rid of
the sand. A future valid reason for going to
see Joan was wasted if she brought the sand
to-day. The sand was flung out of the car. Tot
sand reminded Piggy of gardening and she said to
Jane:

"Are you a gardener too?"

"Too?" repeated Jane, dully.

"Oh, Joan and I work so hard in the garden.
I really do far more at Castlequarter than I do
here. But the soil here is so poisonous."

"Isn't that just too sad?"

"Joan wants me to make a viola garden because my name is Viola, you know."

"How cute!"

"A pity your name is not Wanda, my dear, you might then be some help to me in dividing my primulas," Sylvester put in.

"Oh, I always think Wanda is such a Brave Poor Thing!"

"No doubt you do. Especially after you've been listening to Beverly Nichols on the wireless." Sylvester could have bitten his tongue with vexation at himself for having mentioned his Wanda to Piggy at all. It was a lessening. He was defeated of something that mattered.

Several cars were drawn up in front of Castle-quarter when they arrived. It looked like a large luncheon party, but when you had deducted George's car and Robin's and their own, the crowd did not seem so stupendous after all.

A large lady with gold hair, blue eyes, a blue hat and a blue face stepped out of a new blue motor car and turned to Sylvester with cries of delight. She said, "How do you do" to Jane with a cold stare of surprise, took no notice of Piggy, and continued to talk loudly to Sylvester as they went towards the house.

"I feel awfully naughty, you know, Sylvester; I haven't read your last book yet. I simply can't *afford* seven-and-sixpence. You do understand, don't you? And you will forgive me and lend it to me, won't you? I'd so love to read it."

"Yes, indeed, I understand, Alice, and of course I'll lend it to you. Why should I mind? My dear, if my sales depended on my friends they'd be *so* strangely limited, wouldn't they?"

"Would they? How odd! Oh, Arthur has a lovely bit to tell you, Sylvester. You *must* hear it for your next book. I thought it was good enough for *Punch*. I wish I could remember it, it really was *most* amusing."

"Come on, Jane," Sylvester said. He really was not going to hang about in front of the house all day talking to that paralysing Alice.

"Whoever is that tatty old dame?" Jane asked, following him towards the house. "*Such* a cruel shade of blue her face is, and her legs, Sylvester— *Frightening!*"

"Those legs, my dear, are positively pillars of society in the county. If you ever intend to be a social success here, keep on the right side of Alice. She's a very influential woman. We're all terrified of her, I assure you. Even Joan does not encourage her dogs to bite Alice. You will see."

In the hall Joan was sitting on a divan with her legs folded up underneath her and about seven dogs of different shapes and sizes disposed on and about her person. She was looking lovely and not quite eighteen. She screamed. Lady Drumderry (in blue) shouted. A few of the dogs barked.

"I can't get up," Joan was yelling. "Mother's Bom-Sweet'll bite some one if I do. She hates you, doesn't she, Alice."

"If that little brute bites me again I'll never walk another puppy for you, Robin. And you know I'm the best walk you've got."

"How are the puppies?" Robin was so serious and sweet. "Do let me shut the Bom-pet up, darling."

"Alice—glass of sherry?" It was George walking about with some rather indifferent sherry.

"First Yellows; then Hysteria—they do add to the difficulties of life. No, thanks, George. Yes, please, I think I will."

"Oh, darling, do let me shut Sweetie-Bom up?"

"Oh, Robin darling, don't be tiresome."

"What can one do with a woman like that?"

"Beat her!"

There were yells of laughter.

Weathering this gale of mirth, Piggy, Jane and Sylvester advanced upon their hostess.

"How d'you do?" Joan said to Jane. "Don't think me awfully rude, will you, but if I move you'll be bitten. *Shut* up, Bommy."

Robin immediately took charge of Jane, giving her a glass of sherry, asking her how long she'd been in Ireland. He was quite well off in subject matter for the next five minutes. George was involved with Lady Drumderry. There was no escaping her. She had a story to tell about a

salmon she had caught a few months ago. Sylvester
retired to the window with Lord Drumderry—a
quiet and sensible man who showed not the smallest
ambition to tell him that tale with which Alice had
threatened him. There they were joined by somebody's Land Agent and a peaceful conversation
ensued about the numbers of snipe in certain bogs,
the numbers of partridges in certain localities, the
numbers of foxes in certain coverts, until it was
time to go in to luncheon.

Luncheon. Lobster salad. Roast chicken. Plum
tart. Cream cheese.

Piggy had her wish. She sat beside Joan. "Piggy,
you must protect me from Sylvester. Sit here——"
a childish whisper.

"Oh, Joan, you baby! I believe you're frightened of him."

"Oo, literary people are terrifying."

With it all Sylvester found himself sitting
between Blue Alice and fat Piggy. If he had been
quick he could have sat where George was sitting
on one side of Jane. But he had been kind, not
quick. So here he was, and Alice was going to talk
about books. It was her pride that she could talk
competently to anybody. Even to people like
authors and artists, who knew nothing of hunting
or fishing or racing. Besides, Sylvester was
different. The Brownes were a good old Westcommon family, remember. And Sylvester was
a success. Not like that poor Piggy.

"Have you read Mabel Hautboy's book?" she asked.

Sylvester was extracting a tiresome morsel from the extreme toe of his lobster claw.

"No," he said, "I have not indeed. A memoir, one presumes, of a social and useful life in the early years of the present century."

"Oh, a *capital* book," Lady Dumderry asserted. "So sincere. So clean. I enjoyed it so much."

"I see. No hinting at intimacy with Edwardian Royalty, or anything of that sort."

"Oh, nothing like that. A most sincere book. A book to buy and keep, I thought. So *sincere*."

"And could you afford it, Alice? Eighteen-and-six, wasn't it? You might lend it to me. I have a passion for photographs round about the year 1903. I feel sure Lady Hautboy was an enthralling Edwardian Rose, wasn't she?"

"I believe she was. Of course I was in the schoolroom when she was really at her best. But when I first knew her she was *still* a very lovely woman."

"Where does one obtain this entrancing book? Is it by any sad chance a limited edition which she hoped her friends might buy?"

"I don't imagine so. I ordered it through the Book Society. It was not on their list, which I thought rather surprisin', but they got it for me."

"Are you an ardent member of the Book Society, Alice?—like Piggy, for instance."

"Oh, well—ardent—I don't know. I think there's a lot to be said for the Book Society. They send you your book so nicely done up in green cardboard. Have you read *Worlds*, Piggy?"

"Oh, no. You know I scarcely ever read novels."

Lady Dumderry, who had waded through *Worlds* with much mental tribulation and little pleasure, snorted her contempt for Piggy's ignorance of modern difficult thought and turned to Robin with a question about his yearlings, none of which had reached their reserves in the Blood Stock sales.

George was saying to Jane, "—and *were* you sick in the back of the car last night?"

"Oh, no. I went asleep."

A lovely moment of confidence.

Joan observed it from her end of the table. She was a practised interpreter of George's silences and said to Piggy now:

"How rich is she? D'you know?"

"Very rich, I think. *Joan*, isn't she terrible? Her nails, Joan. Joan, I must talk to you after lunch—or some time."

"Stay to tea. They'll be gone then. Aren't her clothes frightful?"

Piggy glowed and choked over her glass of white wine. Sweet Joan. Beloved creature.

After luncheon other people appeared. An old man, very tidily dressed in a blue suit. His wife, who had sciatica and a gentle, tiresome face, and

their young daughter, very sweet in a blue suit
rather like father's. Her name was Rosemary.
Rosemary wanted to know how her puppy had
entered. She was very girlish and earnest about it
all. Alice wanted to see her puppies too.

"Would it bore you to come down to the
kennels," they said to Jane. "We'll see some of
the hounds. They've been *fed*, of course . . ."

Poor brutes, she hoped so.

More people arrived; a small old man in a
check suit, with the crossest voice Jane had ever
heard. He was very lame and extremely fussy.
And another girl. She and Rosemary flew to each
other.

George and Jane walked down to the kennels
together. The path from the house was used and
narrow. There were rooks in the trees overhead.
The near trees were heavy in summer green still,
but in those at a little distance one could see that
the leaves had turned. Everything was very dry,
twigs snapping underfoot. Everybody walked
solemnly along. Nobody said much. It was as
though they were all going forth to a religious
exercise. Robin walked with the cross, important
old man. Joan was being very childish and sweet
with the elder ladies. Jane went picking her way
along in her high-heeled shoes. She had taken off
her hat and stuffed it in her pocket, without her
hat she looked less like a party at the Berkeley,
but still absurdly another creature from these

women round her. Like the mountains yesterday,
dangerous but not quite wholesome. She was
rather prepared to enjoy herself; no more nervous
of saying the wrong thing or saying nothing at all
than any one of them would have been during an
afternoon at the Zoo.

Rosemary was thinking—I know I won't know
my puppy. What a fool I shall feel. Even Alice
Drumderry, after all her years of outdoor sport,
was feverishly trying to recall the spots by which
she had been used to distinguish Dainty from
Dauntless—those twin queens of the last puppy
show. The old gentleman in the check suit was
one of the few people really prepared for an afternoon's enjoyment. For twenty-one years Master of
a neighbouring pack, his disapproval of all Robin's
theories on breeding hounds or feeding hounds or
hunting foxes, or even killing foxes, was a well-
rooted enjoyment and old satisfaction to him. He
looked forward to a really delightful afternoon's
disapproval and a grand fund of conversation for
days to come.

Strangely enough it was with this notable judge
of hounds that Jane was presently to have a success
that many an outdoor girl might have envied her.
But this was not for some hours yet. Hours during
which she stood, the sun beating upon her head,
her body lapped in a white linen coat, the remains
of a small whip in her hand, while hounds were
drafted through interminably and regarded in a

silence of disapproval or ignorance by the visitors.
A Sunday afternoon in the kennels was pursuing
its usual course.

Jane was interested, though her feet were rather
tired and she wished one could sit down for this
entertainment. The women all stood in one corner.
Joan occasionally made one of them look silly by
her reply to some ill-ventured remark. Occasionally she would say: "Oh, Robin, darling, do let's
have Ajax out now—he's the *only* hound you have
I like looking at." But Ajax was not produced for
a very long time.

"This poor dawg is all pink and itchy—and
why?" Jane asked shrilly. She was a little bored
and wanted to talk.

"Little 'eat in the blood, Miss," the kennel
huntsman told her in a hushed voice. "Ravager,
Ravager." The hound's lovely posing excited
Jane. The strong flight of his lines.

"Grand mover, isn't he?" Joan said to Lady
Drumderry, paying no attention to Jane.

Pieces of biscuit scooted along the flags and
rolled down off a tin roof. Ajax was at last brought
out.

"Oh, what a horrible dawg!" said Jane dis-
tinctly and insistently. She had no reason to
produce for her rude remark. Simply she did not
like him, any more than she had liked Tig. As
it chanced, opinion differed very much about
Ajax, that noble stallion hound. Some judges

liked and others hated him. The old gentleman in the lovely check suit was a sound hater. He started slightly and soon limped over to Jane, from whom there had been after that remark a slight drawing aside of skirts. Here was a sensible girl and a pretty one too, poor thing, and by gad, she was not afraid to say what she thought.

"Well, I rather agree with you meself," he said to her in a hoarse whisper, "I do like to see necks and shoulders."

Jane stared at him round eyed, wondering what sort of answer such a remark required. Luckily she said nothing.

"Quality," the old man insisted, "must have it. Seen a hound to-day that looks like galloping?"

"Oh, no."

"No. Nor have I."

"Darling Jane," Sylvester said as they walked back to the house. "Such success as you had. Have you taken in that *all* poor Robin's hounds ought to be knocked on the head in the interests of fox-hunting?"

"Oh yes, Sylvester. It does seem a pity. I thought they were so very, very lovely myself."

"So they are," said Sylvester, "a noble pack of hounds. Don't mind what any of those old Quags say to you. All the same I'm delighted you annoyed Joan about that glorious dog Ajax. And are you going over to spend a long and happy morning in the kennels with old Johnny Curby?"

"*Yes.*"

"*No!* If you only knew, Jane, how elect and enviable you are—chosen among *all* outdoor girls."

Piggy was saying to Joan:

"I feel rather guilty about having brought her here—but it wasn't really a Piggy's fault, was it *Could* I have imagined George would be so silly?"

"Is he being silly?" Piggy was annoying Joan with her apologies and her obscure tales of yesterday. Stupid ass she was. "Personally I think he's quite right to have a crack at her if he feels like it."

"But she's not his type." Wildly Piggy searched her heart for words that might set forth and emphasise her horror of Jane and all that Jane was.

"She's very *attractive*," Joan stated calmly. "I must write to Cissy Minister and find out more about her. She says she knows her."

Then indeed was Piggy put outside a pale. She, who saw Jane day by day, was set aside and one of Joan's distant exciting friends was to approve or condemn this stranger.

"Anyhow," Joan said, "I shall do nothing till I've sold her my Balmorals."

"Oh, yes," Piggy agreed, eagerly agreed. "I talked to her about them yesterday; but, of course, Sylvester shoved his oar in and told her not to buy them. Joan—do tell me, do you like her?" Stupid, pitiful Piggy.

"I rather take my hat off to her for knowing

she didn't like Ajax and I think she has the most
exquisite legs I've ever seen."

"Americans nearly always have good legs, don't
they?"

"Do they?"

"I think so, don't they?"

"Do you know many Americans, Piggy?"

"Oh, I don't know." There was no reason in
the pain which Piggy had to bear. Her god had
turned his face aside. But this had happened
before. It would not endure. It was but a moment.

Jane and George were walking together again.
Along the edge of a wood, the Sunday party was
on its way back to tea after an inspection of
Robin's yearlings.

"I come down to do a bit of work here," George
said, looking contentedly about him at the familiar
field. "I often gallop here when I can't gallop at
home."

"Oh, whatever do you mean? Do talk so as a
girl can understand some of what you say."

Lovely Jane, unashamed, unposing in all her
ignorance of George's life, of what it meant to
train your own indifferent race horses. She did
not know and she would ask. Entrancing girl!

The afternoon was not complete until a separate
and individual visit had been paid to every sensible
and efficient old hunter in the stables. One by
one their merits were discussed and enumerated.
Some of them were plain old horses enough, but

all brilliant performers. There were a great many
of them, so there was a great deal to say, and the
plainer the horse the longer grew the tale of his
merit as a hunter. To Jane they were all horses
with manes and tails. She grew a little weary
before it was time to go in to tea. Sylvester grew
peevish. This entertainment with Joan invariably
maddened him. Her appalling "me and my best
chum" attitude towards her favourite hunters
made him feel very ill indeed.

"Darling Luck Pot," she embraced the remains
of a common old hunter with childish tenderness.
"Hasn't he a grand sensible old head?"

"He looks as if he had sense enough to stop
when he's tired anyhow," Sylvester said sourly
from outside the door.

"I've never got to the bottom of this horse yet,"
Joan said grandly.

Luck Pot drooped his ugly head and coughed
and rested another leg.

"Dirty cough," said Sylvester, moving on.

Joan said angrily that it was only stomach; he
always had it when he first came up off grass.
But Sylvester had spoiled her best moment with
Luck Pot and stupid Piggy had not been on hand
to say, "Didn't you see every moment of the good
hunt from Kilfeen on Luck Pot, Joany? Was it a
five-mile point or four-and-a-half? And weren't
you and Robin the only people who finished it?"
Ah, if Piggy had been there, then her day might

have improved and other matters fallen out very differently.

After tea Joan said to Robin: "Alice tells me Gwen's not coming to us till Thursday."

"How long is she going to stay?"

"I don't know. You must be nice to her. You swore you would. You were so awful last time. Edward," Joan called her child to her, "do you know who's coming on Thursday?"

"No."

"*Cousin* Gwen. What are you going to call Cousin Gwen, Edward?"

"That *dreary* woman——" Edward was difficult and sulky, standing first on one mammoth leg and then on the other.

"If you ever call her that, Edward, I shall never take you out shooting rabbits again."

"What Daddy said——" very sulky.

Joan tried round in another direction: "Will you go and see her in bed in the morning?"

"I don't know. What will she have for me in her suitcase?"

"Don't be so greedy. There won't be anything for greedy little boys. She'll probably bring John a present because he's going to show her his pony."

"*Yes*, Mummy," said sweet John, ever eager to oblige, "I'll show Cousin Gwen my pony."

"*No*, John. You let Gwen alone."

"Can't I show her my pony, Mummy?"

"Yes. Be quiet, darling. Only presents for little boys who show their ponies, Edward."

"*John* can show her my pony too if he likes. John can get both presents. *Dear* John will give me my present."

"*Yes*, Edward."

"John is too weakly and insufferably good-natured," Sylvester interrupted. "Edward, if I liked you better I might make you my heir."

"What's your heir, Uncle Sylvester? Would I like to be?"

"It's what your mother wants Gwen to make you."

"Sylvester, I won't have you putting sordid ideas into the child's mind."

"What is Heir, Mummy?"

"It's nothing, darling. Uncle Sylvester is a silly ass. You go and tell him that."

"You ask Gwen what an Heir is," said Sylvester, unpleasantly. Go and see her in the morning and ask her what she has in her suit-case and what an heir is, and tell her Mummy said you were to show her your pony. Do you understand me clearly, my child?"

"*Yes*, Uncle Sylvester," said Edward, almost as sweetly and eagerly as John. But Joan, not unnaturally, failed to see that all this was particularly funny. Soon she retired to a distant sofa, gathered her dogs about her and answered simply, "Do you?" to anything that was said to her. She really could cope no longer with these people. She was too young, too bored, too childish to endure them. Would they never go away?

Piggy whispered to Jane: "We must go now. I think Joan's a tiny bit tired."

"Is she?" Jane was tired too. She did not mind how soon she went home now that she had made a plan for seeing George to-morrow. The importance of to-morrow and other to-morrows was suddenly plain to her. That only mattered. That only was her clear desire. "It's fantastic. It's frightening," Jane thought, but she was not one to explore further into her own emotions. She loved. She accepted her state. It made life more difficult and complicated and left her vulnerable to much unkindness, but there it was. She loved again.

"Good-bye, Mrs. Nuthatch," Jane said. "I *have* enjoyed myself and seeing all your lovely hounds has been very, very thrilling."

"Do you?" said Joan faintly. Then, remembering the possibilities of a deal over the Balmorals, she got up from among her dogs. "George tells me he's giving you a horse on Thursday morning. What about clothes? I don't suppose you've brought any with you. Could I lend you anything, I wonder."

"Oh, how very sweet of you!"

"Oh no. Come on, Piggy——" Joan liked to have Piggy about on these occasions. She knew

her part. "We're going to play at clothes. I
rather like that hat you're wearing, Pig. It's not
terribly You, but it might be quite Me."

Presently they were in Joan's bedroom. Delphiniums on the chintz and baskets for dogs in all
directions and Joan was saying, "I'll give you ten
shillings for that hat, Piggy. Will you deal?"

"Yes. Rather." Piggy agreed with slightly
forced heartiness, for she had paid twenty-five
shillings for the hat in question not ten days
before.

"Or, I'll tell you what"—Joan opened a cupboard—"shall we have a swap? I'll let you have
this hat I bought from *Denise*. It's a wonderful
line."

Piggy regarded in silence the confection in straw
which Joan produced. It looked as if it had known
a wet Ascot. Such moments try love almost too
highly, but Piggy's love had survived many such
and still endured. She tried the hat on before the
glass and gazed miserably at her reflection.

"I always say, if you want a good laugh, just
pop a two-year-old hat on your head," Jane said
helpfully, "and I suppose in its day that was
quite a lovely hat."

"*I* always think if one goes to the really good
people it pays one over and over again. Their
things stay right for ever. I bought that hat from
Denise two years ago and look at it now."

They all looked at it. Joan with defensive

pride, Jane with undisguised horror, Piggy with sick despair.

"Are you *sure* you want to part with it, darling? I always thought it suited you marvellously."

"Yes, it's a lovely hat. It looks awfully good on you, Piggy. I feel you *must* have it. It ought to be yours, really. It's so terribly becoming. Now let's look for some clothes for Mrs. Barker."

Having disposed of all hesitations over the hat question, Joan dived into another cupboard, reappearing with a peculiar pair of canvas drawers which laced down the knees and buttoned up the back.

"I wonder if these would be any use to you? If they are you can have them. *Honestly*, I almost never wear them. Try them on. They look *rather* good on her, don't they, Piggy? Have you a high-necked jersey, I wonder? What about my blue one, Piggy? Would it fit her?"

"Do you mean the one Daphne Mullett bid you four shillings for?"

"Yes. I stuck out for six. Daphne's a Jew, isn't she?"

"Oh, that *reminds* me"—Piggy had an idea—"What about your Newmarket boots? Did you sell them to Daphne in the end?"

"No. She tried like anything but she just couldn't squeeze herself in."

"Well—wouldn't they be the very thing for

Jane? You know the misery of riding in shoes and stockings."

"Oh, yes, it's agony, and quite dangerous. Robin won't let me do it, you know. I wonder if you'd like to have these boots? They cost me a tenner, but I only want seven-ten for them. I think I've worn them three times. Or have I, Piggy?"

"Only twice, I think," answered the faithful Piggy.

"No, I *think* I wore them three times," Joan insisted with laudable honesty. "But anyhow, there they are, if they're any use to you, do have them."

"They look lovely," said Jane, helplessly.

"Yes, they're good boots. Try them on."

"*Must* I? I'm so tired. I could take them home and try them when I feel stronger. Albert will help me. Might I do that?" Jane really was tired, and she could not find her way out of the sporting drawers. It was all very exhausting and puzzling. She would have bought anything to save further argument and get herself home to bed. Life was tiresome and difficult at the moment.

"I'll let you know to-morrow evening if she takes them," Piggy murmured to Joan as they went downstairs. "I'll pop over after tea."

"Oh, don't bother, Piggy. Violet Enderly's coming here to-morrow and I *know* you hate her."

"I don't *know* her." Piggy was half-way between tears and temper. Violet Enderly was one of the important people on whom Joan did not inflict her fat Piggy. She kept Violet for herself.

"Do come over if you like," Joan repeated evenly. She stooped and picked up a dog. "Who was mother's darling, sweet? Who was? *Oo* was. Of *course* oo was... Have you got your hat, Piggy?... and the boots?... and the breeches? ... Good-bye... See you soon."

They had gone. Joan said to George: "I like your American girl. She's so attractive and she bought my Balmorals... Shall I ask her to stay here on Wednesday night before cub-hunting? Say if you want me to."

"You always were so sweet," George said gratefully. "I'm frightfully glad you like her."

"And Robin won't complain so much about Gwen if she's there. Robin, darling, would you like that girl to come here on Wednesday night?"

"Oh yes. She's a lovely girl. Didn't you think so, darling? And I can talk to her."

"What did you talk to her about?" Joan asked, idly.

"She was telling me about her dressmaker and about divers and about that nigger fellow who makes the records I like. She knows him quite well. Such a rest from Alice and her eternal chat about her horses."

"Poor old Alice. She's such a bore."

"I thought old Arthur was looking very seedy."

"Yes, didn't he look ghastly? On the drink again, I suppose."

"Oh, darling, do ring for the sherry."

"Oh, darling, do make a cocktail. They drank up most of that filthy sherry before lunch to-day."

"It is bad, isn't it?"

"Darling, you know Violet's coming to look at my brown four-year-old to-morrow. What would you do about that leg if you were me?"

"I'd go out now and cover it in antiphlogistine from the knee to the fetlock."

"All right, I will. I thought it was so brave of that girl to *know* she didn't like Ajax."

"Yes. Lovely of her."

"Robin darling, you *are* going to be nice to Gwen, aren't you? Isn't this rather a severe cock-tail? It's lovely though—Do you promise me about Gwen?"

"Albert, did you buy me a Bradshaw?"

Jessica sat forward in her armchair. Her hair was brushed frigidly back from her face, her hair that grew as though a wind had blown through it and a black frost frozen it into shape. A pair of crutches leant against her chair for she was now able to hop about a little. She had put on a black silk shirt but the flannel trousers were still rather a difficulty. There was a rug over her knees.

"Did you ask me to buy a Bradshaw, Miss? Well, I *am* sorry. It quite slipped my memory. However, I daresay there's one in the house but it's probably out of date."

"Never mind. It will do. At least I suppose it will have to. You really are growing awfully forgetful, Albert. What did you do in the town if you forgot the Bradshaw? That's all you went in for."

Albert looked guilty. He had gone to the town to attend to a secret of his own and he had no intention of telling Miss Houpe-Boswell anything about it.

"Well, the fact is, Miss, I was buying a mouse-trap," he said. "I have a horror of mice, as you know. Mice make me feel all oo-er, they do, really, and my bedroom here is just crawling with them. I mean to say it's simply swarming. Why, I spent most of last night sitting on top of my chest of drawers, really I did. Couldn't get it out of my head there was a mouse in my bed."

"Oh, you're too temperamental. What are you going to do now?"

"Well, I've bought this rather ingenious little trap I told you of and Cook has kindly said she will set it for me and also visit it in the morning to remove the dead mice. I don't think it's healthy having them about."

"What a coward you are, Albert. Can't you even take a dead mouse out of a trap?"

"Touch a mouse? Oh, I *couldn't.*"

"You have a marvellous sunburn, haven't you? I suppose you've been helping yourself to that oil of mine." Jessica was tired of Albert's vapours over the mice.

"No, Miss. I'm using some stuff Mrs. Barker gave me for growing the eyelashes. It's quite useless for that purpose but I must say it's lovely for the skin. Ever so soothing."

"You'll be covered all over in fur if you're not careful. Go and find me that Bradshaw."

Just before dinner Jane came in.

"Reading Bradshaw, darling. How fantastic! What a good brain you have, darling. How does it end?"

Jessica did not answer. She was for the moment remote—the competent Time Tabler. A waggling little finger questing yet assured of ultimate success pursued its way down the columns of names and figures to wrest the ultimate truth from a medley of hours, days, Holydays and Bank Holidays.

Jessica had done her hair in a new way, very calm and saint-like, and she had put on a black shirt like an executioner's which fastened right up to her chin. Slowly the portent of all this dribbled through to Jane's mind. She was not very quick, poor girl, at any time, but now it occurred to her that Jessica wanted to go away, to leave Kilque and Ireland behind and compel Jane to come with her. How to escape. Ah, how to escape? Until such necessity is immediately upon one, how begin to perceive the difficulties which prevent its relief.

"Filthy shirt, sweetie," Jessica said, looking up from Bradshaw, "so 'Great open spaces,' isn't it?"

Jane giggled nervously. Jane who an hour ago had happily poured an incredibly awful smelling liquid rightly called Stinko on to pieces of sheep's wool and shoved the pieces of wool down large holes in a bank—quite why she was not sure, George had told her but she had forgotten, Jane giggled a weak betrayal of her enthusiasms.

"Darling, how funny you are. It is rather filthy. I'll give it to Albert. How are you feeling to-night? I'll say you're looking marvellous. Are you feeling marvellous, sweetie? I'm wild to know how you're feeling, sweetie."

"I'm really better," Jessica looked up from train guide. "So intensely better that I'm looking up the trains that might take me away from here. I've been doing it all day—*such* a lovely entertainment for me."

Jane turned faintly sick. She had not expected this contest to start quite so soon.

"But the doctor said you weren't to go, darling, not for six weeks. And we haven't been here a fortnight yet."

"We've been here exactly fifteen days—a hideous interval of time, you will admit, won't you?"

"Well, but darling, why do you want to go away by train?" Jane whined, evading this question.

"I don't want to drag you away until you're really satiated with all this outdoor fun. You're loving it still, aren't you?"

"Oh, Jessica, you're horrible to me."

"Albert could travel back with me, couldn't he? Could you spare him for a day or so? I mean he'd be some help climbing in and out of trains and buying tickets, and if I got really bad I expect he could find me a stretcher or something. I don't want to make a fuss or be tiresome, but it's so shaming to be so helpless, you don't *know*. I won't take him if you want him, of course."

And Jane sat saying, helplessly, "*I'll* take you away, darling, the moment you want. Really, really I will, the very moment you say."

"Will you, darling? You're lovely to me. So lovely. D'you mind, really? What about Friday? I'm sure I could go by Friday or even sooner. How lovely to be really going. I wonder if the doctor would let me go on Wednesday?"

"Oh, Jessica, I meant to tell you, I've got into such a mess over Wednesday. My dear, I've promised to go and spend a night at that place where I went on Sunday. It's awful for me but

I just couldn't think of an excuse when the woman asked me, I just couldn't think of any reason not to fix it, and then I fixed it. Oh, it was dumb of me, I know, but girl gets caught like that without an excuse and what can she do anyhow. And then, sweetie, the worst of it is I have to go out foxhunting the morning after. Why ever weren't you there to save me from these awful muddles?"

"You do seem to have got yourself involved, don't you?" Jessica said slowly. She must give herself time to take in what all this meant. It could be dealt with. She had not yet failed to deal with Jane, to keep Jane for her own thing, subdued entirely to her ruling, and Jane was not going to escape her now. Did Jane desire so to escape? Ah, if she did, there was another matter entirely. She would not leave Jane whole in any new happiness or in any altered way of life in which she had no part. There would be suffering first for Jane, through which she could never hold her wish distinct or see beyond the present toils of Jessica's unkindness.

But now Jessica would give herself time. She remembered what Sylvester had said to her on Sunday—such a particularly clever woman, Jessica —Yes, she would grant Jane a further indulgence, stand apart and hold her tongue a little longer. Presently she would see . . .

"Darling, they do that sort of thing at the most

indecent hour—did you know?" she said now.
"My poor Jane, it's going to be so awful for you.
I think I'll have to struggle out after you in the
car. Do you think Miss Piggy Browne would
drive me? I could rescue you then before you
quite collapse. Would that be a plan, darling?"

"Oh, Jessica, you are lovely to me, aren't
you?"

"Sweet, am I? Look, Jane, Albert's being
awfully secret and absent-minded to-day. Do you
think he's starting another affair?"

"He can't have an affair here. He just *can't* be
romantic here." Jane was too upset by the idea.
Nasty Albert. His affairs belonged to another life
where they were faintly amusing and anyhow did
not matter. But here—Jane leant out of the open
window into the faint adventurous autumn evening, the sky was the colour of a young mouse and
the air as soft as its skin. Here she would not have
such rudeness. No, she would deny it all, all. This
life and that were a world apart; one could
escape, surely one could escape. Tears ran down
Jane's face as she leant out into the evening, a
flood of tears, she cried without sobbing. Enormous easy tears. The evening filled her with such
vague despairs.

Hester was at work in her garden. It was late.
She should have come in long ago, but she did
not. "Chrysanthemums!" she exclaimed inwardly.

"I must really smoke a cigarette near their elegant turpentine scent, and then smoke goes so properly with their foliage."

Now it was evening. She had known beauty on a dark day. The oyster skies; the earth broken purple and rough; the *Daphne* quickened to untimely flowering—its scent a complete circle, a ring as whole as Love that's not been told or given; the rank true smell of turnips boiling; the scattered papery gold on the jessamine against a wall; leaf-mould on the back avenue—Is it leaf mould on which I nourish these wretched plants or is it pure back avenue, Hester wondered. She was not entirely happy about it, but on the whole she thought it would do.

Piggy sat among her diamonds. She had some lovely diamonds that had belonged to her mother. Some were badly set, heavily buried in gold or arranged for wearing on the head, not a very useful form of ornament to Piggy. But there were two graceful and charming old rings. Piggy was now considering them.

The candles on Piggy's dressing table burnt low in their pink candlesticks, their flames were hooded crookedly, but diamonds and candlelight are romantically correct. Ladies dead and lovely Knights are recalled to a perilous nearness and romance is possible.

Piggy told herself stories, affable, familiar fantasies. She combed her hair and put jewels in her ears and rings on her fingers and red on her mouth. She smiled and grimaced at this strange she in the glass, turning her head and tilting her chin in a dreadful parody, poor Piggy who had nothing. And he said: "Piggy, *can* I have this dance?" and Piggy said: "No. I *am* sorry. Nothing left, not one." Piggy in a black gown that was, with a face as pale as gardenias. Then Piggy in a pink dress, all skirts—a columbine, laughing, laughing . . . Such *success*, my dear . . . She's *rather* marvellous . . . Piggy, dance with me. Piggy, you must . . . Piggy, you're so *wonderful*. Haven't you ever guessed I thought so? Not all this time. Oh, *silly* Pig . . . George, my sweet, my sweet . . . She leant near to the glass and nearer. It was true, this beauty, all romance was here, her eyes fainted back into her eyes, eyelashes like reeds and water pale diamonds. She could never gaze long enough on this lovely Piggy.

Without a knock at the door Jessica stood there, tall and stooping on her crutches, Tig running before her, pattering and snuffing, very fussed. Oh, such confusion, and Jessica standing in the doorway in stark silent amusement before she said:

"Your dog woke me up twice, so I thought I might bring him in to you. D'you *mind?*"

"No. Thank you so much. I'm so sorry. Tig —what's-a-matter? *Strange* dog. Did he come

scratching at your door? How stupid of him.
I used to sleep there, you know."

And Jessica came across the room, swinging
herself grotesquely between her crutches and stood
over painted Piggy, dressed up in diamonds.
Ridiculous Piggy, covered in confusion, hiding
the diamonds in her ears with her fat ringed
hands. It was an awkward moment for her.

"Do you sometimes look at your diamonds at
night?" Jessica said. "How strange! I often do.
Diamonds at night give me the sharpest pleasure."
She could not have told what impelled her to this
moment's kindness. "What a lovely ring! That
really is a good setting."

Piggy was her dreadful self again in a moment,
saying: "Well, diamonds aren't much in a piggy's
line, are they? But I do rather love them for
themselves, you know. Don't you think one does?"

"Why don't you wear them?"

"Oh, they're not very Me, are they? That's
what Joan always tells me. I can't show you
rather a wonderful brooch I have because I've
lent it to Joan. She says I must leave it to her
in my will. As a matter of fact, I've left her this
ring too."

Jessica said, drawing herself apart from all
confidence:

"Joan? Joan? ... Oh, that's the woman Jane
is going to stay with on Wednesday night, isn't it?
Didn't you lunch with her on Sunday or some-

thing? I'm rather vague about it. Jane seemed to quite like her."

Such unreasonable darkness and pain fell upon Piggy's spirit then as may never be understood. In one shocked moment Calamity was on her. Vanity fell headlong, Love and Constancy were wounded and Piggy hurt beyond bearing was left wordless and alone in her pain.

"Does she? Is she?" Piggy said. She did not know what she was saying. Such unhappiness as this was beyond her. Her heart beat and tore within her breast. She was shocked into a terrifying sickness. She could realise nothing except that Joan had betrayed her. This unkindness was all betrayal. Another was chosen and Piggy the faithful and loving was of no more account.

Jessica yawned good-night and turned about to go slowly out of the room again, her shadow hopping evilly before her. Piggy's obvious anguish amused her very much. Quite, quite obscene, she thought. Really *frightening*. How amused Sylvester will be.

Alone in the darkness now Piggy was crying, crying for comfort. Then she would stifle her tears and cry no more. It could not be true. No, Joan had never asked this stranger to Castle-quarter. Anyhow there would be a letter in the morning saying Piggy was to come too. It would be all right. Never could there be such unkindness to Piggy as this. Not from Joan. Joan

who was her world could not fail a poor Piggy
all in a moment. Such things do not really
happen.

"I suppose Jane, you won't go all penitent and
mad for confessions now, will you?"

"Oh, and why?"

"Now that you find yourself in love."

"If we had no hearts—my, Sylvester, wouldn't
we be grand, grand girls?"

"All I want you to promise me is that you
won't distress George and imperil your chances by
any dreary fancy that he should hear about your
past from you."

"Oh, no, Sylvester."

"It wouldn't go with a swing, I warn
you."

"Oh, don't be horrible to me. I've been tough,
I know, and all that I know."

"Sweet Jane. You're a lovely girl. Off you
pop now. Be your natural self and don't say
more than *Oh No* if Joan is saying *Do You* and
you'll have such success I can't tell you."

So Jane got into her car and drove off to Castlequarter.

From her bedroom window Piggy saw her go.
No note had come for Piggy. No word from Joan.
Piggy had seen Jane's green suit-cases carried
down stairs by Albert, and she had hidden herself
in her room, a chilly trembling was on her, a despair

and a disgust of all familiar things. She must hide from them all; from Sylvester who would look at her with malice and sly laughter; from Hester, who understood too much; from Jessica to whom she had boasted with such unthoughtful candour. She would hide away from them all. She would take Tig for a walk. Slipping out by the back door she would go down to the river and cross the high bridge to its further bank, and there where rhododendrons and oak scrub struggled up the steep heights of that valley she would spend the long unhappy afternoon. Hating height as she did, she would still walk all that afternoon on the steep paths that shouldered their corners out over space and loud water far below.

So we despair when no creature loves us. A king said: "I shall despair. There is no creature loves me." This was Piggy's sad case too. And which was worse, she had not one true care to bind her.

CHAPTER VII

IN the end perhaps it is the simplicities of life that most affect us—especially those that live with more dangerous artificiality, such rediscover their inheritance.

To George this mountain road was no more than an unfrequented way of going from Kilque to Castlequarter. No, it was more than that, he

would have said, the view was good. He would
have said, look at the light and shade on the
mountains; or told you that the berries on the
mountain ash were scarlet or the grouse were
scarce. But for Jane there was a wildness here and
a free air, an aloneness which she had never
known. She was a stupid and a savage creature,
Jane, removed by very few generations from
extreme barbarism. Here she was alive suddenly,
keen as a bird. Sweet and unembarrassing to love
and always in loving her that sense of something
lost and gone, never to be found or taken.

It was late.

"Jane, drive carefully, sweet, promise me."

"I will give you a kiss before you go."

"Don't mind me. I'm being tiresome, I
know."

"I'm a tough baby, I know, saying I will give
you a kiss."

"Am I tiresome? We ought to go—we ought to
go now—now we really ought to go."

"I will give you a tiny piece of love so small you
will hardly know."

"You do drive so badly. Do be careful. Please,
please promise me."

The stupidity and tenderness of such a love as
George's encompassed Jane entirely. Savages are
not bored by mountains nor by fire nor by water;
nor was Jane bored by this loving. She was

enthralled and held away from herself. She was
the Jane he thought her to be. She would for ever
protect him from the Jane she was. This she knew
with a surprising shock of strength, and knew too
a gentleness towards him that she might never
dismiss. It was new to her. As new and strange
as these small roads and lonely mountains, as
quiet as a poor little house. There was power in
her to hurt him and she would never hurt him.
His loving was in her hands. Too dear for her
taking, but hers and only hers. What should
defeat her of its keeping?

Jane knew. Jessica would encompass her
disaster. Jessica could break and ruin and reveal
all that Jane had done and all that Jane was.
Jane's lovers and sins made a sad story, and to
George it would be more than sad, it would be
desolating and unholy. Yes, drugs; drink; affairs
—Jane drew in a little whistling breath of terror
as she drove down the mountain road. Fool that
she had been looking for peace and kindness that
were never for her. She was foresworn. No power
of loving could undo such evil as she had known.
And Jessica would tell and tell and tell. Pulling
Jane's house down stone by stone and leaving
Jane desolate in all her frailties.

Little houses she saw, and their small paths of
bitter smoke against the unmerciful beauty of the
mountains, lovely and dangerous, beauty near to
madness in the autumn evening. And beyond and

away from it all poor Jane with strange hands
laid upon her for her love and her undoing.

"It's no good," Jane's despair found small
plain words. She whispered to herself as she
drove along. "I'm tough. I've made a muddle all
of my life. Life is like that. What can a girl do
anyway? What can a girl do? I'll go. I'll go
away again with Jessica. It will be less hurting.
Jessica would hurt him so much—the poor
sweet . . ."

Down from the mountains now among fields of
saved corn, pale fields and little dark woods, loneliness was abroad, it was time to be in a house
again.

Soon Jane was housed and bathed and scented
and some of the unkind truth was lost to her
again. Flattered as in dreaming she saw that all
was possible. One exaggerated. One loved and
exaggerated. Words, just words could not break
and change matters as one so dreaded. Not a
thing as quick and desolately single as this.

After dinner they played cards. Jane, for all
her stupidity, played bridge well, and this was
something more for Joan to approve in her. It
was one of the few things she respected in another
woman, for she herself played bridge with pious
endeavour and retributive vengeance but with
little skill. She gave her whole mind to it. Nothing
childish about Joan's bridge except perhaps her
want of skill. The only time that Piggy had made

a failure of her "Joan, you baby" speech, was in a game of bridge. Then it had not been a success. There had been a cold little scene which had shaken Piggy too sadly.

They did not sit late playing at cards. They went to bed in good time, for to-morrow was a hunting morning. So it was. Jane had forgotten.

"Are you frightened?" George asked her. "Do tell me!"

"Oh, no."

"I believe you are, though."

"My dear, she can't be frightened. She's riding Miss Smith, isn't she?"

"Edward could ride Miss Smith."

"Are you happy about it, Jane? You shan't go out cub-hunting unless you want to."

"No, I do want to. I'm crazy to ride Miss Smith."

"Joan," George said, "Jane and I are going to be married."

"How lovely. I thought you were." Joan really was pleased. On the whole she was rather impressed by Jane and so predisposed to like her.

Robin was less sure. "She's a lovely girl, but is she very much George's sort?" He asked Joan afterwards.

"What d'you mean?"

"George is so full of ideals and plans about how lovely life will be once he's married."

"She won't shatter them. She's not just a nice young girl."

"She won't find him a bore? George is the dearest person in the world. He's not going to be hurt, is he, Joan? One couldn't bear it for any one to think him a bore."

"No. That would be ghastly. But it's all right, Robin. She adores him. One can see she's mad about him."

"It'll be all right?"

"Yes, sweet Robin. Good-night, dear Robin."

The night was sharp as glass. Once Jane heard the hollow sweetness of hounds singing in kennel and could put no name to that wild, unearthly music. She stirred in her sleep to the loud gentle sounds of birds' wings on the water below the house. All would be well yet. But later she woke with sweating hands from a dream. Jessica was holding George's hands in a fire, in a brazier such as Jane had seen on race-courses. There was no escape for George. He was tied and Jessica was holding his hands into the fire. "You getta Hell out of this, Mrs. Bloody Barker," George said to her, like one of her rough American boy friends. She ran away, hiding herself from his pain as one avoids sickness and unlovely death. And all the time George's hands were burning. It was true. Crowds of people went running by her to see the burning.

"Oh, such a horrible dream," Jane murmured.

"It is not fair. Poor, poor Jane—such a dream. I guess I got too much imagination. I think too much, that's why." She felt quite ill and shattered. If only Albert had been here to fix her a Cachet Faivre. After all, one must sleep. There was such a little while till morning. It was pathetic that a girl should have to ride out horseback so early. To ride out mornings was all right, but, hell, why ride out for a fox-hunt in the middle of the night? One must sleep again.

Jane's eyes were hardly closed before it was time to get up. The horrid morning had come indeed. Presently Joan came in with a pair of jhodpurs, for she was determined to do the right thing by George's love, and made Jane struggle out of the sporting drawers and into the jhodpurs, in which it must be said Jane's thin legs looked very well indeed, and so the day was begun.

A little later, but while the hour was still dark, dark as Christmas morning, the headlights of the van in which they drove to the meet caught round and green on the hounds' eyes as they passed them in the road and flashed narrowly on stirrup irons. The servants' voices rated the hounds over and Robin's voice from within the van quietly repeated the rate—as though his hounds should hear him.

Soon in the greying light the van stopped and he who was its driver and lord of the terrier pack was sent on to make a big earth safe.

Waiting . . .

Jane felt nothing. Numb. Quiet. Shocked beyond herself by the awful stillness of the hour, she sat in the front of the van between Joan and Robin with a whip grasped upside down in her hand. She had no idea what was going to happen to her next. Everything was gone from her. Her love of George was not, nor her fear of Jessica. She felt neither brave nor calm nor did she feel actually frightened. Of what should one be frightened? One ought to feel something. She cast her mind back to those books about the chase which had filled her with such enthusiasm, but now she could remember nothing to her purpose from them. Those girls always rode blood-like three-year-olds, bay mares, horses with manes and tails. They never took the field that a stirring gallop did not ensue. Jane wondered very much if she and Miss Smith would ever win a hunt. Very doubtful, she thought. Then there was their incredible success with Masters of Hounds. Jane peeped at Robin, who sat in a silent bundle, buttoned up in an overcoat, and wondered whether this was not a bit of a myth too. Probably they all had lovely wives like Joan. Jane was a simple girl and enjoyed her success with Joan.

"Now, why won't you allow Gwen to be pretty?" Joan said suddenly. "Now I call Gwen a very pretty woman."

"No," said Robin. "She's too hard."

The terriers in the back of the van screamed and snarled.

"Quiet! Quiet! You couldn't see a fox go any earlier than this."

"No. Could you? Did you think that was a good pudding we had last night?"

"Lovely."

"It was a recipe Alice gave me. Her cook makes it better than Mrs. Pryce, though. Are you excited, Jane?"

"*Yes.*" Jane shivered suddenly.

"I'm afraid it'll be a dull morning for you," Robin said kindly. "I must kill a fox here to-day, if I can."

"*Yes.*"

"Do you think you and George will have a pack of hounds somewhere?"

How solid and reasonable it sounded. And quite too unreal. And the reason of this lying at Jane's heart she was suddenly filled with sadness. She rather wished indeed that Miss Smith had been the sort of horse on which one might ride to a glorious death—leaping down a quarry or plunging into a river. But on Miss Smith, Jane rightly guessed, a girl could put no such sensational end to her troubles. Miss Smith would look after everything.

"I'm glad Gwen's coming before the border is *quite* over. There's more colour in it now than there is in Gwen's border in July. Poor Gwen,

her garden's always so *drab*, I'd like her to see
the border."

Robin's silence was rather obviously patient.

"Robin, is Diligent out to-day?"

"Yes."

"I can't think why you don't knock her on the
head. Idle skirting brute. Jane, you know I found
her one morning curled up in the sun, fast asleep,
under a gorse bush."

"Did you? How *cosy*."

"She might enter late. I had a hound once——"

"Look! Here are the hounds."

"No; it's Sylvester and George."

The steep glen, wood partly, partly hazel scrub,
and partly gorse, lifted darkly in the paling hour.
No one paid any attention to Sylvester and George.
Another five minutes passed and the hounds came
round a corner, led horses two and two behind
them.

Jane climbed out of the van and stood in the
road, wondering which of these terrifying horses
was Miss Smith, and thinking how cross and silent
George and Sylvester looked.

George was carved in glum wood until he spoke
to her and heaved her up on a huge roan mare.
Incredible that eight stone should take so much
levering upwards. He shortened her leathers and
very gently put her whip right side up.

"All right? Quite all right? Stay with Joan."
He said to Sylvester, "Come on with me, Sylvester.

We're to watch the top end." They rode away from Jane. She was left all unprotected on Miss Smith, who dived down her head in a sudden and disconcerting manner and proceeded to snatch mouthfuls of grass from the side of the road. Unsympathetic and ungovernable creature she now seemed to Jane to be. Really, she had only just avoided falling off her.

"How d'you like old Smith?" Joan said, turning round in her saddle to watch Jane's progress down the road behind her.

"She's a swell horse," Jane gasped, setting her teeth, for she certainly thought Miss Smith was horrible.

Across a dark shallow ford Sylvester and George splashed, and up a deep cart-track to the top of the glen. On their right and behind them the hounds went into cover. Sylvester heard no unsteady puppy speak, nor any cheering voice.

Through a happy line of gaps Sylvester cantered on to his post. All the world was black and grey, and held in still hands until the hounds opened in the covert behind him—a voice and another voice, and a chorus beautiful. This first half-hour there might be a bit of scent, but the covert was very strong and very full of foxes. A hard place to catch one, but a great place to make young hounds. No doubt Robin would have a royal morning.

Nearer now came the hounds' voices and now

the crash of this music hesitated and was silent till one voice had it when their fox turned short and the chorus again joined full and again lessened away from Sylvester.

A fox was Robin's prey to-day. Alive to this savage importance, Sylvester was aware and watchful in the morning.

A fox slipped out of covert—a little fox, monstrously visible in the thin greyness of the light. Sylvester rode at him, heading him back into the covert, a strong pulse of excitement breaking through his bandage of watchfulness.

He waited again. Hounds were hunting another fox. Further failed their voices. His horse ate grass; midges persecuted Sylvester with assiduous attention. He lit a cigarette. Wan light about him. Pallid the propped corn-sheaves. Silent all birds. Heavy and waxen are the opening eyelids of the morn.

Two and a half couples of hounds came out into the field feathering on the line of that little fox. Robin was below him in the wood and Sylvester rode down with his fox-news.

"This is an awful place to catch one," Robin said in his quiet, unfussy voice. "Did you hear that ass Ned trying to holloa me away on an old fox? What does he think cub-hunting is for? They're hunting another below here." He turned his horse's head down a steep ride.

A black and tan hound nipped up on the fence

like a big cat, out into the field and back into the covert with him.

Robin called: "Is there any one out beyond the farm house? That's a dangerous corner. Go on there and take George with you. Ned can stay here."

That was where a fox slipped past Sylvester. Or had he gone before Sylvester reached his post? Out of the glen below him the hounds strove, their voices proclaiming his idle blindness as they spoke to the line in the open. But they took it back into the covert again. So lucky for Sylvester. He lit another cigarette and wondered why he ever found any life but this of the least importance.

For hours they hunted, changing from fox to fox, scent growing worse, lines crossed and re-crossed. A holloa here, but Robin paid no attention to it, his hounds were hunting another fox. A holloa away at the end of a ride and he damned the screaming lot of them.

Weary at their posts were the watchers; consumed by midges; tired of looking into those coverts; the fine urge which earlier inspired their vigil was gone from them.

Robin and his hounds alone maintained a tough persistence to endure and to catch a fox. In the covert with them, on his feet now, Sylvester had seldom seen a man so hunt a fox with his hounds. A well of energy was in his voice, one might know his hounds got together as they heard it. Heart-ened to effort, grim once more for a fox's blood, they strove on through the steep, strong covert. And he—stumbling and falling and clambering— still with them till some one met him with his horse at a cross-ride. And then it was:

"Woa—*Stand*. Stand-still-you-can't-you?" as he got up and away with him then, his toe still feeling for the off-iron as he went bent double in his saddle under the half-cut-out rides.

Another turn round the covert and hounds were at fault again. Scent was worse. Their fox had turned short and lain down probably. They could do no more with him for the moment.

Out of that hot, foiled glen Robin took them and down to the ford. Here where the narrow dark stream was spilt out wide and shallow his hounds lapped and rolled upon the close grass and looked up when they heard their names spoken.

The morning was so old now that indeed it had turned to daytime, and weary again were the field —weary of fox-hunting; weary their fat fresh horses that gave them no rest; weary of the insistent midges; weary their eyes of looking as they returned, faint-hearted, to whatever point seemed good to them—much help they were now to that persistent huntsman. A broken army they were, half-hearted scouts.

Now his hounds were at it again. A tired cub was close before them, roused horridly from that strong fastness of a thorny, sandy corner where he had laid him down in such safety as a fox may find with earths stopped fast against him.

Old Dominie made a chop at him and missed him as he jumped up. Out of the briar patch they struggled, three couples on his back indeed had this been other than heavy covert.

Over the main ride, Robin was there to view him across, and back again as he turned just short of a blind elbow. A lucky view, and cap in hand he cheered his hounds over again. Another turn—the tapping of whips on saddle flaps held him to the shelter of the covert—and one more, shorter yet, before the crying of hounds was grimly still. They had cracked his back among the cracking briars. So died a fox to crown the morning.

Jane was mad with excitement. She had fallen off Miss Smith twice and had not hurt herself. She was filled with an enormous sense of achievement. Now she must tell George all about it. That was the simple and lovely thing to do.

"My dear, I fell and fell and clutched at everything, and then I was sitting on air and holding on by Smith's head; it was ages before I hit the ground. And then, Honey, I've *got* to tell you—" Jane had a great deal to tell. It had been an enthralling and frightening morning but she had survived it. The perils of her progression on Miss Smith had supplied Jane with a more definite excitement than she had ever known. How can one be bored when one has had two falls, many

frights and a great curiosity as to what is going
on around one?

"Why does he blow his trumpet now? . . . Why
is he scolding that sweet little dawg? . . . Why is
that man shouting? . . . Why do the hounds
bark? . . ."

"Joan! Joan! Look! *Look!* A *Fox*——"

Thus had the morning sped for Jane.

George said now: "But how did you manage
to fall off Smith?"

"Joan took me over a jump. My, I was
thrilled."

"She was mad for leaping," Joan said in-
dulgently. There was no doubt Jane had great
success with her future sister-in-law.

They were standing in the road that had been
so dark and quiet in the morning. Now the sun
was hot on the steep cornfields behind it and hot
on that quiet covert, but between the sun and
the earth the air was thin with autumn. At a
little distance Robin stood amongst his hounds.
He would stoop his head and blow a blast on his
horn, for he was short of a couple of hounds, and
then he would talk with his whipper-in.

Jane and George leant against the hot, loose
stones of a little wall. Jane was quiet now, so
happy and quietened in spirit as she had never
been. Even Joan and Sylvester were at peace
together. He had given her half an apple and was
eating the other half himself. They were quite

embraced by contentment, all of them, and asked nothing of each other but to be still.

Thus Piggy and Jessica found them. Piggy came roaring up the road in her big car, putting on brakes in all directions when she saw the hounds. They stopped opposite Jane and George and Joan and Sylvester, all so quiet and aloof after their morning's endeavour, belonging to the moment and to each other, not to any outsiders. Certainly not to Piggy and Jessica. With Piggy and Jessica they were in no accord.

"You're a bit late, Piggy, aren't you?" Joan said to Piggy. She looked with horror at Jessica, who had put on her grey flannel trousers to-day, and altogether looked too like an advertisement for Austin Reade. Joan walked over to Robin. Really, one could not compete with that sort of thing.

Jane may have looked as aloof as the rest of them. But she was not aloof, she was bound still in a rabbit-like fright. Frozen in anticipation of Jessica's probably immediate anger, she leant against the wall beside George, who was idly picking burrs off her coat. Jane did not move or even speak. She was overcome by a sudden realisation of all that Jessica would take away from her. It must not be. She looked to Sylvester for help and he saw, for the first time almost, pain in her eyes and grief. Poor Jane, who loved now. Alas, poor girl, how she had undone herself.

Sylvester felt profoundly gloomy about it all.
And Jessica here obviously screaming for her
erring lovely—Well, one could keep Jessica quiet
for the moment. Sylvester approached Jessica.
He asked her for a cigarette. He would talk to
her now, winning her to a state of amiable converse and so quieten the moment till the moment
was past.

"So this is it?" Jessica was thinking. "This is
it, is it? But it's not going to be as easy for her
as it looks. My Christ, the *disloyalty*—terrifying.
That's what shakes one. That's what one minds."
She gave Sylvester a cigarette and lit one herself.
But all the time under her hooded eyes she was
watching Jane and George and all the time she
was aware of her own power to undo and destroy.
She was as fully conscious of it as if it was a stone
she held in her hand. She was angry, not desolate,
for it was within her power to defeat them all.
Jane who had deceived her. Sylvester—Sylvester
had fooled her too; he must have known of this—
what did he get out of it?—a vicarious sensation
of some sort no doubt; Sylvester then must be
defeated of his purpose whatever it might be.
Jessica's animosity included them all, Joan and
Robin and George, all of them whose influence
was contrary to Jessica's power. She had no
wishes further than their desolation. Health of
spirit would only return to her through their
desolation, she longed to see them desolate, these

hearty, doggy people. She would break Jane's future with them; she would for one moment shock and disturb their disgusting equanimity. She would require no more of Jane after she had destroyed her. She only required her destruction. One must end a chapter. Then one could go away and laugh and tell of it.

What with one thing and another Jessica had had a wicked morning. First Miss Piggy Browne had wakened her at an unreasonable hour and demanded that she should arise forthwith and drive out to the chase. That, of course, was merely funny. Jessica had advised Miss Piggy Browne to go back to bed and she herself had slept again.

From the first she had been condemned to an outdoor, clean-living day. From the moment when Albert had remarked as he laid out her grey flannel trousers, "I cort a mouse in my bedroom last night, Miss—a fine *dog* mouse," she had known that this was going to be an awful day. She had stared at Albert, incredulous of such breezy unsqueamishness as this over mice, and staring she beheld a change in him. He walked briskly about in a pair of brown shoes that would not have disgraced a golfing professional. His shirt was unbuttoned almost to the navel. The back of his neck was burnt nearly black. Jessica wondered what new and strange departure all this portended. Then she discovered his secret.

Looking from her window she saw upon the

gravel a greyhound bitch to which that horrible
terrier of Piggy's was making unmistakable
advances. Albert saw them too. With a scream
of anguish he was gone from her room and in an
incredibly short moment of time had captured
the greyhound and led her away from all carnal
temptations. Jessica heard him dragging her
upstairs and turning the key of his bedroom
door upon her.

"May I ask what you're doing to that dog,
Albert?" Jessica had demanded on his reappear-
ance.

"It's not a dog, it's a bitch, if you'll excuse me,
Miss," Albert had replied with sulky defiance.

"I don't care which it is. You have no business
to keep it in your bedroom."

"You'll excuse me, Miss, but Miss Browne quite
approves. What's more, she's a lady understands
what it means to a chap like I to own a bitch with
such a chance as mine should have in the Puppy
stakes next month's meeting in Cloneen. Five
miles every evening I walks her and if I can keep
her safe from that nasty terrier of Miss Viola
Browne's, I shall back her that night too."

"You won't be here," Jessica said unpleasantly.
"We're returning to London the end of this week."

"Oh, *no*. Are we?" Albert looked quite ready
to burst into tears.

Really, it was rather much, first Jane and then
Albert given over to this lust for outdoor sport.

Somehow at the moment she resented it almost more in Albert. It was too unnatural. She invented a hundred jobs to occupy his day and then hopped downstairs and set off with a nearly distracted Piggy.

"Of course it's *rather* stupid going now." Piggy changed gear with elaborate skilfulness and drove at high speed.

"Why?"

"Well, the morning's pretty well over."

"Oh, that'll be lovely." Jessica lit a cigarette. "Blood Sports and Huntin' cries make me feel quite *quite* sicky."

"Of course I love hunting. I've been brought up to it, of course," Piggy said indignantly.

"Didn't even that put you off it a bit? *My* father was thirty years a master of hounds. One couldn't hope to survive that, could one?"

This remark rather silenced Piggy, who had always imagined that Jessica's father was a Big Business Man. Obsessed by many dreary and out-of-date affectations, Piggy was inclined to despise what she still called Trade.

And now Piggy sat in her rich motor car, desolate indeed. Quite suddenly hope died in her. On that morning of thin sweet air with the ash trees a pallid gold and those trees still unturned in colour as green as ice, all Piggy's hope and trust in Life died. She looked from George, still silently picking the burrs off Jane's coat, to Joan, who was not coming back to talk to her, and all pretence was quenched within her.

Now there was a hot morning sun and a little fugitive wind. Piggy felt as thin and bitter as the wind, as sick as death. For once she saw her life as her life was—a rotten wooden whistle into which she might puff wind endlessly till she died. There was no note of music in it for her blowing. She felt as wicked as a dog and as weak as a bruised snake; weak and poisonous. But her fangs were choked in dust. The wheels of all happiness passed endlessly across her. Again she was as a house that had no light and no fire. Her crying, too, was spent, and if all her wish towards love was granted her now, it was too late. Her hour was gone but was not spent. She was sick with grieving and a distemper was on her, bitter in her mouth. Now she knew how right it is to say a heart is as heavy as lead. My heart is as heavy as lead, she thought, and what weight is there so dead and cold.

Piggy's poor fat face was shrunken and pinched in this sudden devastating misery that was come on her. Her blue china eyes were hollowed wide with this death of loving. It was too shameful to cry. Too shameful. No. She would not cry. Her heart was beating wildly in her side. Wildly. Sickeningly. It caught at her breath. If she did not have to speak she might endure. Piggy's hands, so squat and without meaning, gripped the steering wheel of the car and through her pain they were translated into a lovely agony in bones. Afterwards Sylvester remembered this and wondered why he had guessed so little from such hysterical tension and so great a change.

George saw that something was the matter with Piggy. He stopped picking burrs off Jane and stared at her unwinkingly for a few minutes. George, the kindest and sweetest creature in the world, could never pass pain by. George's kindness gave him a curious slow sense of perception. He saw things slowly, for he was by nature a stupid young man, and besides his consideration of trouble was always delayed for he never saw it without seriously wondering if it was at all within his power to put the matter right. He said now:

"Piggy, you look as if you had a pain, poor Piggy. Come with me. I will give you a drink."

Piggy was startled indeed from her melancholy reflections. Old habit overcame her to a bridling compliance and then, like a broken watch that ticks when it is shaken and ceases at once, Piggy relapsed into the unnameable tragedy of the moment.

"No, thanks, George. I don't think I want a drink, really."

"Yes, silly Piggy, a drink would do you all the good in the world. Step into my car and I'll drive you down to Mrs. Maher's pub and we'll have a delicious drink up together. Jane—do you want a drink?"

Jane shook her head dumbly. He had gone from her. All her false dream of shelter she must forget, putting it all away from her with crazy hands. Grieving beyond all thoughts of herself, she knew she would submit to Jessica's ruling, would go away again with Jessica, for Jessica should not hurt him. It was better for him that he should suffer through Jane than vilely by Jessica in a sick hour of telling. He could not understand. He was not made so that he should. Jane shivered under the hot sun as George walked away, Piggy bundling along at his side.

Presently Joan came over to say: "Robin and I are starting now. We have to see a man on the way home. Will you come on with George, Jane? Sylvester is coming in the van."

Sylvester was taken away from her too. In a few minutes she would be alone with that silent Jessica. She might run into the woods and hide, but Jessica would come hopping after on her crutches. She was uncannily active on those crutches. She would part the bushes where Jane had hidden with her crutch and lean in, saying:

"We must discuss this, Jane . . . Put it all on a plate, my dear . . ." Yes, it was going to happen just like that, except that Jane did not run into the woods in a futile endeavour to escape. She stayed where she was, her back against that low, hot wall, the wild, poor country behind her and the glen where little foxes lived and died on her right hand, and Jessica, sitting there in Piggy's rich car, Jessica in her lovely severe clothes, her beautiful hands manicured and smoke-stained, her dark face sardonic and uninstructed in any kindness. Yes, she leant out of the car, saying:

"Darling, d'you think perhaps we ought to discuss this a little?"

"Discuss what?" Jane kept opening and shutting her hands. They were dry shells of hands, as a rule, but now her palms were wet with fear.

"Must you talk at a shout? I'd like you to be quite detached about it all if you can. Come here."

"No."

"Come here."

Jane went. Like a fascinated bird trailing broken wings, she went slowly round to the other side of the car and got in.

"Albert's bought a greyhound," Jessica said inconsequently.

"No? Without telling us. What cheek!"

"Yes. I thought it was rather rude of him."

"He can't have it in the flat."

"He has it in his bedroom now."

"My dear, how unnatural!"

"Jane, about this Playfair man. What is the position exactly? *Must* you have an affair with him?"

Now the storm was gathering. Albert and his greyhound were forgotten. They were the sort of nonsense that would be dragged into a desolating moment like this. Jane had no art to evade an issue or pursue a line or in any way to defend herself from the truth. She at once forgot how full she had been of noble thoughts and determinations of self-sacrifice, so she whined as usual:

"What d'you mean? Oh, Jessica, what d'you *mean*?"

"I mean——"

"You're not going to be horrible to me, honey? Say you're not."

That was the way these shattering scenes with Jessica always started—with Jane trying to escape from them before they were begun. Jessica went on. She cared very little for Jane's injunction. This particular kind of wordy cruelty was the breath of life to her. She went on:

"I know you can't realise what you're doing because your stupidity is such that you're practically mental. You can't think for yourself. One gives you that."

"Like hell I can't think for myself." Jane was inclined to resent an aspersion on her intelligence. "I can think for myself enough to marry who I

want for myself. You think I got no mental resources, but you're wrong."

This was indeed an outburst, and that Jane
should so definitely include the idea of matrimony
among her mental resources came as something of
a shock to Jessica. An affair, well perhaps, but
marriage was ludicrous—also easier to deal with.
Now she would be indulgent.

"Marry him! *Tiny*—a huntin' man like that—
My dear, the queer *noises* he'll make, have you
thought? Shall you be able to endure it?"

"Mentally we gotta lot in common," Jane
insisted.

"Oh, don't go *on* about your brain like that,
darling. It's not what you mean in any case."

There was silence between them for a minute.
A silence full of bitter and useless feelings on
Jane's part, and on Jessica's a calm and a sense
of vast entertainment. But behind the calm her
intention never changed. She was going to break
this.

"Jane, you don't think you're in love with him,
do you?" she said at last.

"Yes. I'm crazy about him."

"And he wants to marry you?"

"Yes, he's crazy about me."

"Must you go on like this, sweet? It's all just
a *little* sicky. You'll tell me soon you want to
mend his socks and have fat babies and leave the
rest to Nature. And how much does he know

about you? The you," said Jessica, gently, "that
I know." She stopped and Jane burst into floods
of bitter tears.

"It's important, you know," Jessica went on,
"that the poor young man should know *something* about you. Have you told him anything?"

"I've told him," Jane said with a sort of Victorian dignity, "that I'm—not—worthy of his
love."

"My dear, you haven't! *Disgusting.* I suppose
he loved that?"

"Oh, Jessica, you're horrible."

"No, my dear. Only obvious. I mean, there
are things he might hear for himself and then you'd
feel pretty silly, things like——"

"Oh, be quiet, you—you——" Jane was desperate.
There was nothing left in the world at the moment
but her livid pulsing hatred of Jessica.

"Don't scream," Jessica said. "Don't scream,
Jane. No amount of hysteria is going to change
this thing at all." Jessica was talking levelly, but
her head was thrust forward on her neck, flat,
snake-like. Her eyes were all pupil, terrible and
dark with power.

Jane shrank into her corner and covered up her
eyes like a child.

"Things," Jessica went on, "things like Baby
Smith's party last Whitsun—you remember? *That*
would go with a swing, wouldn't it? Bits about

the Villa—when we had poor Matty Arnold to stay
—D'you remember that party, Jane? It was too
indecently funny. D'you remember? My dear, how
we *laughed*. And Lindy's charades—my God, they
were rude, but they were *brilliant*."

"Oh, I been bad, I know," Jane turned on
Jessica a little wildly. "I know I been a bad,
bad woman, but if you knew the way I feel now,
you wouldn't tell him, you wouldn't spoil everything for me."

"D'you think he'd see the point of Lindy's
charades, or would the story be a bit lost on him?"

"Jessica, don't act this way. Why are you
doing it? What have I *done* to you, anyway?"

"I've a certain sense of justice."

"You're mad, I think. I'll say you're mad."

"And a certain sense of proportion," Jessica
went on, "which means I just can't stand aside
and see you make such an absurd *sentimental* mess
of your life. Of course, if this man should have
enough vision to want you when he has some
idea of the real you, then I've nothing to say."

Jane had no more tears now. All life was
quenched out of her. She said: "What d'you
want, Jessica? What d'you want me to do?"

"My dear, I've awfully little interest in what
you do. As for *wanting* anything——"

"I so hate him to be hurt——"

"You don't believe anything could survive for
you when I've told him, do you?"

"Oh, *no*." That sweet, empty note was grievous and final. "He won't want me any more then."

"And *still* you imagine you could make a success of living with any one so entirely apart from you."

"I'd be so sweet to him," Jane said. "I meant to be so sweet to him," quite vacantly and hopelessly she said it.

Jessica looked at her and laughed a short, terrible gasp of laughter.

Piggy felt better now. She was ever so little drunk and that gave her a certain amount of false conceit again. Her failures and her sorrows became dramatic and tragical to her and thus in a way more endurable.

She and George sat upon two stiff chairs with slippery seats in the private parlour and drank up together.

"I must buy some cigarettes," George said. He left her for a few minutes. It was long enough for Piggy to become divinely obsessed by the sad importance of her lamentable state and overcome by her desire to tell something of it, to ask advice, to gather in sympathy, not pity. For pity is no use, it undoes all small pretence and vanity. Piggy did not want pity, she wanted to be set up again in her own esteem. She wanted to be given some immediate reason to hope, some defence against her own unimportance to anybody.

Piggy took out her powder box and powdered her face. She made long, mournful eyes at her reflection in the lid of the box. It was all faintly restoring. George came back and gave her a cigarette. Poor Piggy. He was fond of Piggy. He hated to see her looking so entirely wrecked. Joan didn't do enough about her. One could do such a lot for Piggy. But Joan was a bit hard about her. Of course Robin found her tiresome and that was difficult. George decided benevolently that he and Jane were going to be very kind to Piggy.

"You look better, Pig," he said, "that drink has done you good, hasn't it? I knew it would. Have another?"

"No, thank you, George. I feel simply *grand* now. I wasn't ill, you know—Just, just worried perhaps——" She stopped, suspended on a breath. Dear, kind George, would he fuss and ask her what was the matter? He did.

"Worried—poor Piggy, who's been worrying you?"

"Oh——" Piggy became incoherent, nearly overcome by her emotion and her readiness to tell and her loss of words. Piggy's candour was indecent and alarming. But George, wrinkling his eyebrows almost into his hair, only wondered how he could help her. What one could do for Piggy. He genuinely liked to busy himself in his friends' lives. Their repetitions and confessions were not

nauseating to him. Not even now when Piggy
was saying:

"—So you see, though she doesn't say very
much, a Pig can suffer—"

It was all very confused. Vague "things" were
different. Joan did not mean to be unkind. Piggy
knew she was not so amusing or so rich as some
of Joan's friends—George was not to forget that
all this was in the strictest confidence—George
promised her he would not forget—Well, then,
there was the thing about Piggy joining the
hockey club. Joan despised hockey herself and so
she had made Piggy's membership of the hockey
club quite impossible. She had gone on about it
till Piggy had given it up. "I don't think she
liked my joining the hockey club," Piggy said
drearily, "so, of course, I gave it up. I've
never knowingly done anything to annoy
Joan."

"I always thought you and Joan were the best
of friends," George said heartily. "And as for the
hockey, Piggy, I shouldn't pay the smallest
attention to her. She never could play games
herself and it bores her for any one else to play
them."

"Yes, she always likes us to have the same
interests," Piggy admitted, an old spark kindling
in her. "Anyhow, I've given up the hockey now.
That doesn't matter. But, somehow, *everything's*
so changed. You can't see it, George, but I can.

Women," said Piggy, generalising grandly, "*know* these things. Even ," she added whimsically, "the Piggies."

With all this girlish confidence being reposed in him, George may be forgiven for going a tiny bit kindly and pompous in his reception of it. Anyhow he took the right line with Piggy, the line which a less kindly and less stupid person might have neglected. He dwelt on Piggy's importance to him, on his reliance on Piggy's friendship, on his appreciation of Piggy's unselfish and useful life. In five minutes of not very subtle converse he provided Piggy with a new idol, a strange and exciting Godhead, a reason to be and to serve. And all these things were summed up in one thing. In a word, in George.

Poor Piggy who was lost was found again. Yet nothing was given to her but the opportunity to love and serve. She was wanted a little. She mattered a little. She would be one of those calm women friends whose devotion is so lovely, so enduring, a thing to whom men turn at the last (for Piggy was no pessimist) saying: "My dear, you've been *everything* to me—almost——" And after that—but this moment was enough. George required her friendship. He knew the strength and value of a Piggy's devotion. Every desire that Piggy had was sublimated into a single wish to serve.

"I'm marrying Jane. You know that, I expect,

Piggy," George said. And Piggy, half-way through
her second drink, only nodded contentedly. Her
goal of living was beyond that, far down the years
beyond it now.

"You'll have to stay with us a lot," George said.
"We'll all have lovely times together."

"Are you going to be happy? Really terribly
happy? Promise me you are." Already Piggy was
that tender indulgent girl-friend. In wine unembarrassed, she bent towards George, urgently
asking him to be happy. In point of fact, all she
wanted was his unhappiness. That she might serve
and he confide. Those would in future be Piggy's
moments in life. But of this she was unaware.
Piggy was swept as near delight as she would ever
go by this new importance.

"I'm frightfully pleased about it, Piggy," George
said. "It's all the most marvellous thing that's
ever happened. If anything happened to upset my
plans now I'd go out of my mind, I think."

"How lovely, dear George, I *am* glad."

George got up. It was time for them to go.
It was rather an emotional moment. But George
did not know that. He did not realise the awfulness of emotional moments anyhow. He only
knew that it was time for lunch and wondered
whether he'd been quite wise in giving Piggy two
drinks. He did not know that he had given her
new life as well or he might have pondered the
wisdom of that too. He had been away from

Jane for half an hour. He would see her again in
a minute. As they drove back down the road, life
was for them both as it had never seemed before.

If Piggy found herself happy and exalted in
George's company it was not strange, when he had
gone, driving a tired poor Jane away with him,
that Piggy should be renewed again threefold in
her new power of loving and giving. When the
actual god is absent in the flesh there is simply no
limit to Fancy's journeyings.

Joan as nothing, hockey clubs and other old
unkindnesses forgotten, Piggy stepped into the car
beside Jessica and lit a cigarette with all her old
swagger. Her poise was restored. She was as
dreadful as ever.

Jessica wanted time to think. Time to be alone.
Time to make and discard many plans. She said
to Piggy:

"This is rather an amusing sort of country.
Would it bore you frightfully to take me for a
nice old-fashioned motor drive? I don't want any
lunch, do you?"

"Oh, no," Piggy assented quite readily. "I
never mind when I eat. We'll buy biscuits at a
pub when the spirit moves us, shall we? What
fun!"

Piggy felt quite pleasantly in accord with Jessica.
She felt now as she had scarcely felt since that
morning weeks ago when she had boasted so

lovingly of Joan, and all that she meant in a
Piggy's life. This was better, this foothold that
her conceit had found was far better and more
enduring. Presently she would tell of it.

Now she drove down sunny roads while but
an hour ago the autumn had seemed to her so
bitter and rotten. This lovely day was taut with
promise. The sweet wind filled the sails of Hope.
Piggy knew a thousand precious thoughts. Forgotten that night when she had sat painted and
powdered before her glass. Then she had not near
as much as now. Now she had more than her
own again. I wonder why I've never *guessed*,
said Piggy to herself, how much he relied on me.
It's so lovely to think that he's trusted me always
—and George had said, "We've always been good
friends Piggy——" He had to tell me first, Piggy
thought, first before any one. I dare say Joan
doesn't know about it yet even. Sad, of course,
to think of him throwing himself away on Jane,
but no doubt in time his mistake would be known
to him. Just in a flash he'd realise——

"Where are you taking me?" Jessica said.

"Would you like to go down to the sea?"

"Yes, I'd like that. Is it far?"

"About twenty miles. It's a charming drive.
Don't you think the light and shade on the mountains is rather wonderful?"

Jessica said nothing.

"Of course I'm a mountain lover myself," Piggy

said, and she hummed a little song about the highest mountain.

"You seem very gay," said Jessica resentfully.

"Oh, I think life's such a wonderful adventure. Don't you ever feel that? You know that 'What's round the corner' feeling?"

"No, I don't, thank God."

"Oh, what a cynical outlook! I feel just like a child over it. All the surprises *le bon Dieu* has up His sleeve—as my old French nurse used to say."

That hot-blooded governess who had reigned so briefly at Kilque was often translated into "my old French nurse" by Piggy and held accountable for many strange little phrases. There had been a time when Piggy had taken to emotional religion and *le bon Dieu* and *La Sainte Vierge* had figured often and familiarly in her conversation. In the matiest way in the world she talked about them.

"This is a lovely bit of road for speeding,"Piggy said now. "I must step on the gas. You're not nervous, are you? George always says I'm very safe."

"George always says——" the change was established now indeed.

In spite of what George may have said, Jessica thought many times before they neared the sea that Piggy's other friend, *le bon Dieu*, must have kept a protective eye upon their progress. For

nothing could have been more uncertain than
Piggy's driving. Jessica did not know about the
two drinks nor about Piggy's other causes for
hysterical elation.

"There," said Piggy, slowing down at last,
"that's my favourite *peep*. You're honoured
really. I don't show it to every one."

On their right, dark shaley hills came steeply
down to the road. Dark with gorse and stained
bright with bracken, the hills ran steeply down,
and below them the sea that was as blue as dark
delphiniums washed deeply in against the cliffs.
A broken wall, a little space of nipped grass, then
height and deep water. The sun went in and the
sea and the hills were dead. Shale and indigo
and a cold wind blowing.

"I think it was George who first showed me
how lovely this corner is," Piggy invented boldly,
snuggling down in the car and feeling a delightful
sensation of superiority over Jessica, who had no
such romantic friends as George, she was sure.

Jessica lit a cigarette.

"George?" she said, "George?" as she had
said, "Joan? Joan?" on another evening. "Oh,
George. Oh yes, you mean the nice huntin' man
Jane thinks she's going to marry."

But this time Piggy was not disturbed in spirit.
"Yes," she answered dreamily. "George took me
away this morning to tell me about it. I think I
must have been the first person to know, don't

you? I do hope it'll all be a marvellous success. He's quite mad about her."

Oh that frightful, that ghastly Miss Piggy Browne! Somehow she must be shattered into a lasting silence. Jessica said:

"As it happens, I'm not going to let Jane marry him. I think the whole thing's quite too absurd and monstrous."

"You what?" Piggy's mouth fell open. She looked more stupid and unattractive than usual. A passion of defence for George blazed through her. Her voice was thick and nervous. "Do you mean you don't think George——?"

"I think they're absurdly unsuited in every way and I'm going to stop it. That's all." Jessica blew smoke out through her nose, flattening her nostrils in a queer tempersome way.

"And how do you think you're going to stop it?" Piggy asked insolently. She was trembling with anger. A thousand hot reasons for George's happiness came and went in her mind.

"That, if you don't mind my saying so, is quite entirely my affair."

"You can't stop it anyhow," Piggy said. "How can you?"

"I can and I will——" Jessica's temper was rising now too.

"Nonsense," said Piggy roundly.

"Look here," Jessica turned round and gripped

Piggy by her fat arm. "Look at me, Miss Piggy Browne."

Piggy looked. Stupid Piggy. She saw in Jessica's eyes such hate and such resolve as she had never even dimly guessed to be possible. Jessica still held her arms, her fingers bruised into Piggy's fat arms. "Do you understand now?" she said in a very low voice, "you fat, hungry virgin——" she whispered low.

"Virgin yourself!" Piggy shrilled at her. "Leggo my arms. Oo, let go," she moaned. "You've gone mad," she said.

Jessica let her go. "Now, will you shut up, you squalling fool," she said. "Now, have you taken in that I intend to do as I say?"

Piggy sat shivering and trembling in her corner. Here was something beyond her power of understanding. She only knew that a force, certain in its strength for evil, was set loose. No, not loose, but directed most surely at George—at George's happiness. Beyond all thought of herself, Piggy's gift of service was in her stronger than she knew, and to-day George had quickened this gift towards himself with an almost divine intensity. All Piggy's poor dreams of future loving were lost and gone in her actual conviction of George's need and danger. She did not know what Jessica might do nor how Jane might fail and fall short of George's stupid ideals. To Piggy, George's need of Jane was as real a thing as her present sure knowledge that it lay in Jessica to destroy him and leave his loving barren and ugly for always. Stupid unreasoning Piggy held the truth in her hand and did not question it.

"Show me a way," she prayed to *Le bon Dieu.* "Oh please, please show me a way to stop her; I must, oh please help me." She started the engine and let in her clutch. Spikes of heavy rain were driving into the sea, gulls mewed forlornly overhead. The malign little hills were dark in the coming rain. Piggy pressed the knob of the windscreen wiper, for the glass was drenched in the drive of rain, and in the sudden wet arc of clearness she saw the way out—a broken gap in the stone wall and the invisible drop to the sea below.

Piggy did not think. She only felt and knew. Her blind gift for serving when she loved cast out all fear. She put her foot down on the accelerator and the car leapt forward and dropped.

THE END

Also of interest

THE LOVE CHILD
by Edith Olivier
New Introduction by Hermione Lee

At thirty-two, her mother dead, Agatha Bodenham finds herself quite alone. She summons back to life the only friend she ever knew, Clarissa, the dream companion of her childhood. At first Clarissa comes by night, and then by day, gathering substance in the warmth of Agatha's obsessive love until it seems that others too can see her. See, but not touch, for Agatha has made her love child for herself. No man may approach this creature of perfect beauty, and if he does, she who summoned her can spirit her away...

Edith Olivier (1879?-1948) was one of the youngest of a clergyman's family of ten children. Despite early ambitions to become an actress, she led a conventional life within twenty miles of her childhood home, the Rectory at Wilton, Wiltshire. But she wrote five highly original novels as well as works of non-fiction, and her 'circle' included Rex Whistler (who illustrated her books), David Cecil, Siegfried Sassoon and Osbert Sitwell. *The Love Child* (1927) was her first novel, acknowledged as a minor masterpiece: a perfectly imagined fable and a moving and perceptive portrayal of unfulfilled maternal love.

"This is wonderful..." — *Cecil Beaton*

"*The Love Child* seems to me to stand in a category of its own creating...the image it leaves is that of a tranquil star" — *Anne Douglas Sedgwick*

"Flawless — the best 'first' book I have ever read...perfect" — *Sir Henry Newbolt*

"A masterpiece of its kind" — *Lord David Cecil*

THE SHUTTER OF SNOW

by Emily Holmes Coleman
New Introduction by Carmen Callil and Mary Siepmann

After the birth of her child Marthe Gail spends two months in an insane asylum with the fixed idea that she is God. Marthe, something between Ophelia, Emily Dickinson and Lucille Ball, transports us into that strange country of terror and ecstasy we call madness. In this twilit country the doctors, nurses, the other inmates and the mad vision of her insane mind are revealed with piercing insight and with immense verbal facility.

Emily Coleman (1899-1974) was born in California and, like Marthe, went mad after the birth of her son in 1924. Witty, eccentric and ebullient, she lived in Paris in the 1920s as one of the *transition* writers, close friend of Peggy Guggenheim and Djuna Barnes (who said Emily would be marvellous company slightly stunned). In the 1930s she lived in London (in the French, the Wheatsheaf, the Fitzroy), where her friends numbered Dylan Thomas, T.S. Eliot, Humphrey Jennings and George Barker. Emily Coleman wrote poetry throughout her life — and this one beautiful, poignant novel (first published in 1930), which though constantly misunderstood, has always had a passionate body of admirers — Edwin Muir, David Gascoyne and Antonia White to name a few.

"A very striking triumph of imagination and technique... The book is not only quite unique; it is also a work of genuine literary inspiration" — *Edwin Muir*

"A work which has stirred me deeply...compelling" — *Harold Nicolson*

"An extraordinary, visionary book, written out of those edges where madness and poetry meet" — *Fay Weldon*

PLAGUED BY THE NIGHTINGALE

by Kay Boyle
New preface by the author

When the American girl Bridget marries the Frenchman
Nicolas, she goes to live with his wealthy family in their
Breton village. This close-knit family love each other to the
exclusion of the outside world. But it is a love that festers,
for the family is tainted with an inherited bone disease and
Bridget discovers, as she faces the Old World with the
courage of the New, that plague can also infect the soul...

Kay Boyle was born in Minnesota in 1902. The first of her
three marriages was to a Frenchman and she moved to
Paris in the 1920s where, as one of that legendary group of
American expatriates and contributor to *transition*, she
knew Joyce, Pound, Hemingway, the Fitzgeralds, Djuna
Barnes and Gertrude Stein: a world she recorded in *Being
Geniuses Together*. After a spell living in the bizarre
commune run by Isadora Duncan's brother, she returned
to America in 1941 where she still lives. A distinguished
novelist, poet and short-story writer, she was acclaimed by
Katherine Anne Porter for her "fighting spirit, freshness of
feeling." *Plagued by the Nightingale* was first published in
1931. In subtle, rich and varied prose Kay Boyle echoes
Henry James in a novel at once lyrical, delicate and
shocking.

"A series of brilliant, light-laden pictures, lucid, delightful,
highly original" — *Observer*

"In delicate, satirical vignettes Miss Boyle has enshrined a
French middle-class family...The lines of the picture have
an incisiveness and a bloom which suggest silverpoint"—
Guardian

Other *VIRAGO MODERN CLASSICS*

ELIZABETH von ARNIM
Fräulein Schmidt & Mr Anstruther
Vera

EMILY EDEN
The Semi-Attached Couple &
  The Semi-Detached House

MILES FRANKLIN
My Brilliant Career
My Career Goes Bung

GEORGE GISSING
The Odd Women

ELLEN GLASGOW
The Sheltered Life
Virginia

SARAH GRAND
The Beth Book

RADCLYFFE HALL
The Well of Loneliness
The Unlit Lamp

WINIFRED HOLTBY
Anderby Wold
The Crowded Street
The Land of Green Ginger
Mandoa, Mandoa!

MARGARET KENNEDY
The Constant Nymph
The Ladies of Lyndon
Together and Apart

F. M. MAYOR
The Third Miss Symons

GEORGE MEREDITH
Diana of the Crossways

EDITH OLIVIER
The Love Child

CHARLOTTE PERKINS
  GILMAN
The Yellow Wallpaper

DOROTHY RICHARDSON
Pilgrimage (4 volumes)

HENRY HANDEL
  RICHARDSON
The Getting of Wisdom
Maurice Guest

BERNARD SHAW
An Unsocial Socialist

MAY SINCLAIR
Life and Death of Harriett Frean
Mary Olivier
The Three Sisters

F. TENNYSON JESSE
A Pin to See The Peepshow
The Lacquer Lady
Moonraker

VIOLET TREFUSIS
Hunt the Slipper

MARY WEBB
The Golden Arrow
Gone to Earth
The House in Dormer Forest
Precious Bane
Seven for a Secret

H. G. WELLS
Ann Veronica

ANTONIA WHITE
Frost in May
The Lost Traveller
The Sugar House
Beyond the Glass
Strangers

Other *VIRAGO MODERN CLASSICS*